SECONDARY TARGET

THE SECRETS OF KINCAID

SECONDARY TARGET

ANGELA CARLISLE

BETHANYHOUSE
a division of Baker Publishing Group
Minneapolis, Minnesota

© 2024 by Angela Carlisle

Published by Bethany House Publishers
Minneapolis, Minnesota
BethanyHouse.com

Bethany House Publishers is a division of
Baker Publishing Group, Grand Rapids, Michigan

Printed in the United States of America

Library of Congress Cataloging-in-Publication Data
Name: Carlisle, Angela, author.
Title: Secondary target / Angela Carlisle.
Description: Minneapolis : Bethany House Publishers, a division of Baker
    Publishing Group, 2024. | Series: Secrets of Kincaid
Identifiers: LCCN 2023046611 | ISBN 9780764242502 (paperback) | ISBN
    9780764243233 (casebound) | ISBN 9781493446643 (ebook)
Subjects: LCGFT: Novels. | Detective and mystery fiction.
Classification: LCC PS3603.A752874 S43 2024 | DDC 813/.6—dc23/eng/20231006
LC record available at https://lccn.loc.gov/2023046611

Scripture quotations are from The Holy Bible, English Standard Version® (ESV®),
copyright © 2001 by Crossway, a publishing ministry of Good News Publishers. Used
by permission. All rights reserved. ESV Text Edition: 2016

Emojis are from the open-source library OpenMoji (https://openmoji.org/) under
the Creative Commons license CC BY-SA 4.0 (https://creativecommons.org/licenses
/by-sa/4.0/legalcode).

Cover by James Hall, JWH Graphic Arts
Cover images from Adobe Stock

Published in association with Books & Such Literary Management, BooksAndSuch
.com.

Baker Publishing Group publications use paper produced from sustainable forestry
practices and postconsumer waste whenever possible.

24   25   26   27   28   29   30   7   6   5   4   3   2   1

To my parents,
who instilled in me the love of words and story
long before I could read them myself.

1

SECURITY ALARMS SHATTERED the autumn morning's tranquility.

The mechanical shrieks pierced Corina Roberts's consciousness, dissipating any lingering fog of sleep.

Not again.

She threw back the covers and rolled from the bed, revolver drawn from the nightstand before her feet touched the polished oak floor. She shoved the holster into her pocket but didn't bother searching for her phone. Her dad's security system was configured exactly like her own and would send a notification to the police within thirty seconds of being triggered if they didn't shut it off. Help would be here soon enough. In the meantime, she'd be prepared to protect herself if necessary.

As she reached for the bedroom door, her German shepherd howled, creating a dissonant chorus with the wailing alarm. Shivers chased themselves up her spine. Her hand tightened around the revolver's rosewood-and-steel grip, and a fraction of her tension melted away. The .38 Special LadySmith fit her hand perfectly.

Hopefully, she wouldn't need it.

She sucked in a deep breath and glanced over her shoulder. "Houston. Quiet."

The howling broke off abruptly, but agitation continued to radiate from him. Before she had the door fully open, he burst through it, nearly knocking her off-balance in the process.

She slipped into the darkened hallway after him and caught sight of her father already standing at the front door, his own gun held in a ready position as he peered out the peephole. He would have checked the security monitor as soon as the alarms started. Whatever triggered them must be somewhere along the front of the house. The bright glow of motion-sensing lights beyond his position confirmed it.

"What is it?" She raised her voice to be heard over the alarm.

"I don't know yet. Stay back." He didn't look her direction as he crept from the peephole to the edge of a nearby window and parted the blinds with his finger. Seconds passed. They were well past the requisite thirty now. "Turn the alarm off."

Keeping to the perimeter of the entryway, she did as he asked. Sudden silence engulfed the home, but her eardrums still pulsed with the electronic rhythm of the previous few moments.

She glanced at her dad, and he signaled her to wait. Together they listened, but no sound carried through the door. Whoever had set off the alarm had probably been frightened away. Or were they merely biding their time?

Her dad bent down until his lips were close to her ear. "I'm going out the back to have a look around."

She latched onto his arm as he started to turn away. "Wait for the police, Dad."

"If anyone's still out there, the police will scare them off."

"Then let them get scared off." Her voice rose on the last words, and he pressed a finger to her lips.

"Shh. I know what I'm doing. I'll be back in a few minutes." He extracted himself from her grasp as he spoke.

Something akin to panic wrapped around her chest as he strode down the hallway. She had to stop him from doing something reckless. Something that could get him killed.

She followed him to the spare bedroom and found him unlocking a window. Even with the alarm off, he couldn't use the back door without setting off the motion sensors. A window was his only option. But a window wouldn't do much good if he needed to make a quick reentry.

"Don't go out there, Dad." Corina tried to still the slight tremble in her voice. She hated sounding weak, but more than that, she knew it would only feed her dad's protective instincts.

"I need to, Corina."

"Why? So you can play hero?" She refused to cringe at the implication of her words or take them back. Her dad didn't play hero—and they both knew it. But she never understood why he was always adamant about investigating threats on his own. Almost as if he didn't trust the police to do their jobs.

He didn't answer her. Just started easing the window upward. He wasn't going to listen, so she said the first thing she could think of. "Fine. I'm going with you."

Her wild shot hit its mark. Her dad stopped midmotion and turned back to face her. Even in the near darkness, she could see the steel in his gaze.

"No. You're not. Stay here and keep Houston close." Quiet finality rang in his words, but she lifted her chin in defiance, tamping the fear that threatened her control.

"I'm not a child, and if you're going, so am I."

"Corina, I know you're not a child, but I don't have time to argue with you. Stay. Here." He fixed her with a look that had once made hardened criminals sweat.

She met it. Matched it. And waited.

The faint sound of a quickly approaching vehicle interrupted their glaring match and saved her further argument. The car stopped at their house, strobing lights announcing the police had arrived.

Her dad frowned and brushed past her to let them inside. He wasn't happy, but he was safe. She'd stalled him long enough.

Breathing a sigh of relief, Corina leaned back against the wall as red and blue lights bounced around her. She slipped her revolver into her pocket holster, then clasped her arms across her chest to hide the trembling in her hands.

Buried memories surfaced, and she fought a wave of nausea. *Not now.* She clenched her fists and forced herself to focus on the present until the feeling subsided. She'd dwell on the past another day. Maybe.

BRYCE JESSUP'S HANDS stilled in the middle of his fifty-third rep. Police lights flashed outside his front window, and they weren't just passing by. Not normal for sleepy Kincaid, Kentucky, especially at four in the morning. He lowered the barbell to its resting place and removed the headphones pumping upbeat music into his ears.

He tossed a towel around his neck before moving to peer outside. His heart skipped a beat at the sight of a cruiser parked across the street. *Corina doesn't live there anymore*, he reminded himself. His sister had assured him of that.

Her father hadn't moved, though.

Concern for the overly private man prompted him to step outside. He ignored the midforties temps and focused on the two officers from the local PD standing on the Robertses' porch. With their backs to him, he couldn't identify them. Truth was, he might not know them anyway. It had been several years since he'd spent more than a week or two in his hometown. Change in a small town might be stilted, but it was still inevitable.

Will Roberts stepped into view, leaving the door open behind him. Okay, so he was safe. Bryce held his breath, trying to hear the low voices, but he was too far away.

A flash of fur caught his eye as a familiar—though now fully grown—German shepherd pushed around Will to investigate the officers and the mess littered about the porch. A mess Bryce hadn't noticed until now. He eyed the upturned trash can.

"Houston. Inside." The command came from somewhere behind Will. The feminine voice was one Bryce knew all too well. His gaze settled on a shadow in the darkened doorway. His jaw tensed. So Corina was there after all. Why would Allye tell him she'd moved if she hadn't?

When his mom had offered to rent him their old home upon his return from active duty, he'd put her off with excuses, not caring to voice the real reason behind his hesitation. Allye wasn't fooled, though. At least she'd had the decency to wait until their mom was out of earshot before flatly informing him that Corina had moved. She hadn't called him a coward, hadn't even insinuated it. But he'd felt like one just the same as he took his mom up on her offer.

Now he just felt like a fool.

He truly intended to seek Corina out at some point—try to make things right. But he had no intention of seeing her day after day in the neighborhood where they'd shared so many memories. That was asking too much.

Far too much. He cleared his throat, and Houston's head shot up. *Now you've done it, Jessup.*

"Houston." Corina's call was slightly louder this time.

Houston glanced at the doorway. Back at Bryce. Back at the doorway. In an instant, he was off the porch and making a beeline for him. Bryce braced himself for the impact of paws against his chest. "Oof!" Houston had definitely grown since the last time he'd seen him.

He grunted and pushed the excited animal off him. "Down." Without taking his eyes off the scene across the street, Bryce bent to ruffle the fur on the dog's neck. "So you remember me, huh, boy?"

One of the officers turned, and he recognized Mike Broaddus, a senior member of their small department and one affectionately dubbed "Officer Mike" whether on or off duty. Although Mike was the type to keep a bag of candy in his patrol car just in case he had a chance to treat the neighborhood kids, he could also hold his own against any criminal likely to show up in this town.

As the man began walking toward him, Bryce straightened and pointed at the Robertses' house. "Go home, Houston." The dog sauntered off, taking his time but headed in the right direction.

"Well, if it isn't Bryce Jessup. I'd heard you came back."

"Yes, sir."

"Glad to hear it."

Bryce nodded, then gestured to the Robertses' home. "Some excitement this morning?"

"Yeah." Officer Mike scratched his head. "Something triggered his alarm system. You didn't happen to see anything, did you?"

"Sorry, no. I was up but didn't look outside until just now."

"Figures. Eric's taking a look around, but there's no evidence anyone made it inside—or even tried to, if you discount the alarms." The man sighed. "I'd better get back over there."

"You mind if I come with you?" Bryce could have kicked himself the instant the request popped out of his mouth.

Officer Mike quirked an eyebrow. "You and Corina back together?"

"No." His lips firmed, and he was thankful for the darkness that hid the heat rising in his neck. Officer Mike and everyone else had been aware of their previous relationship. And why it ended.

"Sorry. Didn't mean to hit on a touchy subject."

Bryce waved him off. "Not touchy. That ship sailed a long time ago." Five years ago next month to be exact.

"Understood." Officer Mike turned away. "I suppose it won't hurt. Just don't touch anything."

"Thanks." Bryce followed the officer across the street, still trying to figure out why he'd asked to come. He paused at the edge of the Robertses' porch and glanced at the still-open door. No Corina. He wasn't sure whether he was more relieved or disappointed. As much as he dreaded their inevitable meeting, he couldn't help wondering how the last five years had treated her.

Will had his back to him and didn't seem to notice his presence, but the other cop who'd arrived with Mike caught his eye and nodded. Eric Thornton. Of all the guys he'd attended high school with, Eric was the last one Bryce would have expected to hang around Kincaid this long. Maybe things had changed even less than he'd thought.

Bryce returned the nod, then allowed his gaze to travel the area. Might as well be useful while he was here. His eyes landed again on the upturned trash can. This was garbage day, so it had probably been full—hence the mess. But he saw nothing that should have set off the alarm. Nothing unless . . .

On a hunch, he circled the outside perimeter of the porch, paying careful attention to a muddy patch near one corner. Yep. There they were. He motioned to the men. "Hey, I have some footprints over here."

2

CORINA SURVEYED what she could of the front porch from her position just inside the doorway. It wasn't much, and she couldn't see the impressions Bryce Jessup was chuckling about, but a raccoon had apparently been a recent visitor.

Why is Bryce even here? She peeked around the corner and caught a glimpse of him in an undershirt and sweats. His shoulders were broader than she remembered. Her already racing heart hit the accelerator, and she promptly wrote it a speeding ticket. She'd prefer to revoke its license. The traitorous thing. Hoping he hadn't noticed her, she ducked back out of sight.

Last she'd heard, Bryce was stationed out of the country. She tried to recall how long it had been since that news. Six months—a year, maybe? She shook her head. No matter. But it was strange that Allye, his sister and her semi-housemate, hadn't mentioned his return. Not that Corina had asked about him, but if she'd known he was in town, she might have done things differently. Like schedule a vacation in Florida while her side of their duplex was being renovated instead of arranging to stay with her father.

"How likely is it for a raccoon to set off an alarm?" The skepticism in her dad's voice pulled her attention back to the present.

Eric released a laugh so brief it was barely more than a breath.

"I don't know how likely it is, but it's entirely possible. One broke into my attic through a loose window once and made it through more than one closed door in its search for food. They can turn a knob almost as easily as a human."

And her dad's system was purposely wired to respond to even the slightest provocation. He'd chosen the specifications with care.

"I still want to take a look around." Her dad was clearly unwilling to pin their wake-up call on a woodland creature until he'd exhausted every other possibility. And as a former PI, he had to be part of the investigation.

"No problem. We'll do the same." Eric didn't sound bothered by her dad's interference. The local police were used to it by now.

Corina breathed a sigh of relief as the voices faded and the group moved to the backyard. Despite what her dad thought, she was convinced any other evidence would confirm the raccoon theory. It had all been a false alarm, as it always was.

Her dad would be fine.

She started to close the door, then realized Houston was still outside. Without a fenced-in front yard, she couldn't leave him out there running loose. Why hadn't he come when she called? Usually he was better behaved, but if there was a raccoon to track, there was no telling how far he'd go before coming home.

She muttered under her breath as she opened the hall closet and snatched a dark denim jacket from its hanger. Houston *would* choose to run off at a time like this. Without taking the time to retrieve socks, she slipped on a pair of boots and stomped outside.

And almost into Bryce's muscular arms. Sidestepping to avoid him, she tripped over the garbage can lid. His reflexes saved her balance but not her pride.

"Sorry if I scared you," Bryce said as she pulled away. A tight smile pulled at the corner of his mouth, hinting at the familiar dimple in his left cheek.

Straightening, she shoved her hands into her jacket pockets

and ignored his comment. And the dimple. She wasn't about to explain her reaction. "I'm looking for Houston. Have you seen him?"

The smile disappeared. "A few minutes ago, but he was headed this way."

"Well, he didn't come back inside." She pushed past him, careful this time to avoid the obstacle course on the porch. Unsure which way to go once she reached the street, she paused beneath a tree and cupped her hands around her mouth. Just as quickly, she dropped them. It was still early. If any of the neighbors had managed to get back to sleep after the ruckus they'd caused, she didn't want to wake them now by yelling her dog's name. Again.

A whistle pierced the air, and she turned a sour look on Bryce. "What?"

Before she could say anything, she heard Houston's bark—immediately followed by the crack of a gunshot and a pained yelp.

"Houston!"

BRYCE TACKLED CORINA as the cry tore from her lips. Covering her with his body, he scanned the area. At this hour, not even the faintest tinge of amber colored the horizon. Motion-sensing lights still shone on the Robertses' house, but their glow didn't penetrate this area of the yard. Good.

But that meant he couldn't see anything close to them either. And he had no idea where the single shot had originated. Canine whimpering indicated its destination, though.

"Get. Off." Corina struggled beneath him.

He shifted his weight so he wasn't squashing her and received an elbow to the chest as thank-you. Corina's only response to his grunt was to push him farther away and stand.

"Wait." He grabbed her arm and pulled her back down.

"Houston's out there," she hissed.

"I know, and so is someone with a trigger-happy finger."

She pursed her lips, then focused on something behind him. He turned to follow her gaze. Nothing more than darkened houses met his eyes, but Corina took advantage of his shifted attention. With a quick twist, she broke his grip on her arm and took off at a run.

He stood and puffed out a breath as he headed after her. They should have waited for Officer Mike and Eric to join them. That's what he would have told her if she'd taken the time to listen. Now no one would know their position when they came to investigate.

It was too late for that now. He couldn't let Corina go off alone with an active shooter on the loose. At least she had sense enough to keep to the shadows as she searched for her pet. With her dark clothing, only her long blond ponytail stood out against the blackness surrounding them.

When she disappeared around a bend in the road, Bryce quickened his pace to catch up and almost bowled her over when he made the turn himself. Crouching next to Houston under a dim streetlight, Corina murmured soothingly in the German shepherd's ear. Her fingers probed his fur, searching for wounds.

Bryce ran his eyes over the dog, evaluating him as best he could in the light they had. Houston was standing—shaky, but standing. And the blood on the pavement appeared to be minimal. Maybe he wasn't hurt badly after all. *Please, God.* It would crush Corina to lose her dog.

"How is he?"

"I don't know yet."

Houston yelped as Corina moved to his back legs. Blood marked the hand she snatched back. "Found it," she muttered.

"Can you tell how bad it is?"

She shook her head. "I think just a graze, but I can't be sure in this light." She yanked off her jacket and reached for the injured leg again. "Hold still, Houston."

Bryce arrested her hand. "Wait. Use this." He pulled the towel from his shoulders and offered it to her. He'd almost forgotten it was there.

She hesitated only a second before accepting it. With gentle quickness, she wrapped it around the wounded limb, securing the ends together with an elastic band pulled from her hair.

"Thanks." She slipped back into her jacket. "Who would do this?" Disgust coated her words as she surveyed the surrounding houses. The homes of their longtime neighbors.

Bryce followed her gaze. Who indeed? And why? There weren't many good reasons to fire a gun within city limits. Did the shooter hate dogs? Mistake Houston for a coyote? Or did he have something to hide? Like an attempted break-in.

Maybe they'd been too quick to blame everything on the foraging raccoon.

One thing he was sure of. Whoever it was hadn't gone far in the last couple of minutes. The three of them needed to get out of the open. Besides, the cops would be searching for the shooter by now, maybe even calling in backup. And they didn't know he and Corina had left the house. Dodging friendly fire was not something Bryce wanted to do ever again.

And as soon as Corina's dad noticed her absence, he'd work himself into a protective frenzy. The man's temper was volatile when it came to his daughter. That overbearing protectiveness was the only thing Bryce hadn't missed after he and Corina broke up. He understood it to a degree—he'd be protective himself if he had a daughter, especially one like Corina—but Will took things a little too far.

They needed to get back. The sooner the better.

Bryce looked at Houston. "We need to get him back to the house and get a better look at that wound."

"I know, but I'm not sure how well he can walk." Corina reached into a pocket, then frowned. "And I don't have my phone. You don't happen to have yours, do you?"

Bryce shook his head. There had been no need to grab it before leaving the house. He hadn't planned on going anywhere.

"Why don't you head back and get my dad to drive up here and get us?"

And leave her alone in the meantime? Did she not realize the shooter might still be close by?

"I don't think so." Without waiting for a response, Bryce bent and lifted Houston onto his shoulders, taking care not to touch the wounded area. The dog whined but didn't fight him. Good thing too. He wasn't a small animal—probably weighed close to eighty pounds. At least they only had a quarter mile or so to go.

Corina stood with him. As they turned back the way they'd come, a tingling feeling settled on his back—the unmistakable sense of being watched.

He spun and stared into the darkness.

"What's wrong?" Corina's voice barely reached his ears. Her hand inched toward a slightly bulging pocket. Was she carrying? Probably.

He wished he were.

He shook his head and held his position a moment longer. Nothing moved, and only Houston's heavy breathing disturbed the predawn quiet. But the feeling didn't go away.

"Something's off," he finally said. "We need to go. Now."

His jaw twitched as he turned his back to the potential threat and ushered Corina around the bend. Back toward the safety of her home. If he were alone and armed, he would investigate. But he wasn't alone, nor did he own a gun. And he wasn't foolish enough to walk around in the dark while the cops were searching for an active shooter.

He blew out a breath.

"You okay?" Corina asked, glancing at him.

"Fine." He didn't expound further. They didn't have far to go now and were close enough to see the increased activity around Will's property. A third police car had joined the pair already parked at the curb, and another was just pulling onto the opposite end of the street.

As they neared the house, a bright light suddenly switched on, partially blinding them.

"Freeze. Police." Eric's voice rang out from behind the light.

"It's just us," Bryce said, complying with the demand.

"Bryce? Corina?" Eric grunted and lowered his flashlight. "What are you doing wandering around? You could've gotten yourself shot."

"Somebody shot Houston," Corina blurted before Bryce had a chance to respond.

"Houston?" The officer turned his light to the dog, who still rested on Bryce's shoulders. "How bad is it?"

"Leg wound. Probably not too bad, but he'll need a vet to check him out."

"Where'd you find him?"

"Up the road a bit. Let me drop him off, and I can show you."

"All right." Eric let them continue on to the house.

When they arrived, Corina held the front door open and directed him to place Houston on a towel in the large master bathroom.

"Thanks," she murmured.

"You're welcome." He wanted to tell her how risky it had been to go after the animal, but watching her retrieve a first aid kit and tend to her pet, he didn't have the heart to.

He headed for the porch, where Eric waited. As he exited the house, he heard a frantic voice behind him.

"Where have you been?"

Will.

Bryce winced and glanced over his shoulder at the nearly shouted words. The question hadn't been aimed at him. The man was focused on the bathroom.

Bryce almost turned back to defend her actions, even though he didn't agree with them, but it wouldn't do any good. Corina was Will's only living child, and she'd put herself in danger.

Eric caught his eye and gestured toward the road. "Show me."

Bryce nodded, tuning out the argument behind him. Corina could hold her own. She always did.

Right now, it was more important for the police to figure out what happened this morning, and taking them to the spot they'd found Houston was the best thing he could do to help. The dog might have moved after the shot, but if he had, the police could follow the blood trail to find his original position. Then they could work on determining where the shot had come from.

And who fired it.

3

IT WAS EARLY AFTERNOON before Bryce had a chance to visit Kincaid's recently opened Western Outfitters. He surveyed the storefront property before climbing from his car. This place had been empty the last time he'd been in town, but it used to hold a cozy mom-and-pop restaurant. He and Corina had had their first date there after the county high school's Drive Your Tractor to School Day.

That had been, what, a decade ago? Seemed like yesterday. Seemed like forever. He pushed his way inside, hoping the memories wouldn't follow him.

A doorbell signaled his arrival as he stepped across the threshold. At first glance, he appeared to be alone. No other customers browsed the shelves, and no employee stood behind the register.

His eyes bounced about the room. To his left, a wall had been removed, doubling the business's size. The place looked nothing like he remembered, but the setup was intriguing. Pale yellow walls texturized to look like stucco held a scattered array of cowboy hats, spurs, and traditional leather holsters. Black-and-white photographs of various Wild West movie stars adorned the wall above the register.

He'd bet Corina loved this place. He frowned. So much for leaving the memories outside.

But everything about it screamed her name: the décor, camping and sporting gear, racks of jeans and Western-style shirts, and shelves of cowboy boots.

Sounds from a room beyond the checkout counter caught his attention a second before a woman backed through the doorway, a large box in her arms. She dropped her load on a shelf behind the counter and wiped her hands. "Welcome to . . ." The words trailed off as she turned to face him.

Corina. Again.

He took in her outfit. Though less flashy than the costumes pictured on the wall, her clothes blended in with the business. A fringed vest over a red checkered button-up, sleeves rolled to just below the elbow. Her ever-present cowboy boots.

Typical Corina.

"Afternoon." He mustered a smile.

Without returning his greeting, she crossed her arms and leaned against the wall. "What are you doing here?" So she was happy to see him too.

He raised an eyebrow and pointedly glanced around at the racks and shelves. "Shopping. You work here?"

"I own the place." A trace of pride colored her matter-of-fact statement. "Allye didn't tell you?"

Allye knew? Of course she did. Allye knew about everything that went on in town. And he was starting to think they needed to have a talk about the secrets she'd been keeping.

"No, I had no idea. I was curious about the new shop, and after this morning, I figured a gun wouldn't be a bad investment."

Corina's stance softened slightly at his admission. She looked relieved. Had she thought he'd tracked her down? That was the last thing on today's to-do list.

"Are you looking for anything specific?" Her tone hinted at apology, though she made none. She started to round the counter, but he waved her off.

"I want to browse a bit. I'll let you know if I need help."

"Sure. I'll be here." She pivoted back to the shelf behind her and began unpacking the box of merchandise.

Moving to the nearby display case, he waited a moment, then sneaked a glance behind him just in time to see her swing her ponytail over her shoulder. The motion triggered memories of running his fingers through those silky strands. Of her snuggling next to him on the couch as they watched a movie while her dad pretended not to be watching them more than the TV screen.

Focus, Bryce. The sooner he got out of here the better. Releasing a sigh, he turned back to study his options.

The shop's stock of firearms consisted of a small number of sporting rifles and shotguns. Fitting for an outfitters' supply, but not ideal for self-defense. He spotted a binder of catalogs on the countertop. Maybe he could have Corina special order something for him.

The jingling doorbell announced a new arrival, and Bryce glanced that direction. A young couple entered. They looked familiar, but he couldn't place them. Corina seemed to know them, though, and welcomed them in, her demeanor a total 360 from two minutes earlier. The contrast stung. This warm personality was the old Corina, the one he knew and—

He wasn't about to finish that thought. Tuning out the chit-chat, he quickly flipped through the catalogs. Although he'd like to try one of the slimline Glocks, the Sig Sauer P320 was similar to the model he'd carried in the army. Familiarity called to him.

Satisfied with his choice, he turned back to see Corina dragging a single-person kayak from the back room. A tandem model already leaned against the checkout counter next to the couple.

"I'm sorry for the delay on these." Corina stood the kayak next to the first. "You won't get much use out of them this year."

"Not your fault the ones we wanted were on back order. They'll be ready and waiting for next summer. And we'll be able to squeeze in a trip before it gets too cold."

The woman huffed. "It's already too cold, Jamie."

Jamie. No wonder they looked familiar. Jamie and Collette had been two years ahead of him in school. The couple had dated all the way through high school and gotten married right after graduation.

"Naw. I'll keep you warm." Jamie put an arm around his wife's shoulders. "Or keeping up with Jake will."

The three of them laughed, and Bryce found himself smiling as well. Jake must be their son. Now that he thought about it, they had been expecting when he'd left town. Or had their child already been born? He couldn't remember. So much had happened around that time.

"Let's get you loaded up." Corina grabbed an end of the tandem kayak, and Collette reached for the other. Bryce straightened his drooping shoulders and pushed off the display case. "You all need an extra hand?"

The couple looked his direction as if just noticing him. Jamie squinted as if trying to place him, but before he could respond, Corina shook her head and started moving. "We've got it."

Jamie shrugged and hefted the single seater over one shoulder. Collette didn't look quite so sure, but she didn't argue as Corina led the way to the door and awkwardly worked it open.

Okay then. Bryce propped himself against the display case and watched through the large front windows as they loaded the kayaks onto a trailer and strapped them down.

A few minutes later, Corina reentered alone, all business as she met Bryce's gaze. "Have you made a decision?'

"Yep." He slid the binder toward her and tapped the glossy image. "I'd like to order one of these."

She took the binder and examined his choice. "Do you need any accessories?"

"Probably."

Together, they figured out what else he might need, and while she processed the order, he studied her for the first time since he'd returned home. She had lost weight in the last five years—

and she'd already been on the lean side. Dark circles were etched under her eyes. Were those just from this morning?

"Your total is—" She looked up and caught him staring. "What?"

"Nothing."

She frowned but didn't press the issue as she stated the amount.

He handed her his card and stuck his hands in his pockets. "So did the police department come up with anything new on this morning's incidents?" He'd hung around a bit after showing Eric where they'd found Houston, but there'd been no further shots fired or any sign of the shooter when he'd headed home an hour or so later.

She shook her head.

"Nothing at all?"

"No." She sighed. "Well, the cameras confirmed a raccoon got into the trash on the porch, but he wandered off well before the alarm was triggered. But at the time the alarm went off, the footage doesn't show anyone or anything around. Maybe the system just glitched."

"But someone did shoot Houston."

"The police are still looking into that. None of the neighbors they spoke with saw anything. There are a couple of houses they weren't able to get a response from, but those are elderly residents with hearing issues." She pursed her lips and slid his card through the reader. "Officer Mike and Eric planned to run by again this afternoon, but if those neighbors couldn't hear the cops knocking on their doors this morning, I really doubt the alarms or gunshot woke them up."

Figured. So unless something random turned up, they'd probably never know exactly what had happened or who had shot her dog. "How's Houston?"

She sighed and glanced toward the back room, where the tip of a tail was visible. "He's fine. It was just a graze, like I thought. The vet gave him three stitches, prescribed antibiotics, and handed me a bill the size of Texas."

"Good—that he's okay, I mean. Not that you have a big bill."

For the first time since he'd come back, she directed a smile his way—a half smile maybe, but it still warmed him. "I knew what you meant." She returned his card and handed him his receipt. "I'll contact you when everything comes in. Have a nice day."

CORINA DROPPED her half-finished book on the counter. Four hours had passed since Bryce left, and she still couldn't concentrate. His broad shoulders and military haircut looked even better in the daylight than they had early this morning. And that fact made his presence dangerous.

"You are *not* falling for him again." She wasn't falling for anyone again. Ever.

Houston raised his head at her voice, and his tail thumped the floor. "That's right, boy. You're the only company I need." And she'd almost lost him too. She shuddered. The small bandage on his leg was the only indication of how close he'd come to a serious injury.

She stood and slipped on a jacket. "Come on, let's go home." She smiled as the dog stretched and yawned. "I guess you have a right to be tired," she said, scratching him behind the ears. "Even though you didn't work a lick today." He wagged his tail, unoffended by her evaluation.

She swung her purse onto her shoulder, then secured the roll bars over the windows, flipped the lights off, and reached for Houston's collar before arming the alarm system. She'd forgotten his leash, and a repeat of this morning's escapade was not an option.

Outside, she inserted her key into the lock, but something in the old building must have shifted in the cold. The dead bolt refused to move. She grunted and released her hold on Houston. "Stay," she warned him as she lifted the doorknob with her left hand and turned the key with her right. The bolt finally clicked into place.

"I hope I don't have to wrestle that thing all winter," she muttered. "All right, Houston, I'm ready now." She turned her back to the door.

Houston's posture stopped her. He stood stock-still, the fur on his neck bristling.

"What's wrong, boy?" she whispered, scanning the area for herself. Nothing seemed out of place except for a burnt-out streetlamp near the mechanic's shop across the road. It was early evening, but things were quiet tonight. Almost too quiet.

Don't be silly. Quiet is a good thing. Still, standing alone in the deserted parking lot, she couldn't help feeling like a target. She backed farther into the shadowed doorway while she evaluated her surroundings. The area immediately around her was well lit, but the darkness beyond seemed sinister, almost mocking as it concealed its contents. A low growl emerged from Houston's throat.

Goosebumps prickled her arms. Since soon after the store's grand opening in June, she'd periodically felt unsettled, like someone was watching her. Nothing tangible was ever out of place, though, and she'd never seen anyone around that didn't belong, so she'd begun to chalk it up to her imagination. But Houston wasn't imagining things.

Of course, he could also be reacting to a possum or a skunk. She eyed the distance to her truck. She had parked at the edge of the lot to save the best places for customers—what precious few of them she'd had today—but it still wasn't far.

She reached for Houston's collar and walked briskly across the lot. No sense in drawing extra attention by running if there was somebody or something out there. The remote on her keychain unlocked the doors mere seconds ahead of them.

Before opening the door, she glanced into the windows, assuring herself no one hid inside. "Up." She let Houston jump in ahead of her and take his place in the copilot's seat. Two seconds later, she was inside with doors locked and engine running. A sigh of relief escaped her.

A look at Houston put her on edge again. Instead of sitting to enjoy the ride like he usually did, he was standing on the seat, staring out the window, teeth bared in a silent growl. She'd never seen him act like this. Not even in the excitement this morning.

She fished inside her purse for her cell phone, refusing to turn on the vehicle's interior lights to aid in the search. Surely she hadn't left it in the store, had she? She needed to let someone know where she was. Just in case.

Houston scrambled over the center console to the back seat just as her probing fingers touched something metallic. There it was—underneath her wallet. She pressed the power button as she pulled it out. Nothing.

Really? Of all the times for a dead battery. She shoved the charger into the port and tried the power button again. The startup tones sounded as she pulled onto the street.

Barely glancing at the screen, she typed in her password and speed-dialed her dad. She tapped her index finger impatiently on the steering wheel as it rang. "Come on. Pick up," she murmured, eyes darting between her mirrors and the road before her. The ringing stopped, and the call went to voice mail. She hesitated but decided to go ahead and leave a message. It couldn't hurt.

"Hey, I just left the outfitters." She glanced up as headlights appeared in her rearview. "Just got an odd feeling as I was leaving—"

She paused, distracted. Those headlights were coming up too fast, and the engine was loud.

"Got to go. There's a speed demon behind me." She tried to add a chuckle to the end of her sentence, but it sounded more nervous than amused, even to her own ears. Disgusted, she hung up and dropped her phone into the cup holder.

4

BRYCE USED A TORTILLA to scrape the last bit of refried beans off his plate. They were starting to get cold, but he wasn't willing to waste a bite. Besides, focusing on the food helped hide the way his thoughts kept straying to a certain blond business owner.

"Bryce? Hello?" His sister reached across the table and waved her hand in front of his face. "Are you even listening? What's wrong with you tonight?"

So much for hiding his distraction.

"I'm just tired. Moving is exhausting." He ended the last words on a yawn, hoping she wouldn't press him. He really was tired. After several trips from his storage unit to the house, he'd taken care of his business at Corina's shop, then detoured to check on his uncle's farm in Butler since Jesse and his wife were celebrating their thirtieth anniversary in the Smoky Mountains. Normally Bryce's cousin would have taken care of things, but Hailey was on bed rest with a complicated pregnancy. The lot had fallen to Bryce. He didn't mind, but it was one more thing on top of an already packed day.

Once he'd finished there, he spent the remainder of the afternoon unpacking what he'd removed from the storage unit. Now the house resembled the aftermath of an IED.

So did his thoughts.

He pushed his empty plate aside and glanced at Allye's. She was only halfway through her entrée. This could take a while.

He flipped through the dessert menu, then waved down a waiter.

"Can I get an order of fried ice cream?"

"Of course." The waiter turned to Allye. "Anything for you?"

"A box, please. And an extra spoon. He's sharing." Allye grinned as the waiter walked away.

Some things never changed.

Allye studied him, her grin fading. "What's really the matter?"

He sighed and rubbed the back of his neck. As much as he wanted to confront his sister for lying to him about Corina, the middle of a restaurant was not the place to do it.

"I told you, I'm tired."

"Mm-hmm. And perturbed about something. Spill."

He dropped his hand. "There was some excitement in the neighborhood early this morning. The Robertses' house alarm went off."

"Is everyone all right?" Allye didn't sound as concerned as he expected. But then again, that alarm had woken them all up several times during the first couple of months the Robertses lived there. Will had finally relaxed the settings *slightly* after a neighbor threatened to report them for disturbing the peace. Maybe he'd upped them again in the years Bryce was gone.

"Yeah, they're fine." He toyed with his nearly empty glass. "But imagine my surprise when Corina walked out of the house in her pajamas."

"Corina left the house in her pajamas?" Allye didn't try to hide her amusement. Or respond to his implication.

He tried to keep the edge from his voice. "Not *left* left. Houston got out, and she was trying to find him."

"Oh." She took another bite of her enchilada.

"That's all you have to say about it?"

Allye looked up at him. "What do you want me to say? If Houston escaped, I guess Corina had a good excuse for being outside in her pajamas."

"That's not my point, Allye, and you know it."

"Then what is your point?"

The waiter returned, a box and the check in one hand and a bowl of delicious-looking fried ice cream in the other. Bryce wasn't in the mood anymore, but he picked up one of the spoons anyway and waited until the man was out of earshot.

"You told me Corina moved."

"Yes." Allye raked her food into the takeout box, then set it aside.

"Why?"

"Because she did," she said slowly. Her eyes widened, then narrowed as they met his skeptical gaze. "Is that what this is about?"

He nodded, his fingers tightening around the spoon.

Allye rolled her eyes. "She doesn't live there anymore, Bryce. The other side of my duplex became available two years ago, and she moved in. She's just staying with her dad for a few days while the landlord is having repairs done. Sheesh."

Bryce leaned back in his chair and exhaled audibly. "She lives next to you now? You never mentioned that detail."

"As I remember, you told me back when you first deployed to stop giving you updates about her."

Only because they'd hurt too much. But he wasn't about to admit that.

"You're right. Sorry, Allye." He reached for the ice cream, but she pulled it away from him and took a bite. "Hey, that is mine, you know."

"Debatable," she said around a mouthful.

"Come on. Truce?"

She eyed him for a long couple of seconds, then slowly slid the bowl across the table.

"Thanks."

She was quiet for a moment. A dangerous thing for his sister.

"You know, it wouldn't be such a bad thing for you and Corina to talk things out."

Like that would go over well. She could hardly bear to look at him. Although somewhere in the time he'd spent at the outfitters, her demeanor had changed from hostile to professional. When he left, she seemed more resigned than anything.

"I don't think so."

"She's still hurting, Bryce," she said softly. "She put up a wall even I haven't been able to get past. Not really."

"But you're still friends?"

"I didn't give her a choice." She gave him a rueful smile and stole another bite of ice cream. "But it isn't like it used to be. I miss her."

He'd never stopped missing her. Yet another thing he didn't intend to admit.

Allye scooped up another bite of his dessert and checked her watch. "Yikes! I've got to get to the studio." Her chair scraped against the floor as she scrambled to her feet. She pulled a twenty from her purse, tossed it on the table, and took off for the door.

"Hey, what's your hurry?" he called after her.

She barely paused to look over her shoulder. "I have an appointment in ten minutes. I'll call you later." Then she was gone.

Bryce chuckled and finished off the ice cream. Allye was always running late for something. And leaving things behind. He eyed her takeout box. *Might as well take that home.* He picked it up and grimaced. Her cell phone lay underneath.

He glanced toward the door, but he knew Allye was long gone from the parking lot—he'd heard her tires squeal as she pulled out. Sighing, he tucked the phone into his pocket. He'd have to drop it off later.

CORINA GLARED into her rearview. The other vehicle was still tailgating her. She should have turned off sooner and let him pass, but as close as he was now, she wasn't sure she'd be able to brake enough to turn without getting clipped. She reached for her phone again and hit the speed dial for Allye. "Back off, buddy," she muttered under her breath. Aggressive drivers were the worst. She pulled the phone from her ear to search for the Bluetooth option. Should have turned that on sooner.

"Hello?"

The call connected before she found the right button—and just as the vehicle behind her edged closer. She sucked in a breath, her fingers stilling over the screen. From the position of the headlights, it looked like some type of SUV. Her stomach turned a slow loop. *It's okay. It's just a vehicle.* Right. Just a vehicle. The kind that scared her to death. She tapped her brakes just enough to make the lights flash. Maybe the guy would take a hint. The second he backed off, she'd look for a place to pull out of his way.

"Everything all right?"

She sucked in a breath. That was Bryce's voice coming through the line, not Allye's. She swallowed and put the phone back to her ear. "Hi, it's Corina. Is Allye there?"

"No, we had dinner together, and she had to rush off. She left her phone."

Of course she did. "Can you have her call me later?" The mirrors drew her gaze again. The other driver hadn't paid any attention to her warning attempt.

"Sure." Bryce paused. "You sure you're all right? You sound nervous."

"I'm fine. Just dealing with an aggressive driver, and something felt off when I left the shop a few minutes ago." She clamped down on her lips. Why did she say that?

"What happened?"

"Houston was acting funny." Her cheeks burned. She felt foolish saying it out loud. After all, *she* hadn't actually heard or seen anything out of the ordinary. "Don't worry about it. He probably just smelled another raccoon or a cat or something. Sorry to bug you."

There was a slight pause, then "Don't feel bad about letting someone know what's going on. Especially after this morning."

"Yeah." She stole another glance in the mirror. The SUV had backed off a little, but it was still following too closely.

"Where are you now?"

"I'm just passing—Hey!" The other vehicle struck her from behind. She jerked against the seat belt. Houston started barking.

"Corina! Corina, are you okay?" Even though it sounded like he was shouting, she could only vaguely hear Bryce's voice on the line. It took her a second to realize she'd dropped her phone in the collision.

"I'm fine!" she yelled, hoping he could hear her. The SUV behind her slowed and put on its hazard lights. *Great.* Now they had to exchange insurance information. Call the police for a report. This could take a while.

She pulled off the road and turned on her own hazard lights. *Better get the police on their way.* She bent down to retrieve her phone. Just as her fingers closed around it, she heard a sickening crunch, and her head smacked the radio as she was thrown forward again.

5

"BRYCE!" SHE SCRAMBLED to put the truck in drive again, fumbling with the gearshift twice before getting it into the right position. "He's ramming me!" Somehow she managed to hit the Bluetooth button as she gunned the engine. She dropped the phone into her lap so she would have both hands free for the wheel.

"Who? Corina, where are you?" His voice came through the truck speakers now, demanding and insistent. And worried.

Her tires screeched on the pavement. Houston jumped into the back and pawed at the rear window, barking frantically. A quick look in the mirror revealed the other vehicle was gaining again. She braced herself, but a small cry still escaped when it hit them. The force threw Houston to the floor. She lost the phone to the darkness at her feet again.

"Corina! Talk to me." She faintly heard a car door slam on his end of the line.

"I'm just past the bank."

"I'm coming. Stay as far in the lead as you can. Try to lose him."

She tried to think beyond the next few feet of pavement. It wouldn't be easy to lose anyone on these roads. If she turned quickly enough to catch him off guard, she'd run the risk of hitting a building or parked car. Even if she made the turn, all the other driver would have to do was turn down the next street and cut back across.

Wait. Just ahead there was a spot where some of the local cops liked to pause on their rounds. *Please, God!* She desperately needed one of them to be there now. Risking letting go of the wheel with one hand, she blared her horn, hoping to draw attention.

They rounded a bend and—*Yes! Yes!*—she could see metallic silver and blue reflecting in her headlights. Barely a second passed before red and blue flashers lit the darkness.

The vehicle behind her seemed farther away. She breathed a shallow sigh of relief as she pulled in behind the patrol car and peered over her shoulder. Just in time to see the headlights coming again.

She let out a strangled scream as the impact threw her truck forward and into the back of the cruiser.

Watching the mirror, she reached for the gearshift, ready to try to outrun him again. But just as quickly as he'd eaten the distance between them, the driver backed up and swung a turn onto a side road. She tried to make out his plates but couldn't get a good look. Then he was gone.

She sat still and forced herself to focus on simply breathing normally. Slowly, she began to register Bryce's voice. Their call must still be connected. She'd just tuned it out.

"I'm—" She swallowed and tried again. "I'm okay." Tears filled her eyes, and she blinked them back. "I'm—there's an officer here."

She tried to let him know exactly where she was, but adrenaline was muddling her brain, and Houston's frantic barking wasn't helping. "Just look for the lights, Bryce. You can't be far from me now." She turned her head. "Houston. Down." The worst of the racket stopped, but the dog whined his protest. She reached a hand toward him. "I know," she whispered.

The officer—she tried to place the plate number with a name,

Eric?—hadn't gotten out of the car yet. He was probably radioing for backup. She didn't blame him.

Headlights illuminated the road beyond the officer's car. "Is that you, Bryce?"

"Yeah."

The line finally cut off as Bryce pulled off the road in front of the squad car. She saw his interior lights come on, but he waited a few seconds before exiting the vehicle. Probably giving the officer a chance to identify him before exploding out the door to check on her. She was glad he had the foresight to wait. The police department had enough to think about in emergency situations without trying to decide in a split second if the guy running toward them was dangerous.

She flipped on her own lights and stepped carefully out the door. Her legs buckled with unexpected weakness as adrenaline's aftermath kicked in, and she grabbed the open door to steady herself. In an instant, Bryce was beside her, his bear hug providing all the support she needed to remain upright. She buried her face in his chest.

"What's going on?" Eric Thornton's voice cut through the air. His words were calm, but there was no mistaking the force behind them. The officer was ticked.

Corina turned her head to the side to look at him. She could make out the sound of a siren headed their direction. Eric's backup most likely. Once he realized who was causing the commotion, he must have decided not to wait for it.

Bryce pulled back enough to look into her face, evaluating her condition. Then he turned toward Eric, keeping her tucked close to his right side—effectively sandwiching her between his body and the truck.

"Someone just tried to run Corina off the road." His voice was low, dangerous.

"And into me." Eric raised his eyebrows. "You okay?"

"I think so. He rear-ended me a couple of times before I got to you." She eyed his cruiser. "I'm so sorry—I had no idea he'd keep coming once he saw you."

Eric's eyes flashed. "Not your fault. Did you see the other vehicle? Can you identify the driver?" He tapped the scrunched area that used to be his trunk. "I didn't have a chance for a good look."

"No." She frowned. "It looked like an SUV or something big. He had his brights on. I really couldn't see anything else."

Eric shook his head and walked around the back of her truck to survey the damage there. He let out a low whistle. She stayed where she was. She wasn't ready to see what that jerk had done to her truck. At least she had been in a truck this time, not a compact car. She shuddered, and Bryce pulled her closer.

The other squad car finally pulled in behind them, better illuminating the area. The officer flipped the sirens off and exited the vehicle.

"What you got, Thornton?" Corina recognized Mike Broaddus's voice.

"Road rage. Or a hit-and-run."

On steroids.

Corina tuned out the officers' conversation as Houston pushed past her out of the truck. He yelped as his feet hit the ground. Blood seeped through the bandage on his injured leg. She hoped the stitches hadn't pulled loose.

"Houston, heel." She pulled away from Bryce and reached inside her truck for the roll of paper towels she kept under the driver's seat. It was closer to her gas pedal now. Tearing off a long strip, she knelt and wrapped it around her dog's leg, tying the end off loosely. She'd replace the dressing later, but for now, this would have to do.

"Corina." Eric rounded the vehicle to join them again. "I'll need to get your statement, then you should probably get checked out. Just in case."

"I'm fine, really." She took a deep breath as she stood. A sharp pain shot through her chest, taking her off guard. Bryce reached out to steady her. Irritation rose at her failure to hide her reaction, and she yanked her arm away from him. "I'm fine," she said again, this time through her teeth.

"You need to get looked at." Bryce sounded so much like her dad that she barely resisted the urge to roll her eyes.

Ignoring him, she focused her attention on Eric and cleared her throat. Strange. She hadn't noticed it was so dry. Water sounded wonderful. She shook her head, then wished she hadn't. Now she felt dizzy too.

He needs a statement. Pull yourself together. She squeezed her eyes shut and gathered her thoughts. "I was on my way home from the shop—well, actually something seemed off even before I got in the truck." She closed her eyes again, forcing herself to remember details that were already growing foggy.

She recounted the events up to when she spotted his patrol car. "You know what happened from there. I pulled in, parked, and"—she flung a hand toward his trunk—"that happened."

"And you can't remember noticing anything else about the other vehicle?" Officer Mike prompted.

She pursed her lips. "His engine was loud, almost like he had a hole in the muffler or something." She could thank Bryce and his love of cars for that possible diagnosis. Or she could be completely off. She started to shake her head again but caught herself in time. "I don't know. Maybe it wasn't that bad. It just seemed odd that I heard it over my own engine. The truck isn't all that quiet."

She leaned back against the side of her vehicle as Eric reviewed his notes, clicking his pen as if the action would spur his brain into making sense of the situation.

Finally, he looked up. "If that's all, we'll get to work on this. You can't drive your truck—not in its current condition. Need a ride?" He glanced from her to Bryce.

"Y—"

"I've got it covered," Bryce answered over her.

She glared at him but didn't protest. He did live right across the street from her dad, so it made sense to accept the ride. Still, his assumption grated.

She turned back to the officers. "Thanks anyway, Eric, Officer Mike."

"Anytime."

Steeling herself against the pain it took to stretch, Corina retrieved her purse and phone before leading Houston to the familiar sports car that Bryce's mom had saved for him after his dad was killed in action during the Iraq War. Bryce already had the passenger door open and the front seat pushed forward to allow Houston access to the back. She signaled him to jump in. "Come on. Time for your first ride in a Camaro."

BRYCE FLEXED HIS HANDS on the steering wheel, the action the only visible sign of the tension running through him. Hearing Corina in danger had scared him more than he was willing to admit. Things like this didn't happen in Kincaid. At least, not in the Kincaid he knew.

Corina jerked in the seat next to him, and he looked to see Houston's nose retreating back to the rear of the car. He stifled a grin. Apparently, he wasn't the only tense one.

"Hey, you missed the turn."

He turned his attention back to the road. "Not going that way."

"I know you just moved back here, but that"—Corina jerked her thumb behind them—"is still the quickest way to my dad's."

"I'm not taking you home yet. We're going to the ER."

"I told you I'm *fine*. What part of that statement is so hard to understand? I've been in accidents a lot worse than—" She snapped her mouth shut and turned toward the window.

"I know," Bryce said softly. When Corina didn't respond, he sighed and pulled into a parking lot. He gently turned her face toward him and brushed a thumb over the red spot above her eyebrow. "Corina, you've got a bump the size of a Ping-Pong ball coming up on your forehead, and you can hardly move without gritting your teeth. If you really want me to take you home, I will, but you're *not* fine."

She squeezed her eyes shut, and he waited for her to make a decision. As much as he wanted to, he wouldn't make her go. After a few moments, she crossed her arms and uttered a single word: "Fine." She still didn't look at him.

But it was all he needed. Bryce pulled back onto the road leading out of Kincaid and headed toward the nearest city with a hospital.

"This is a waste of time."

Bryce barely caught the muttered words. He just shook his head. Corina was a lot of things, brave, spunky—definitely stubborn—but right now, she wasn't fine.

It was about half an hour to Harrison Memorial in Cynthiana, but an uncomfortable silence fell between them, endowing the minutes with a power normally reserved for hours. Maybe Bryce should have taken her home. Her dad would have seen to it that she was taken care of. The man was nothing if not protective.

Strains of Tchaikovsky's *Firebird* filtered from the glove box, where he'd deposited Allye's phone after leaving the accident site. He considered letting it go to voice mail, but his sister was probably frantic trying to find it since the device was for both personal use and her freelance photography business.

He tugged open the compartment, grabbed the phone, and pushed it toward Corina. "Do you mind checking that?" A deer darted across the highway a couple of yards ahead of them, confirming his need to pay attention to the road.

Corina sucked in a breath, but before Bryce could ask why, she answered the phone with a "Hi, Dad."

"Corina? What's going on? Why aren't you answering your phone?"

Bryce could clearly hear Will's voice from his side of the car.

"Everything's fine. I'll fill you in later. I didn't think to grab my charger when I left the truck. The battery was low, and it probably died again. Bryce is taking me to the ER to—"

"ER? What happened?" Will's voice rose. Bryce winced at how loud it had to be in Corina's ear.

"Calm down. There was a little accident, and Bryce insisted I get a quick checkup, but I'm fine."

"Let me talk to Bryce."

"Dad, I'm *fine*." Irritation slipped back into her tone as she spoke the words yet another time. "I'll give you the details when I get home."

Streetlights loomed ahead of them, marking the outskirts of Cynthiana.

"Corina—"

"We're almost there. I need to go." She ended the call without a good-bye.

Bryce glanced sideways to see her massaging the uninjured side of her forehead.

"He didn't sound happy."

"I forgot I left him a message before I got hit. He'll be okay."

"How'd he know to call Allye's phone?"

"Probably figured she was the most likely person to know where I was and what was going on."

Ironic considering Allye had no idea, but it made sense. The two had been inseparable almost since the day Corina and her dad moved to Kincaid. Actually, it had been the three—or four—of them until . . .

He refused to follow that train of thought. Those days were long gone, but the memories were still painful. Now wasn't the time to revisit them. He took in a deep breath and let it go. Slowly, a muted regret edged out the remnants of his grief.

He couldn't tell if Corina noticed his renewed tension, but she made no effort to pick up the conversation, and they finished the drive without another word.

6

FOR ONCE, there was no line in the emergency room, and they'd been able to take Corina back almost immediately. After the initial paperwork, an examination, and finally x-rays, she was left alone to dress and wait for the verdict. Corina tried not to fidget, but she couldn't help kicking her foot back and forth like a little kid. She wasn't worried. She just didn't like hospitals, and at this point, she only wanted to collapse in bed.

A rap on the door preceded the ER doctor, and Corina stilled her nervous motion. Petite, with curly dark hair, Dr. Sims beamed a too-sunny smile her direction.

"All right, Ms. Roberts, I have good and bad news for you. The good news is, the x-ray showed no definite broken bones, and that bump on your head shouldn't cause you any trouble worse than the headache you already have."

"And the bad news?" She rubbed at her forehead.

"The bad news is your ribs are bruised from the seat belt, and one has a possible hairline fracture. It's difficult with ribs to tell for sure. Either way, they'll heal on their own but will continue to be painful for up to a month, barring further injury. I recommend against lifting anything over five pounds for the next two weeks. If you need an exemption for work, I can take care of that for you."

Corina shook her head and tried to hide a grimace. *Great. Up to a month of this pain? And two weeks without lifting?* The shelves at Western Outfitters would have to be restocked long before then. Gus, her part-time employee, would help, but some of the heavier items were too much for the elderly man. Maybe her dad would be willing to come in a couple of times a week. Or maybe Bryce—not that she wanted him there. The memory of his arms around her invaded her thoughts and brought warmth to her cheeks. *Forget it.*

"—run a much higher risk of contracting pneumonia."

She blinked and pulled her attention back to Dr. Sims's recommendations. She couldn't have missed much. Or maybe she had. What had the doctor said about pneumonia? As Corina tried to recall the beginning of that sentence, Dr. Sims flipped through the papers on her clipboard and pulled off an information sheet. "Here's a reminder list of dos and don'ts."

Corina glanced at the paper as she took it. The first line jumped out at her: *Breathe deeply.* The ache in her chest sharpened at the thought, and she folded the page to read later.

"Do you have any questions?"

"No." She attempted a smile. "Thank you."

"You're very welcome. If you have any abnormal symptoms— shortness of breath, wheezing, fever, anything at all that causes you concern—either contact your primary doctor or come back in here. Don't just let it go." Dr. Sims arched an eyebrow.

"I'll pay attention," Corina promised.

"All right. Let me just get your prescription sent off. What pharmacy do you prefer?"

Corina gave her the information, then waited for a nurse to clear her with final paperwork.

At last, she made it back to the waiting room where she'd left Bryce. She spotted him first. He sat facing the door, magazine in hand, but he didn't appear to be reading.

Her mind flashed back to five years before. Bryce sitting in another waiting room, head in his hands, his mother and Allye next to him. All wrapped in their own grief. Grief she shared. Grief she was responsible for. Grief she couldn't deal with.

She'd walked out, refused to answer his phone calls, and ignored his texts. She hadn't even been able to bring herself to read them. Whether they would have eventually worked things out was a moot point. A week after the funeral, he left town to stay with a cousin and "clear his head," according to Allye. Next thing Corina heard, he'd re-upped—this time opting for active duty rather than the reserves. He shipped out without saying good-bye. And it was for the best in more ways than one.

Bryce stood and walked toward her, and she realized she'd been standing in the hallway, staring. A tear threatened, but she blinked it back. She swallowed the lump in her throat and willed herself to forget. For now.

"You okay?"

"Bruised ribs, possible hairline fracture, a marvelous headache—nothing that won't resolve itself with a little time." She tried to cover the slight tremor in her voice.

Bryce let out a low whistle. "I've dealt with bruised ribs before. Not fun."

"Tell me about it." She held up a hand and brushed past him. "No, don't. I just want to go home."

"Uh, you might want to hang around for a few minutes." Something in his tone warned her she wasn't going to like what he said next.

"Why?"

"Your dad's on the way."

She turned around to glare at him.

Bryce raised his hands in a placating gesture. "Hey, I'm just the messenger. It's not like I could reach through the phone and keep him from getting in the car."

"You could have tried." She knew she wasn't making sense. She didn't really care. "Why didn't you tell him I was fine and to chill?"

"You seriously think I'd tell *your dad* to chill?" His cheek twitched the way it always did when he was trying not to laugh.

She used to think that was cute, but now it made her mad. *Air.* She needed air. Instead of answering Bryce, she beelined toward the exit. She wasn't sure what she'd do when she got outside, but she'd figure it out.

Before she got halfway across the room, her dad burst through the door. One look at the wild expression on his face, and Corina braced herself for the third degree that only a parent with a law enforcement background could give.

"What happened?" He nearly shouted the words, and she felt her shoulders slump in defeat. There would be no leaving until he knew everything. At least the waiting room was empty, so there would be no strangers to witness her interrogation.

She lowered herself into a nearby chair to tell her story for the third—or was it the fourth?—time in the past couple of hours. Weariness was setting in, and both her head and rib cage clamored for relief. But the only way out was to tell him, which she did—as succinctly as possible.

"So as you can see, I'm fine, and the police are looking into it."

"Who took your report?"

"Officer Mike and Eric." Poor guys would probably get grilled for information tonight.

"And the other driver, he never came up beside you?"

"No, he only hit me from the back." A new thought occurred to her. "He never clipped either corner. Every time it was a direct hit, dead center. It's almost like he wanted me to stay on the road," she added slowly. "Even when he pushed me into Eric, it could have just been a ruse to make sure he wouldn't be followed."

"So he was toying with you?" Bryce cut in for the first time. He sounded incredulous and nearly as upset about that possibility as he had been about someone trying to seriously hurt her.

"Maybe." She didn't know what to think. It *could* have been some high school troublemaker trying to give someone a good scare. Of course, whoever it was had inflicted some pretty heavy damage on his own car. She opened her mouth to say so, but a look at her dad's face stopped her. It had drained of all color, and panic-edged shock shone in his eyes.

7

THE BACK OF AN AMBULANCE was larger than she'd imagined. A first responder whose name Corina couldn't remember rechecked the straps securing her to the stretcher. She didn't react when the doors slammed shut, blocking her view of the scene.

The images remained.

The EMT asked her a question, but the words muddled together in her brain. She couldn't summon the energy to even look at him, much less ask him to repeat himself. She let her eyes fall to her lap, her gaze fixing on her hand. The uninjured one. The one still covered in blood.

Blood that wasn't hers.

The ambulance doors opened from the outside, and EMTs wheeled another stretcher in beside her. A sheet covered the face of its occupant.

Panic replaced the numbness in her heart. She tugged at the straps holding her in place and was surprised when they fell right off. She swung her legs to the side. Folded the sheet back with her good arm just enough to see curly red hair framing a boyish face. A face devoid of all color except for the freckles he hated so much. Her gaze flew to the EMTs, seeking assurance that he wasn't dead—he couldn't be dead—but they weren't paying her any attention. Didn't seem to notice her presence at all.

She looked back down. Her breath caught in her throat. Derryck wasn't on the stretcher any longer. Two faces stared up at her. Lifeless faces. Eyes wide open. Lips parted in terror.

She screamed.

Corina bolted upright in bed, adrenaline masking the pain she should have felt at the sudden motion. The ghost of a muffled scream faded into the night as she groped for her revolver.

A moment passed, then two, as she listened for a repeat of the sound, but it didn't come. All she heard was the playlist she'd started before going to bed and Houston's nails clicking on the hardwood floor. Gradually, her breathing slowed, her head cleared, and she became conscious of the pain in her chest and a burning in her throat.

Her throat. She blew out a frustrated breath and set her still-holstered revolver back on the nightstand. It had been her own near-scream that had awakened her. Again. She'd thought she'd kicked the distorted nightmares a couple of years ago, but every once in a while, they popped up like sardonic jack-in-the-boxes at the least provocation, dredging up the grief from Derryck's death and often combining it with the loss of her mom and brother seven years before that. She should have known tonight's accident and ER visit would be a trigger.

She cradled her left arm against her body. The double fractures in the humerus had long since healed, but it always ached after that nightmare. It nearly rivaled the pain from tonight's injury. But it was nothing compared to the ache in her heart.

Her composure crumbled, and she bit back a dry sob. Houston nudged her hand, whining his sympathy at her grief.

"Up," she choked out, patting the mattress next to her. Houston jumped onto the bed and lay beside her, muzzle between his paws as if he didn't want to overcrowd her.

She twined her fingers in his fur and stared at the ceiling. *God, why didn't you care? Derryck was just a kid, but he loved you. So did*

Mama and Colton. Why couldn't you protect them? Why wouldn't *you protect them?*

She caught herself before she went any further. The prayer was more an old habit than anything. She didn't expect an answer from the heavens any more than she expected Houston to develop a friendship with the raccoon prowling the neighborhood.

Wasn't going to happen.

8

SEVERAL HOURS LATER, Corina stood before her bedroom mirror, examining her visible injuries from the night before. The goose egg on her forehead had receded, but the area was still discolored. Not as much as her rib cage, though. Blues and purples abounded.

She touched one of the areas and grimaced. It could have been much worse. Had God been protecting her last night? She wasn't sure he cared enough to have gotten involved.

She'd like to believe it, but she just couldn't quite wrap her mind around the idea. Oh sure, she still believed in God. In fact, she'd clung to him as a teenager when her mom and brother were murdered. She'd found some comfort in that childlike faith. But when tragedy hit again with Derryck's death, ripping open all the old wounds and adding more, she hadn't found any comfort.

She'd prayed over and over in those first few weeks—begged, even—for him to make the pain stop. To wake her from the nightmare that had become her life. But none of it was a nightmare. Everything was real. Her mom was gone. Colton was gone. Derryck was gone. And, effectively, so was Bryce.

Her prayers had been met with silence, and once she'd gotten through the initial grief, she'd accepted that was for the best. After all, the past couldn't be changed, and there was no explanation that would make everything all right again. God apparently didn't care enough to protect her heart, so she'd have to do it herself.

Even now, the thought filled her with a sadness she couldn't explain.

But now wasn't the time to deal with that. She shook her head, irritating the lingering headache and the knots in her neck and shoulders.

Turning away from the mirror, she selected an outfit that wouldn't require too much maneuvering to get into. Her customers would have to be content with casual clothes today.

She grabbed the jacket she'd worn last night and slipped it on. She wouldn't leave for a while yet, but she was cold. It had to be midsixties in here. For a born-and-bred Texan, her dad never did keep the house warm enough.

As she stepped out of her bedroom, his voice filtered down the hallway. She jumped when something—probably his fist—struck the table and rattled dishes.

"Are you positive?" Silence. "I don't like it, Mike. It's too much like what happened in Texas. And with that bottle—" He lowered his voice, causing her to miss the next few sentences.

She crept toward the kitchen. What was he talking about? Her dad rarely talked about their home state—and never to anyone but her. She stopped just outside the doorway. His back was to her, and she wasn't sure yet if she wanted him to know she was listening.

". . . might be coincidence, but it feels off." Another pause, longer this time. "Let me know if you get anything else. . . . Yeah, thanks." The phone clattered onto the table, and her dad shoved both hands into his still thick but now totally gray hair. He didn't seem to hear her as she walked up beside him.

"What was that about?"

He started. "They found the vehicle from last night."

"And?"

"And it was an SUV like you thought. Apparently, the driver

stole it from Bud's Auto right before the accident, then abandoned it after the collision."

That explained the burnt-out streetlight. Or had her attacker merely taken advantage of an already dimly lit area? Either way, Houston had noticed his presence. How long had they been watched? Western Outfitters' picture windows were great for attracting customers, but they didn't offer much privacy to anyone in the front room. She shivered and crossed her arms over her chest, barely remembering her injuries in time to avoid contact with the bruised area.

Her dad finally turned to face her. "Mike said the inside of the vehicle reeked of alcohol. Could the driver have been drunk, you think?"

She chewed on her lip as she considered that. "That could explain the tailgating and multiple hits, but he wasn't weaving at all, and his retreat wasn't sloppy. After he rammed me into Eric, he backed up and made a controlled turn onto a side street." She shrugged. "It's possible, I guess, but I don't think so."

Her dad didn't answer immediately. She could almost see his brain processing the information.

"Were there any other clues? Prints?" she prodded.

"Lots of prints. Just no helpful ones." Disgust laced his words. "No matches in the database. The police suspect most of them belong to the mechanics at Bud's. They're working on a comparison there."

"And he didn't leave anything behind?"

"An empty whiskey bottle on the floorboard. Printless."

"It was chilly last night. He could have been wearing gloves," she offered.

"Maybe." He grimaced. "If that's the case, none of the other prints are likely to be his." He lapsed into silence, his fingers drumming a slow beat on the tabletop.

She studied his face. Something in his expression bothered her, and it was more than concern over a hit-and-run or a reckless prankster. Her dad was afraid. Last night, she could have attributed it to the immediate danger of the situation. Today, she might have expected him to be frustrated—angry, even—but not still afraid.

And he'd mentioned Texas. A chill ran through her as she remembered his reaction to Bryce's speculation last night. It was exactly how he'd acted the day they left her childhood home twelve years ago. After her mother and brother had been killed in an armed burglary when she was thirteen, her dad had gotten understandably overprotective. But it wasn't until a month later that he'd snapped. He'd come home, gone through the mail, and got that wild expression on his face. Within a couple of hours, they had packed everything they could into the back of his pickup and simply left in the dead of night. No good-byes. No last graveside visit.

They'd never been back.

And he'd been paranoid ever since.

Corina watched in silence as he peered through the closest window, then tightened the blinds and closed curtains he probably hadn't touched in months. Then he walked down the hallway to the alarm box, verifying it was armed. Her niggling feeling of dread grew stronger with every action. This was exactly how he'd been those first three or four months after they moved. Always looking over his shoulder, checking the rearview mirrors, scanning the windows.

Something had triggered a drastic reaction in him that day so many years ago—something more than the hounding news media or bad memories he used to blame. No, something else had happened, and she was willing to bet that something was back.

"What's bugging you, Dad?" she asked as he reentered the kitchen. He set his jaw and busied himself filling the coffee maker. A faint tremble marked his usually steady hands, and some of the water sloshed onto the counter. He didn't seem to notice.

She waited, but when he still didn't answer, she moved in

front of him, arresting his gaze with her own. "What aren't you telling me?"

His shoulders drooped. He opened his mouth. Shut it. Shook his head. "I don't know yet."

"You don't know, or you won't say?"

Again, he didn't answer, but the agony in his gaze tore at her, pleaded with her to trust him. And that scared her.

"Dad?"

"I just need to think some things through." He reached over her head and pulled two mugs from the cabinet, offering one to her. "You want a cup?" He forced lightness into his tone with the last sentence. A total redirection of the conversation and mood. Typical Will Roberts avoidance.

That ploy more than anything else told her he knew more than he was willing to admit.

Her concern turned to irritation, and she set the cup firmly on the counter. "No, I don't want coffee. I want to know what's going on."

He released a sigh and placed his hands on her shoulders. Her bruises screamed at the touch, but she refused to wince. She wouldn't give him any excuse to change the subject again.

"Corina, I'm probably overreacting to the accident last night. You're all I've got left, and I can't stand the thought of someone intentionally hurting you." A miserable attempt at a smile crossed his face. "Just do your best not to go out alone for a while—for my peace of mind."

She held his gaze for a moment longer, then gave a terse nod.

Nothing else was said as he poured coffee for them both and flipped on the morning news.

Corina's eyes flicked between the screen and her dad's profile. The anchorman droned on, but his words were lost on her. She could read her dad better than anyone else. There was more to last night's incident than he was letting on. And he knew exactly what it was.

9

BACK IN HER OLD BEDROOM, Corina checked her watch. Nearly seven. Two hours until she needed to open the store. Two hours she could use to do some snooping—after her dad left, of course.

"Corina." Her dad's voice outside the door startled her.

"Yes?"

"Do you need me to take you to work, or are you going to take the day off today?"

Why would she need him to—*Oh*. Her truck. She grimaced. The front end had fared tolerably well compared with Eric's trunk, but the back end was another story. Her taillights were practically nonexistent, the bumper completely gone, and the bed visibly out of line—and that was just the damage she could easily see last night when her dad drove by after they left the ER. The poor vehicle might not be long for this world, though she was hoping that wouldn't be the case. Regardless, it definitely wasn't drivable at the moment.

But if she let her dad take her, she'd have no time to investigate things here. She pursed her lips and moved toward the window. She split the blinds with her finger. A few lights were on in Bryce's house across the street, and his Camaro was parked out front.

"Corina?"

She let the blinds close. "No, thanks. I'll catch a ride with someone later." Hopefully she'd be able to get ahold of Allye or Gus, but if she had to, she'd call Bryce.

"Okay. Take it easy, and take Houston with you." The German shepherd perked his ears at the mention of his name. "Call me *before* you head home tonight." No missing the emphasis there.

"Got it. Bye, Dad."

"Good-bye." He cleared his throat. "I love you."

She sighed and glanced over her shoulder at the closed door. "Love you too."

The sound of his footsteps faded, and barely five minutes later, the front door signaled his exit. She was alone. Well, except for Houston, who had already curled up in his favorite spot beside the bed. For the first time, the lack of human companionship left her feeling uneasy. She pushed the sensation away. Whatever was going on, she was safe here.

"Right, boy?"

He snuffled and tugged at her comforter until it fell on top of him. Hands on her hips, she glared at him until his head reappeared, but as soon as their eyes met, he ducked back under. She shook her head. "Fine, then."

Leaving Houston in his cocoon, she headed for her dad's home office. Her mother's cuckoo clock signaled the top of the hour as she pushed open the door. There was plenty of time to search.

Her hand faltered over the light switch. What exactly was she searching for? She didn't have much to go on. It wasn't like her dad would have a file box labeled "The Real Reason We Left Texas." Was she seriously about to invade his privacy on the hunch that he was keeping something from her?

She thought back over his behavior last night and this morning. It wasn't normal. Maybe for when they'd first left Texas, but not for any time in the last decade or so. She straightened her shoulders and flipped the lights on. There had to be something he was hiding. And if it had to do with her safety, then she had a right to know.

A knock at the door interrupted her thoughts.

Startled, she slapped the lights back off and yanked the office door closed. Snooping was one thing. Getting caught doing it was another. She quickly moved to disarm the alarm system so she could answer the door, but her brain caught up to her hands, and she stilled. Who was out there this early? If her dad had forgotten something and had to come back, he would have called first, and he wouldn't have knocked. No one else would have a reason to visit at this time of day.

She dropped her hand and stopped to listen, but the knocking wasn't repeated. In fact, no sound came from the front porch. She edged toward the door to check the peephole. Nothing. Unease reclaimed its place in her stomach. The memory of yesterday's hectic beginning flew through her mind. Only this time, she was alone, and a hungry raccoon wouldn't knock to announce his presence.

She wasn't about to open the door to someone who was trying not to be seen, but she didn't want to ignore it either. And she couldn't check the security cameras quickly since she'd recently upgraded phones and didn't have her dad's account information saved anymore. Without thinking, she settled her hand over the weapon in her pocket. Something crinkled.

Focus still on the door, she pulled out the slip of paper and glanced at it. Bryce's number. He'd scribbled it down for her last night. She'd fully intended to toss it when she got home but had forgotten about it.

Should she call him? He'd given her an open invitation to contact him if she needed anything. Or if something else happened.

She bit her lip and took a few steps back from the door, tugging her phone from another pocket. She dialed the number. It rang twice. Three times. She hoped she wasn't waking him—no, there had been lights on when she looked out a few minutes ago.

"Hello."

Nerves assaulted her at the sound of his voice, but it was too late to back out now. "Bryce? This is Corina."

"Hey. I didn't expect to hear from you so soon." Was that a hint of teasing in his voice? Doubtful. He probably hadn't expected to hear from her at all.

"I need a favor. Someone knocked on my door, but I can't see anyone through the peephole. Do you mind looking out a window to see if anybody's there and hiding?" She closed her eyes, hating how paranoid she sounded. "I'm sorry, but after everything yesterday—"

"No problem." All traces of levity were gone from his voice. Something creaked in the background, then all she could hear were muffled footsteps.

BRYCE CRACKED THE BLINDS on his front door. Corina's porch was empty, as were the driveway and the yard. He stepped outside and looked up and down the street. The neighborhood was quiet. Not even a passing car broke the stillness.

"Well?"

"I don't see anyone."

"Someone knocked. I didn't imagine it."

"I didn't say you did." He swung his gaze back to her porch, and something caught his eye. "Hold on. There's something on your door. Give me a sec, and I'll check it out." He ended the call and slipped the phone into his pocket.

When he was barely halfway across the street, Corina's door opened. So much for waiting on him. She gave him a halfhearted wave, then turned to what he could now see was a small envelope taped just above the doorknob. He quickened his steps as she tore it open. Her expression gave no indication of the contents.

He took the porch steps in one bound. "What is it?"

"A warning, I think."

"You think? What does it say?"

"'Consider yesterday a preview.'" She handed the note to him. "That's it. No signature, no explanation, no 'ha-ha.'"

"It could be from whoever rear-ended you last night. You should probably call it in to the police." He turned it over. The back was blank, those four words the sole contents of the page.

"No."

His head snapped up. "Why not?"

"Because leaving notes isn't a crime."

"It is if they threaten violence."

"I don't even know for sure what the reference is. It may have nothing to do with the wreck." He held her gaze, and she lifted her chin. "Besides, I have things I need to do before I open the shop. I don't have the time or energy to fill out another police report right now."

He returned the note to her. "Suit yourself, then. But call me immediately if anything else happens—and I mean *anything*." He didn't believe for a moment that the note was less than a threat that should be reported. But Corina had made up her mind, and from the set of her jaw, she would be impossible to convince otherwise. He turned to leave.

"Hey." The hand she placed on his wrist sent tingles up to his shoulder. How could her touch still do that?

He turned back to face her. "Yeah?"

"Thanks for checking things out—and for coming last night." She chewed on her bottom lip as if considering her next words. "Would you, um, like to come in for coffee?"

The invitation surprised him. He'd been expecting more of a "Thanks for your concern, but you can exit my life now."

Coffee sounded much better.

He smiled. "Coffee would be great."

Corina led the way inside, tossing the note into a small garbage can. He fished it out and slid it into his pocket to examine later.

As he followed her down the hall, Houston emerged from a side room. "Hey, fella." He stooped to ruffle the fur behind the dog's ears, earning himself a slobbery greeting. Wiping his hand on his jeans, he looked up to see that Corina hadn't stopped. "Come on, or she'll leave us behind."

"You better believe I will," Corina called over her shoulder.

He grinned down at Houston. "You heard the lady."

The kitchen was just as he remembered it, but then again, it hadn't changed in the years before he'd left town either. Will and Corina weren't the kind of people to change things for the sake of change.

Well, not normally, anyway. Their move from Texas to Kentucky was a notable exception. He'd once asked why they moved, and the only reason Corina had given him was that her dad thought they needed a change. The explanation had sounded lame even then.

He leaned back against the corner counter and watched Corina dump the remains of an old pot down the drain.

"You still prefer dark roast?" she asked, already reaching for the canister.

"Yes, ma'am." He shouldn't be surprised she remembered, but he was.

While the coffee brewed, Corina tapped her fingers on the countertop. She had a faraway look in her eyes. If he didn't know better, he would think she'd forgotten he was there.

He cleared his throat. "I hope I'm not keeping you from whatever you were needing to get done."

She started, and her cheeks flushed as she met his eyes for a brief second. "No, it's fine." She looked as if he'd caught her at something. "I was just . . ." Her voice trailed off.

"You don't have to explain." Except now he was curious.

She sighed and focused her gaze on the liquid gold dripping into the coffeepot. "I can tell you—just don't make fun of me."

"Never." He crossed his heart and lifted his hand in a scout's salute.

She took a deep breath, and he didn't miss the wince she tried to hide. "Well, you saw my dad last night."

He sure had. Will had freaked. Sure, the guy was known to overreact, but last night was something more.

"This morning we got an update from the police. They found the vehicle that hit me, but it was stolen, and the driver didn't seem to leave much evidence behind."

"Nothing?"

"They're still checking out the fingerprints, but it doesn't look promising."

"And he didn't take that well."

"No." She poured them each a cup of coffee and circled Houston to get to the table. "He knows something about what happened last night, and it's got him scared—scared like he was when we left Texas. I even overheard him mention something about Texas when he didn't know I was listening. But when I pressed him for answers, he clammed up." She added sugar and a hefty amount of cream to her mug.

Bryce left his black. "What are you going to do?"

"Go through the files in his study. See if anything catches my eye. If he won't tell me what's going on, I'm going to have to find out on my own—one way or another."

"Would you like some help?"

Her forehead wrinkled. "I don't even know what I'm looking for."

"Come on, I can look aimlessly just as well as you can." He tried to sound offended but couldn't completely hide his smile. "We could even call Allye over. It would be like old times."

10

YEAH. OLD TIMES. Except back then Bryce and Allye's little brother, Derryck, would likely have tagged along too. A lump formed in her throat, and she fought it down with a mouthful of coffee still a bit too hot despite the amount of cream she'd added.

"Well? How about it?" Bryce's voice was softer, as if his thoughts had taken the same turn hers had.

"I don't want to put you out." Ignoring the burn, she drained her mug and placed it in the sink. "Besides, don't you think Allye's still asleep?" Unless she had an appointment or photo shoot scheduled, Allye wasn't likely to be up for another couple of hours. She claimed to be more productive in the evening and did most of the touch-up work for her photography business then.

"I don't mind, and you know Allye as well as I do. She'd rather be woken up than left out."

True enough. "Fine, if you want to try, go for it." She pinned Bryce with a meaningful look. "But *you're* the one making the call. I refuse to wake the grizzly."

He laughed. "You've got a deal."

Leaving Bryce to contact his sister, Corina went to the office. Any document her dad deemed even slightly important would be in this room. Exactly where he'd keep it was the question. Her eyes fell to the most logical place—the filing cabinet to the right of his desk. She pulled open the top drawer. Unlabeled and totally packed with papers and folders. Such a contrast to the orderly system her dad had once employed. The other drawers were the same way. She released a sigh, dreading the time this was going to take.

A few minutes later, Bryce's footsteps sounded on the hardwood of the hallway. "Allye said she'd be here in a couple minutes." He stopped at the doorway, surveying the room with undisguised curiosity. "Wow."

"You've never been in here, have you?"

"Nope."

Not surprising. Her dad usually kept the door closed. She glanced around, viewing the room as a newcomer would. Six-foot bookshelves lined the back wall, every available space filled with a variety of new and old volumes. Old family portraits and her school pictures hung neatly across the two adjoining walls. The massive oak desk her dad had found in an antique shop dominated the center of the room. The top of the desk was immaculate, holding a single notebook and pen lined up carefully in one corner, but she had a feeling the drawers were as disorganized as the filing cabinet seemed to be.

One thing at a time.

Still, she took a moment to flip through the notebook. Most of it seemed to be work-related, but in the back was a handful of account names and passwords. She spotted the log-in info for his security system account. Once they were done in here, she could check the footage from earlier and see who had left the note on the door.

"Do you have a method for this?" Bryce asked.

"Sort of. I figure we can start at the top and work our way down." She pulled an armful from the front of the drawer and plopped it onto the desk.

Bryce followed her lead, settling his stack on the floor in an empty corner. "Sounds promising."

"Not the word I'd have chosen." She straightened her stack of files. "What did you tell Allye?"

"Just that we were working on a project and needed help. After grumbling about working during reasonable hours, she agreed to come."

"Told you it was too early for her."

"And I told you she'd come anyway." Bryce chuckled, and she felt her own lips tipping upward. They both knew Allye wouldn't consider not being involved.

"Well, I'm going to go ahead and get started." She opened the first folder and found product manuals and hand-scribbled notes.

Great. The only way to determine what had value and what didn't would be to go through it all. She dug in, wrinkling her nose as she pulled apart two booklets that were stuck together. Ugh. Whatever her dad had spilled on the Crock-Pot book was still gummy. She set it aside and tried not to think about which meal that had come from.

About fifteen minutes passed before they heard a knock at the door.

Bryce stood. "That should be Allye. I'll get it."

"Thanks."

He reappeared a moment later, Allye behind him carrying a purse, camera case, and an extra catch-all bag in one hand and a monstrous cup of something—probably highly caffeinated tea—in the other.

"All right, the party can start now." Allye's words were chipper enough, but her eyes said she needed a few more hours of sleep.

Guilt twinged through Corina. "I'm sorry we got you up."

"Nonsense. I have this." She held up her mug and let the bags slide unceremoniously to the floor. "I'll be fine. So what is this project Bryce mentioned?" Her glasses slid down on her nose, and she pushed them back into place with a practiced motion.

"We're going through my dad's files. He knows—or suspects— something about what happened last night, but he's not talking, so we're trying to figure it out ourselves." She pointed to the papers splayed in front of her.

"Hold up. What happened last night?" Allye's gaze darted between them, and Corina moaned. She'd forgotten Allye didn't know.

Bryce headed for the door. "I'm going to grab a water. I'll be right back."

"Thanks a lot."

Allye put her hands on her hips and raised her eyebrows. "Well?"

As briefly as possible, she ran through the details, purposely omitting the part about her injuries.

"Why didn't you call me?"

"Bryce had your phone."

"He didn't say anything when he dropped it off last night."

She sighed. "There wasn't anything you could do." Other than keep her from getting any actual rest. Allye was a regular mother hen.

"Next time, let me know anyway."

"I don't plan on there being a next time." She opened a folder to find receipts of some kind. Important or not? She sighed and set it aside. "I'm starting to wonder if my dad has ever organized this, or if he just threw anything remotely important in the front of the drawer as it accumulated."

Allye dug through one of her bags and unearthed a hair tie. "Do you have any idea at all what we're looking for?" she asked as she whisked her coppery mane into a ponytail.

"Dad mentioned Texas when he was on the phone with Officer Mike. I got the feeling that whatever he's upset about is connected to something that happened there, probably right before we left. I'm just looking for anything from that time period."

Allye watched her for a minute, then leaned in close, eyes sparkling. "I didn't realize you two"—she nodded over her shoulder—"were on speaking terms. Bryce didn't let on at dinner last night."

Corina stole a glance at the door to make sure he was still gone. "Don't read too much into it." She matched Allye's low tone.

"Me? Never."

Sure she wouldn't. If anyone had a matchmaker's heart, it was Allye, and she wasn't shy about putting her "talents" to use. Even while grieving her own little brother's death, she'd been adamant that Bryce and Corina could work things out. Apparently she'd never stopped hoping.

"Seriously, Allye, I didn't even know he was back in town until yesterday. He's just been helping me with a few things."

"Mm-hmm." Allye practically skipped to the cabinet to pull out her own stack of folders.

Corina rolled her eyes and tossed a crumpled envelope at her friend. Let her think what she wanted, but things were over between her and Bryce. Over. Done. Dead. And she wasn't going to resurrect them. Even if she was enjoying his company.

Kind of.

She followed him with her eyes as he reentered the room and settled in.

After a few seconds, he looked up. "You all right over there?"

Caught. "I'm just . . ." She fumbled with the pages as heat rose in her cheeks. "Thinking."

He nodded and turned his attention to the stack in front of him. She'd better do the same.

And she did for the next hour. Occasionally, Allye or Bryce would offer her a file for inspection, but they mostly worked in silence. As they neared the back of the bottom drawer, Corina began to accept that they were not going to find anything today. Not here, anyhow. Perhaps the desk would prove more promising.

"This is a dead end." She heaved a sigh and closed the folder she held.

"Maybe so, but there's still one left." Allye reached for it. "Hmm . . . It's caught on something."

"Let me try." Corina knelt before the drawer and gave a soft tug on the folder. One corner refused to budge. The folder looked older and was made a bit differently from the others. Afraid she might rip it, she felt around the offending edge with her fingertips. The hanger was lodged in the drawer's sliding mechanism. She tried to shut the drawer to see if the file would dislodge itself, but the jam didn't give.

She rocked back on her heels and glanced up at Allye. "The last folder would be the one to give us trouble."

"Naturally."

"I wonder if the whole thing will come out without causing any damage." Corina studied the drawer as she spoke. "One way to find out, I guess." She positioned her hands with one under the drawer to support it and the other wrapped around the upper edge. An upward-and-outward tug had the drawer, and the folder, free.

Her heartbeat quickened, then slowed as she opened the file and scanned the few pages contained in it. Her shoulders drooped. It was a dead end. The pages staring up at her were nothing more than the family birth certificates and her parents' marriage license.

"So much for the filing cabinet," she whispered, unable to hide her disappointment. She wasn't sure what she was looking for, but birth and marriage records were not on the list.

"Maybe, maybe not." The tone of Bryce's voice brought her head up. He was reaching into the space left vacant by the drawer. "The base has a hollow center." He looked a bit smug as he pulled out a black case. "Wouldn't you say this is something out of the ordinary?"

11

CORINA STARED AT THE BOX. It was only a few inches deep, but it appeared to be about the right size to hold legal documents.

Allye reached for it and tried the top. "It's locked. Looks like a miniature fireproof safe." She passed it over for Corina to examine.

"Would he have left the key in here?" Bryce asked.

"I don't know." The keyhole was circular. It would be easy to distinguish the proper key from any others they might turn up. Unfortunately, she couldn't recall having ever seen one like it.

She shook the case. It didn't make a sound. It must either be empty or crammed full. Probably the latter, judging by its weight. Not to mention the hiding place. She set it aside for the moment.

Corina tried to think like her father. If he left the key in here, she didn't expect him to keep it in an obvious place like the desk drawers. Still, she checked them anyway while Bryce flipped through the keys hanging just inside the door, and Allye went to check the junk drawer in the kitchen. The desk was in slightly better shape than the filing cabinet—still messy but with some semblance of organization. Making a mental note of a drawer with yet more documents to go through, Corina closed the last one and blew out a breath. No key.

She turned her back to the desk and scanned the room. Her dad was tall, so maybe on top of the bookshelves lining the back wall? Worth a try.

She climbed atop his computer chair for a better look. And lost her balance when it swiveled. Throwing out an arm, she managed to latch onto one of the shelves. A sharp cry forced its way through her lips. The reflex had saved her from a nasty fall, but the pain from the sudden motion was excruciating.

"What are you doing?" Bryce was at her side in an instant, helping her down.

She blinked away unbidden tears as she lowered herself to the floor, arm clutching her chest. "That wasn't such a good idea," she muttered through clenched teeth.

"No, it wasn't." The words were brusque, but she could tell from his tone that she'd scared him.

"Are you all right?" Allye's voice sounded from the doorway.

Biting back frustration, Corina waved away the concern. "I have bruised ribs from last night. Nothing that won't heal on its own, but I'm supposed to be taking it easy." She forced herself to take slow, shallow breaths to minimize the pain.

"And you're doing acrobatics?"

"Not exactly on my list of approved activities."

"I would say not." The worried expression didn't fade from her friend's face. "Have you taken anything for it recently?"

She shook her head.

"Did they prescribe anything?"

"Ibuprofen. It's on my dresser," she added, anticipating the next question. Without another word, Allye went to retrieve it, leaving Bryce standing over her. "Stop looking at me like that. I won't disintegrate." She squeezed her eyes shut, counted to three, then looked back at him. "Sorry for growling. I just need a minute."

"Take all the time you need." He turned away to renew his search, but not before she caught a glimpse of some unreadable emotion in his eyes. Something that made her wish she hadn't been quite so quick to insist she didn't need him.

She didn't, though.

Couldn't.

And she wasn't going to think about it. Corina forced her mind to return to the locked box and missing key. Where would her dad have hidden an oddly shaped key? She hadn't gotten a good look at the tops of the bookshelves, but nothing had caught her eye. She let her gaze travel slowly back over the room.

A photograph from her parents' wedding snagged her attention. A picturesque outdoor scene with her parents in the forefront and a cozy chapel in the background. The joy on their faces brought fresh tears to her own eyes. *I wish you were here, Mama.*

She studied the portrait. After their move to Kentucky, her dad had replaced the old gilt-edged frame with a bold, more modern style one. Layered turquoise and gray matting provided an exaggerated depth to the portrait's setting, making the entire thing nearly the same thickness as a shadow box.

A shadow box. She cocked her head. The frame was deep enough to hide something in. Would he have? Curiosity aroused, she gripped the edge of the desk to rise to her feet, gritting her teeth against the pain that hadn't yet subsided. Hopefully that wasn't a bad sign.

"What are you doing?"

She turned to find Allye in the doorway with a bottled water and the prescription vial.

She glanced again at the photo. "I want to check out that frame."

"Sit." Allye pointed to the chair.

"But—"

"No buts. You've already done too much." She set the bottles down and gently guided Corina to the chair. "Take the ibuprofen. Bryce will get the picture."

Seeing he was already moving toward it, she sank reluctantly into the seat and reached for the tablets. She shook one into her hand and stared at it with distaste.

"Just do it," Allye called over her shoulder.

She rolled her eyes and popped the pill into her mouth. The water washed it down almost painlessly. Almost. She made a face. "There. Happy?"

"For the moment." As soon as Bryce placed the picture face down on the desk, Allye nudged him aside and began to bend the flexible points holding the backing in place. She gingerly pulled the backing away, revealing the mounting board beneath it. She pursed her lips and slid a fingernail under the edge to pry it loose.

"Bingo." Allye gently set the photograph aside and tilted the frame so Corina could see it better. A hole was cut in the bottom corner of the matting, and a key rested inside the hollow. "Look, he cut through all but the front layer. You can't tell from the outside that anything is there." She tugged the key free and offered it to Corina.

Its circular shape and hollow center looked as if it would fit. She tested it in the lock and felt her nerves return when the soft click met her ears.

Folders full of papers greeted her as she lifted the lid. She caught her breath at the label on the topmost: *Case Notes—Elaine and Colton Mathis.*

"WHO ARE THEY?" Bryce didn't know how to interpret the look Allye shot him. Why would Corina's dad hide old case notes? And why did both women seem to recognize the names?

Corina's eyes never left the stack of folders, but her voice dropped to a pained whisper. "My mom and brother."

Oh. Big oh.

He knew the basic story—how her mom and seven-year-old brother, Colton, had been killed in an armed burglary, but *Mathis?*

"Were your parents divorced?" That was news to him. And not the most sensitive question to ask, judging by Allye's eye roll and mouthed *Shut up*.

"No, Mathis is—was—our last name. Dad changed it to Roberts when we moved." Still staring at the folder, Corina spoke the words matter-of-factly, as if she were talking about someone else. But then she glanced at him, and the haunted look in her eyes nearly did him in. She withdrew the case file with a trembling hand. "He said he didn't want the publicity following us, so he had it changed. He wouldn't let me talk about it."

Publicity? He opened his mouth, but before he could get anything out, Allye had closed the space between them and was digging her thumb and forefinger into his arm. "Hey!" He jerked free and met her warning stare with one of his own.

Corina didn't seem to notice the interruption. "It was a hot story. Similar to some other recent break-ins, only no one was home at the other houses. They never found out who did it." She traced a finger along the edge of the still-unopened folder. "I didn't know Dad had these."

"Do you need some time?" Allye asked before Bryce could say anything else.

"No. Yes." Corina pushed the safe toward them and stood. "You two go through the rest if you want. I'll be back in a few minutes."

Bryce frowned as she made her way to the door, one hand clutching the murder file, the other held protectively across her chest.

Allye waited until Corina was out of earshot before voicing her opinion of his questions. "That was smooth."

"How was I supposed to know?" He yanked a folder from the miniature safe. At one time, he'd thought he knew just about everything about Corina. *Everything except the fact that her last name isn't her last name.* Yeah. Little details. He turned toward his sister. "You knew?" He couldn't believe Allye would have kept that kind of secret—not from him, anyway.

"Not until a few months ago. At Western Outfitters' grand opening, Corina made a dedication to her mom and brother. It was mentioned in the paper, and there's a plaque hanging over the register. I *discreetly*"—she waved a folder his direction—"gathered enough details later to figure it out."

He rolled his eyes. At least she'd had something to go on. He'd been paying too much attention to the store itself to notice the plaque when he was in there yesterday. Okay, the store *and* its owner. Definitely not something to share with his sister.

Still irritated, he flipped open his folder and paced with it. Looked like another murder file. He glanced at the front again for the victim's name. Alan White.

CORINA SAT CROSS-LEGGED on her bed, the case file in her lap. Now Bryce knew their big secret—not that it really mattered anymore. After twelve years, there was no publicity to run from. Hopefully, he'd understand. If he didn't, it was his problem. She dug her teeth into her lower lip. That might be best anyway. Maybe he wouldn't try to renew their friendship if he was angry. It would save her a lot of trouble.

She stared at the file. Judging by the thickness, it held far more details than her dad had ever shared with her. She couldn't totally blame him for that—after all, she had been only thirteen when it happened, and the murders had devastated them both. They rarely talked about it, even now. But she had always wondered exactly what happened. What kind of clues had been left. What progress the investigators made. Why it had eventually been declared a cold case.

Now that she had at least some of the answers available, she was almost afraid to find out.

Distraction came in the form of a scratching at the closed door. A low whine met her ears.

"Hold on, Houston."

The scratching continued. It was let him in now or listen to him complain until she did.

"Coming. Coming." She slid the folder off her lap and stood, stifling a groan. The ibuprofen hadn't quite kicked in yet. She stood to the side of the door as she opened it. Houston entered, sniffed her leg, circled the room, and went back the way he came. *Really?* She pursed her lips and sat back down, this time leaving the door cracked in case he changed his mind again.

She glanced from the folder she'd set aside to her alarm clock. Eight twenty-five. Almost time to head to the shop. Did she have time to read the file, get ready, and get there in time?

If you quit stalling, you will. She needed to do this. Face this. Otherwise, she'd struggle to focus on anything else today.

Sighing, she opened it and scanned the first couple of paragraphs. She straightened. Read them again.

This wasn't the account of a burglary gone wrong. She flipped through the pages until she reached a series of photographs. Her stomach constricted, but she couldn't look away from the gruesome images. By the time she reached the last, a lump the size of Houston's tennis ball had settled in her throat, and her morning coffee threatened to revisit.

Good luck making it past the tennis ball.

She acknowledged the thought as illogical, then dismissed it. She probably should be hurling her guts out. But she wasn't. Should be slamming the folder shut on the crime scene photos. But she couldn't move. Couldn't get past the shock of what she was seeing. Being told about a murder as a child was one thing— seeing it in gory detail . . .

Eventually, someone calling her name pulled her from the fog.

"Corina?" Allye tapped on her door, then pushed inside without waiting for an answer. "We found something you need to see."

She tore her eyes from the picture in front of her. "What?" Her mind felt numb, barely able to form the one-word question.

Silently, her friend extended another folder to her, and a deeper sense of dread settled in her midsection. As Allye released her hold, the name on the label registered. Her name.

"Read the first page." Allye sank down beside her.

Mechanically, she turned back the cover. As the words sank in, her vision began to blur and a tingling sensation crept up her arms.

12

A SERIAL-KILLER STALKER? Corina struggled to wrap her mind around the idea as she reentered her dad's office after calling Gus and asking him to handle the store opening today. She'd go in this afternoon—or sooner if he needed her—but right now, she had to get answers. Had to get a handle on what really happened in her past and whether it had anything to do with her dad's reaction to last night.

A serial-killer stalker. Or was that just a serial killer? She shook her head. Not important.

What mattered was why her dad hadn't ever told her. Yes, he'd said they needed to get away, but she'd never dreamed he meant it literally.

She dialed his number again. She'd lost track of how many times she'd called in the last thirty minutes. This time it went straight to voice mail. He never ignored her like this. She waited for the beep and left another message.

"Dad? I really need to talk to you. Now. Call me."

She hung up and tossed her phone on the desk. Sinking into the oversized chair, she pressed a hand against her eyes as long-dormant memories intruded on her consciousness.

Mama turning pale after a phone call, then laughing nervously and avoiding the question when asked who was on the line. Dad reminding them what to do if anyone ever tried to break in. Mama rushing into the house and locking the door behind her. Dad constantly looking over his shoulder, tensing when the same pair of headlights followed them for too long.

She had noticed but never put the pieces together. Now everything made sense. The fear, the overprotectiveness, the name change and spontaneous cross-country move with a lengthy detour before they arrived at their destination.

Grief she thought she'd dealt with years before rushed back at her. Its strength surprised her, as did the accompanying anger. What she'd once processed as a random, perhaps even unintentional, shooting had really been a carefully planned attack.

And she was supposed to be the next victim.

Little wonder her dad had freaked out about last night's assault. Could it have been unrelated, or was it connected to their past? Surely that wasn't possible. Was it?

Bryce pulled an extra chair next to hers. "Hey, you okay?"

"Yeah, sure. I love being lied to and finding out I used to be on a killer's most-wanted list." She cast an accusing glare at her still-silent phone. Her dad had a lot of explaining to do. After she lambasted him.

"What are you going to do?"

"Do?"

"You might want to consider the possibility that you're still on that list."

"I am considering it." Sort of. "But I'm not going to overreact to a *possibility*. I don't have all the information." And she couldn't bring herself to read the rest of the file just yet.

A chill crept up her spine at the thought of being tracked down after all this time. Surely after a dozen years the murderer had either given up or been caught in some other crime. Even if he was free and had somehow stumbled across them, would he still hold a grudge he was willing to kill for?

Maybe. But the crime scene photos didn't look like the work of a halfhearted killer. She blinked, refusing to allow those images to suck her back into a black hole. Had Bryce seen them? She wasn't sure where the folder had gone after Allye tugged it from her fingers.

"Did Allye tell you what we found in the other files?"

She shook her head. She wasn't sure she wanted to know.

"Do you recognize the names Alan and Miriam White?"

"Yes, Alan is my dad's stepbrother, and he worked for Dad's private investigation business. Well, until a couple of months before . . ." Before her mom and Colton were killed. She swallowed back the nausea that followed an attempt to say the words. "He and my dad had a fight, and Alan decided to go into business for himself, so he and Miriam moved to Dallas. We never heard from them again." She reached for her phone. Why hadn't her dad called her back yet?

Bryce blew out a breath. "Did your dad tell you how they died?"

She stilled, then slowly raised her eyes to his. "They're dead?"

"I'm sorry," he said gently. "I didn't realize you didn't know."

"When? How?" Words failed her again. Her uncle and aunt were dead, and her dad hadn't told her? She'd never been close to them, but they *were* family.

Bryce took her hand, his fingers warm over hers. She should pull away, but his touch felt good in a world that had suddenly gone cold.

"They were killed about a month before your mom and Colton. Miriam first, then Alan a couple weeks later." His voice softened even more. "All of them look like the work of the same killer."

"Alan and Miriam were . . . ?"

He held her gaze. "I scanned all three files. The method, the body placement."

She winced.

"It was way too similar to be coincidence."

So they had a common killer. And if he'd targeted her uncle, aunt, mom, brother, then her, what was the connection—the motive? She let her mind track the questions. Anything to make sense of these new revelations and keep her brain from settling on the photographs she'd seen or envisioning Alan's and Miriam's bodies in a similar state.

"If there was any doubt left, the killer's notes sealed it," Bryce continued.

"What notes?" She didn't remember anything about that in the little bit she'd read.

"Notes of victory left with the victims. I don't remember exactly how it was worded, but something about not losing again and being one step closer to someone paying a debt."

"What debt?"

"No one could ever figure that out—at least I didn't see anything in the files to indicate they had. I could have missed it, though, since I was just trying to get the gist of the situation."

That was the motive, then. Some kind of debt. But who owed it? The victims? Or someone close to them?

WHEN HER FATHER still hadn't called back by eleven, Corina decided to try his work number. It rang a few times before the receptionist answered.

"Hello, it's Corina Roberts. Could you transfer me to my dad, please?"

"I'm sorry, but your dad called a while ago to say he would be late today."

"Did he happen to say why he would be late?" If he wasn't at work, then where was he?

"Just that there was a car accident last night and he had some details to take care of."

"Okay. Could you please have him call me when he comes in? There's been a bit of an emergency, and I need to get ahold of him."

"Of course I can. Are you all right, hon?"

"Yes, I'm fine," she assured her. "But it is urgent."

"I'll have him call the minute he gets here."

Corina thanked her and hung up. What was he doing? He wasn't listed on her title or insurance, so it couldn't have anything to do with her truck. Was he following up on a lead from last night? And why the secrecy?

Her phone rang, and she quickly answered without looking at the caller ID. "Hello?"

Silence met her greeting.

She tried again. "Is anyone there?"

The call cut off, but not before she caught the slight sound of a breath on the other end. Frowning, she pulled up the call history. Her stomach contracted at the private listing.

Allye looked up from the photos she was editing. "Wrong number?" Somehow, Corina had convinced her to go home earlier and retrieve her laptop so she could at least work on some of her projects while she hung around. Besides giving her something to do, the laptop had the effect of distracting Allye from her other project: Corina.

"I don't know." She hoped Allye wouldn't catch the slight wobble to her voice as she shoved the phone into her pocket. She welcomed the reprieve from her friend's hovering and didn't want to incite another round. "I had the calls from the shop routed to my cell so Gus wouldn't have to deal with them. Maybe they were trying to get through to the store."

Allye wrinkled her nose and turned her eyes back to the computer screen. "They could at least be polite about it."

"Yeah." She tried to sound nonchalant, but this wasn't the first hang-up call she'd gotten recently. Over the past few weeks, there had been several, but most of them had come during busy times of the day, and she'd forgotten them as soon as the flicker of annoyance wore off.

Her breath caught in her throat as she remembered the calls

her mom had gotten in the weeks before she and Colton were killed. She shook her head. Not going there. She would not be spooked by the past without confirmation that it was back. *There's nothing to fear.* And she'd keep telling herself that until she believed it.

For now, she needed to relieve Gus at Western Outfitters. The man was capable, but it wasn't fair to leave him to run the shop alone all day. Sitting here wallowing in the past while waiting for her dad to call back wasn't appealing anyway.

But before she made it out of the house, she received a text from Gus.

> Everything going fine, business slow. Why don't you stay home and rest?

She wavered. When her dad did finally call, she'd much rather have that conversation in private. And though she was sure she could force herself to focus on the store and her customers, the morning's revelations had shaken her. Not to mention her limited physical abilities, as evidenced by the office incident.

> Are you sure?

> Yep

She worried her bottom lip. She could spend the time studying the files she'd been avoiding the last couple of hours. No telling what her dad might do with them once he knew she'd found them.

> OK. But only if you promise to let me know if you need me.

> Promise, sweetheart. Get feeling better.

She managed a smile as she pocketed her phone. Gus was the real sweetheart. She wasn't sure how she'd managed things alone before hiring him for the part-time position. Her shop was in good hands.

Her smile faded as reality hit afresh. For once, Western Outfitters was the least of her concerns. And as much as she'd like to bury herself in her business, she had answers to find. Ignoring the dread clinging like a barnacle to her insides, she updated Allye, then settled in the living room with one of the files.

The afternoon passed uneventfully. And quietly—other than Allye's mother-henning, making sure Corina ate a few bites at lunch and took another dose of ibuprofen when the first wore off. There were no more hang-up calls and no return call from her dad.

A little after five thirty—past when he would normally have been home—she punched in his number again, not really even hoping for an answer at this point. His phone again routed her directly to voice mail. She didn't bother leaving another message.

Her knuckles popped, protesting the tightness of the grip she had on her phone. Something was wrong. Her dad never went more than an hour without returning her calls, and he *never* let his phone stay dead this long.

Missing work wasn't like him either. She had called his office again just before closing time, and the receptionist claimed she hadn't heard from him since the initial call that morning.

Houston whined from his position beside the recliner. Her tension was bothering him. She stroked his head, her movements automatic. The whining stopped, but his gaze continued to flick between her and Bryce, who had left for a couple of hours this afternoon but returned with takeout a few minutes ago.

"I wonder if I should call the police," she said, more to herself than to Bryce.

Allye entered the room in time to overhear her words. "Don't you have to wait twenty-four hours before you can file a missing person report?" She set a can of Dr Pepper and a much-too-large plate of food on the side table next to Corina.

"No, actually, you don't. You just have to have a reasonable concern that something is wrong. And I'm starting to get really concerned." She reached for the drink and popped the tab. Caffeine, she could use right now. Food? Well, her appetite hadn't yet made an appearance—which was why she hadn't retrieved her own food from the takeout containers.

Bryce set aside his plate and leaned forward. "It can't hurt. The worst thing that can come of it would be to find out everything's fine and have to call back and let them know it was a false alarm."

Still, she hesitated, second-guessing the idea. "I just hate to get them involved if I'm wrong."

"They're his friends, Corina. They won't mind." He attempted a grin, but it looked tight. Forced. "Besides, if you don't want me and Allye spending the night here, you need to get him home."

She recognized his attempt to make her feel better, but she couldn't bring herself to return his smile. *What would you do if I were missing, Dad?* Easy answer. He'd be combing the streets already, along with the entire on-duty Kincaid police force, and probably would have enlisted the county sheriff's office too. Despite leaving his PI work behind in Texas, her dad had developed a close relationship with local law enforcement here, and he had a way of mobilizing people and getting things done. But she didn't have that gift or any idea where to start. He'd left her no clue to where he was going this morning.

A thought made her straighten in her chair. "Officer Mike."

"What about him?"

She pulled out her phone to make sure she still had his number preprogrammed. "Dad told me once that if anything happened to him, I should call Mike Broaddus."

"Do that, then," Bryce encouraged, picking up his plate again. "He'll let you know if a missing person report is a good idea."

She took a few seconds to gather her thoughts before pressing the call button.

"Hello?"

At the sound of his voice, she realized she'd been holding her breath. Exhaling a bit too quickly, she winced and shifted the ice pack Allye had insisted she use.

"Hello. Officer Mike?" she asked a little breathlessly.

"Yes. Is this Corina? How are you feeling after all the excitement yesterday?" Concern tinged his voice.

"Fine. I'm taking it easy."

"Good. Glad to hear it. What can I help you with?"

She took a deep, painful breath, then blurted, "I can't get ahold of Dad, and he never made it to work today."

A long pause followed her revelation. Finally, he cleared his throat and spoke slowly. "When did you last see him?"

"Early this morning. He left about his usual time."

"And you haven't talked to him since?"

"No." She shook her head, although she knew he couldn't see it. "The first few times I called, it rang, but now it goes straight to voice mail, and he's not calling back. It's not like him."

"You're sure he didn't have an out-of-town meeting or something?"

"No, he called the office and told them he'd be late, but then he never showed up. They were expecting him today."

She thought she heard him sigh. "I'll look into it," he assured her. "Can you remember what he was wearing?"

Their conversation this morning seemed like such a long time ago. She closed her eyes, trying to force the memory back. "A green polo, maybe? And khakis. He probably would have his brown leather jacket with him too."

"Okay, we'll go with that for now. Let me see what I can find out, then I'll call you back."

"Officer Mike?" She wasn't ready to let him go yet.

"Yes?"

She swallowed hard before asking her next question. "Did he tell you the truth about what happened to my family before we moved here?" There was no mistaking the sound of his quickly indrawn breath. He knew.

"What do you mean?" He spoke the words carefully, as if he were uncertain whether to divulge information.

"I found his files this morning."

Again, silence reigned for a moment before he replied. "Yes, he thought someone in the department needed to know. Just in case something happened."

"Why didn't he tell me?" she whispered.

"That's a question you're going to have to ask him."

"Find him and I will." The words barely made it past her constricted throat.

"We will," he promised. "And don't hesitate to call me for anything in the meantime."

Unable to answer, she ended the call.

13

IS WILLIAM MATHIS DAFT?

Silently clenching and unclenching his fist, he stared out a window facing his target's residence. He had found the perfect vantage point and hideaway in the form of a nearby vacant house. A year's rent had secured the place. The owner had asked few questions—seemingly glad to pocket the cash.

It had been unoccupied for a while, judging by the dust-covered furniture that met his eyes when he moved in. No matter. He'd scoured every surface while formulating the details of his plan, and he'd thoroughly clean it again before he left. Once he was gone, there wouldn't be so much as a fingerprint on the doorknob. Not that anyone would connect this place to him. He'd been too careful. Had let enough time lapse that his arrival shouldn't be suspicious—and he'd stay a reasonable amount of time after he was finished to avoid drawing attention with a sudden departure. Everything was planned out perfectly.

Except William didn't appear to be cooperating.

He blinked against the burning in his eyes, a testament to his lengthy vigil. Looked from the window to the camera feed on his dimmed laptop screen. Back to the window. Still no movement.

He could go to bed, but they'd disappeared right out from under his nose once before.

There was a delicate balance to maintain here. His actions were supposed to scare them—terrify them, really—but not to the point they would attempt to flee again. He'd placed trackers on both William's and Corina's vehicles when he first arrived in town, but he wouldn't rely completely on them. Too high a chance of discovery with William's background.

And that brought him back to the immediate problem. William should have reacted to yesterday's events and today's note. He should have panicked or at least started taking precautions. But what was the man's reaction? To leave Corina home alone all day and—he glanced at his watch—half the night now too. It was after midnight, and still there was no sign of his returning home.

To be sure, Corina hadn't been completely alone—one or both of the Jessup siblings had babysat her all day, and they still hadn't left. Hardly a security force, despite the young man's military experience.

Perhaps they were helping her out because of the accident. He rubbed at his chin. No way he'd hurt Corina that badly. He'd only rear-ended her vehicle, and the hospital hadn't bothered to admit her. She hadn't opened the shop herself today, though. And he'd kept a close eye on the cameras. She hadn't even left the house other than to retrieve his note from the door.

Had they checked the footage for that yet? He'd considered looping the video feed so he wouldn't appear on it at all, but he didn't want them to figure out he had hacked into their system. No one appearing on the footage when the note had been left would have raised red flags—especially combined with his remote triggering of the alarm yesterday morning. So he'd worn a disguise and kept his head down. They'd see him, but no one would recognize him.

He stared out the window at his target's mostly darkened house. If he didn't *know* she was inside, he would've started wondering if they had ditched William's car and given him the slip again. That would explain William's absence and the fact that his car hadn't moved since this morning, according to the tracker.

But she was there. No doubt about it. And William was not.

Short fingernails bit into the fleshy part of his palm, and his knuckles protested the tightness of his balled fist. William shouldn't still be absent after the clues he'd left. Especially if his precious daughter had been injured.

They weren't taking this seriously. Weren't taking *him* seriously.

He'd even made sure the SUV from last night had been easy to find—the bottle of Baby Blue in plain sight. He hadn't so much as taken a sip of the famous Texas whiskey—that wasn't the point. But it had been a favorite of a certain now-deceased blabbermouth he and William both knew, and he'd bet William was well aware of that fact. Even if he wasn't, William was smart enough to know the assault had nothing to do with a drunk driver. Or at least, he thought he was. Apparently none of it was enough of a hint—the phone calls, the triggered alarm, the collision, an obvious reference to Texas. Even today's not-so-subtle warning note hadn't gotten through.

Fine, then. If William was that dense, he was more than happy to make things clear.

He lowered the blinds. Taking his computer with him so he could continue to monitor any comings and goings, he retreated downstairs to the kitchen. A box of disposable rubber gloves sat next to his briefcase on the table. He tugged a pair free and slipped them on before beginning his work.

They *would* take him seriously.

14

THE WHIR OF A FLYING OBJECT woke Bryce the next morning an instant before the item collided with the back of the couch and crash-landed on his face. He flung up a hand to swipe it aside. Allye's giggles filled the room.

"Hey." The word emerged as a half growl, half croak. He reached blindly for the cotton-filled weapon but couldn't find it.

"Hey, yourself." The pillow thudded on his stomach.

He opened one eye to glare at his sister. Allye looked far too awake for whatever time of morning this was. "Shouldn't you still be asleep?"

"It's after eleven, Bryce. Even I don't sleep this late," she said dryly, placing her hands on her hips.

Groaning, he sat up and rubbed his eyes. "Seriously?" His gaze shot to a wall clock. "Where's Corina?"

Allye's amusement faded. "Talking to Officer Mike. I don't think he's found anything yet."

He nodded slowly. Yesterday's revelations had kept him awake far into the night—probably why he'd overslept. He had hoped the morning would bring Will's return. The man's continued absence didn't bode well.

"I have an appointment to take senior pictures in Cincinnati today. Are you good to stay with her alone?"

"Yeah, we'll be fine." He suppressed a grimace. Well, they'd be fine if Corina didn't decide to freeze him out again. Her thawed attitude toward him yesterday had been a surprise, but she had been preoccupied with everything going on. Today might be a different story. "When do you leave?"

"I need to head out in about a half hour. We had planned to take the pictures at Friendship Park, but unless this rain clears up, we'll have to move to an indoor location." She wrinkled her nose. "I hope things dry out before we get there. Plan B means more drive time."

"Good luck." A thought occurred to him as he stood to stretch. "Oh, be careful what you say to Mom if you see her."

Her eyebrows lifted. "I thought you talked to her last night. Didn't you tell her what was going on?"

"Part of it. I don't want to worry her, though." He hadn't given her many details when she'd called to invite him to dinner—just let her know Will was out of town and Corina needed someone to stay with her since she'd been injured in a car accident.

It was enough of the truth to get by. And the mention of a car accident was enough to distract her from any other details. Once he'd assured her for the third time that Corina had been the only one in the vehicle and wasn't badly injured, she'd settled enough to let him talk her out of coming over herself.

Allye frowned but agreed. She was close to their mom and usually shared everything with her. But the siblings had made an unofficial agreement years ago to avoid telling her unnecessary details that would only serve to worry her. This fell into that category.

He grabbed the extra set of clothes he'd brought over last night and headed for the guest room shower. Over the last few weeks, his mom had been open about how happy she was to have both her remaining children home again—and out of danger, if he read between the lines correctly. Unless they had a good reason to ruin that, they weren't going to.

Hot water helped clear the remaining fog from his brain, but as he threw a T-shirt over his head, he caught a glimpse of his reflection. He quirked an eyebrow. It was a wonder no one had commented on his face. After Corina called him yesterday, he'd never finished shaving. The lopsided look was definitely not him.

And he hadn't thought to pack a razor.

Bryce opened several drawers, hoping to find one of Will's, but his search came up empty. *Oh well.* He shrugged. It hadn't seemed to bother anyone yesterday. He'd take care of it later.

WHERE ARE YOU, DAD? Corina sat at the table and rested her face in her hands. Officer Mike said the BOLO on his vehicle hadn't turned up anything yet. He couldn't have just dropped off the face of the earth. An involuntary shudder passed through her. With all the hills and winding roads around here, that might be a possibility.

God, please, let him be okay. She wasn't sure she believed God cared, but she knew he heard. She had never doubted that fact. Maybe he would listen for her dad's sake at least.

"Morning."

She looked up as Bryce entered the room. "Hey." She chose to ignore the fact it was now afternoon. "Allye just made a fresh pot of coffee if you want some."

"Definitely." He poured a cup and sat across from her. She wrinkled her nose. How he drank that stuff black would always be a mystery to her.

"There's creamer in the fridge." She knew what his response would be but couldn't help offering. Old habits died hard. She and Bryce had shared quite a few coffee dates in the past. Invariably, she teased him about his lack of imagination and taste buds. His answer was always to smile, take another sip, and simply say—

"I'm good."

The corners of her lips tipped upward. He hadn't disappointed her.

"How are the ribs today?"

"Tolerable." As long as she avoided moving. She picked up her phone again, checking for the thousandth time to see if somehow she had missed a call or text. But there was only an update from Gus, who had graciously agreed to open for her again today but was closing up now to make it to his doctor's appointment. She should probably get a ride over to Western Outfitters to avoid losing business, but when her dad returned, he'd be coming *here*. And if she received news about him and needed to leave quickly . . .

A noise sounded from the hallway. "Allye still here?" Bryce asked.

"Yes, but I think she's about to head out. She had me disarm the alarm a few minutes ago." A slamming door confirmed her statement. "She's running a bit late."

"Naturally." Bryce's grin lit his face.

For Allye to leave at anything but the last minute—or later— would be quite a feat.

A knock sounded on the door. Corina started to stand, but Bryce was already out of his chair, motioning her to wait. "I'll get it."

She rolled her eyes and followed him to the edge of the kitchen anyway. If it was anything important, she'd need to be on hand.

"It's just Allye," he called over his shoulder before opening the door. "Miss us already?"

"Not you." Allye stuck her tongue out at him. "I just thought Corina might want the mail brought in before the box overflows." She pushed a handful of envelopes and catalogs at him, then turned to hurry off the porch, almost dropping one of her bags in the process. "Gotta run. Bye!"

"Bye." He closed and locked the door behind her. "There's mail—lots of it," he remarked, returning to the kitchen and handing it to Corina.

"Great. I hadn't even thought about it." She set the stack on the counter for her dad to go through later.

Bryce hadn't retaken his seat. "Have you already had lunch?"

She shook her head.

"Breakfast?" he pressed.

"Umm, no."

"Then I guess we can eat together. Do you want to go out somewhere or eat here?"

She glanced back at her phone. "I'd prefer to be here when Dad gets back." She refused to say *if*. He would come back.

Bryce nodded understanding. "Fine with me." He opened the refrigerator and peered inside. "So"—he glanced mischievously over his shoulder—"are you cooking, or am I?"

That deserved a smile. "Since when do you cook?"

"I make a mean grilled cheese," he offered, voice dripping innocence. "And charcoal is good for you."

"Really, now?" She pretended to consider it. "Sounds appetizing, but maybe we should reserve your expertise for another time."

He threw up his hands in mock surrender and backed away. "Whatever you say. But just remember, I offered."

"Noted." She took his place in front of the refrigerator and searched for something promising. By the look of the shelves, grocery shopping needed to be bumped up on her dad's to-do list.

She pulled out a jar of pimiento cheese and checked the date. Not expired, at least. "How about a pimiento-chicken panini?" *If Dad's not out of bread and chicken*, she added silently.

"That sounds amazing."

"Let's see if I can pull it off," she mumbled to herself as she set out to find the other necessary ingredients. Luck was on her side. There were four slices of bread left. She located the chicken and got started.

"Canned chicken?"

She shot an amused look his direction. "Don't knock it till you try it. Besides, it's better than sardines."

He made a gagging sound. "I'll take your word on that one."

A smile played about her lips as she started on the sandwiches. When they were teenagers, she and Allye had often tried out new recipes in this kitchen. Bryce, a typical guy, was always happy to taste test their creations.

Except for the time they'd made shrimp scampi and found themselves missing a key ingredient. Apparently, sardines packed in mustard didn't make a good substitute for shrimp. Who would have guessed?

Although they weren't dating yet, she suspected Bryce already had a crush on her back then. He'd put on a good show at dinner, taking seconds even when everyone else—her dad included—declared it unfit to eat.

He'd also ended up sick to his stomach and spent most of that night in the bathroom, according to his sister. To her knowledge, he'd never touched a can of sardines again.

She puckered her lips, trying to hold back the smirk that memory always brought with it. They had a lot of good memories together.

And some really bad ones.

Her smile faded.

She sighed and lifted a corner of one of the sandwiches. Done enough. She transferred them to a cutting board and sliced them diagonally. Three halves went on Bryce's plate and one on hers.

"Order up." She placed the dishes on the table.

He frowned at the distribution. "You need to eat more than that."

"I'm not hungry." She jerked her plate away as he reached for it. "Oh no, you don't. I don't know if I can even eat this much."

He grunted but settled back in his chair and let the matter drop. Good.

She slipped into the seat across from him and lifted her sandwich to her lips. Just before she bit into it, she realized Bryce had his head bowed. She felt her cheeks flush, but he didn't seem to have noticed her omission. Still, she paused and studied him while he uttered his silent prayer.

Funny how he seemed to have kept his faith all these years while hers had shattered. What made the difference?

She'd always thought her faith was strong, but after what she'd experienced, what she'd lost . . .

"What is it?"

She blinked and more heat flushed her cheeks. She hadn't noticed Bryce end his prayer, and she was still staring at him, sandwich suspended halfway to her mouth.

"Nothing. It's . . ." She shook her head. "Nothing."

She took a bite of the panini and almost gagged. It tasted fine, but her stomach was turning before she even swallowed. If Bryce weren't already making an issue out of her eating habits, she would have tossed the rest to Houston. It was going to take some serious willpower to eat until her dad was home safe.

Being watched didn't help her appetite any.

Maybe she could convince Bryce to go home for a while. He and Allye were trying not to impose—she knew that—but she already felt smothered. With both of them gone, she could channel her energy into figuring out where her dad was. Without a doubt, she would be able to think more clearly if Bryce weren't so close by.

It wasn't like she'd be helpless here alone. She was armed and had the alarm system and Houston. She could take care of herself.

It couldn't hurt to try.

"Everything seems quiet," she said carefully, as Bryce stood to refill his coffee.

"Very."

"You know you don't have to stay here, right?" She broke off a bit of crust and slipped it to Houston.

Bryce didn't answer immediately, but when he returned to his seat, he met her gaze. "No, I don't know that. Until your dad gets back, I want to know you're safe."

"I appreciate the concern, but I'll be all right here. It's not your responsibility."

"Five years ago, you wouldn't have said that."

"Things were different then." And they weren't going back to the way they were before.

"I'm still going to protect you." He lifted his cup as if dismissing the conversation.

So much for some time alone.

The thought of Bryce's protection was comforting and disconcerting at the same time. She stood to place her plate in the sink. Now was not the time to unravel that tangle of emotion.

The unopened mail caught her attention, and she reached for it, needing something to do that didn't involve sitting across the table from Bryce. Automatically, she separated the catalogs into their own stack, then moved to the regular mail. She flipped through the envelopes a bit more carefully, sorting as she went. *Junk. Bill. Bill. Junk.*

She paused at an envelope stamped *URGENT*. It was addressed to her. Odd, since she'd moved out two years ago. There was no return address, though. She turned it over. Nothing on the back. *Probably more junk.*

She almost tossed it but decided to open it on the off chance it was something legitimate. Sliding a finger under the flap, she tore it open and removed the contents—a single sheet of trifolded paper and a business card. She flipped the card over. One of hers from Western Outfitters.

Why would someone send her one of her own cards? Perhaps the letter would explain.

Something fluttered to the floor as she unfolded the paper to reveal a blank page. Even more puzzled now, she set it aside and reached for whatever had fallen.

Newspaper clippings? She turned them over. And paled at the images staring up at her. Her legs threatened to give way, so she reached for her chair and sat down. Hard.

15

IT'S HIM. Every doubt Corina had clung to since finding her dad's files fled the instant the photos registered.

"What's wrong?" The alarm in Bryce's voice penetrated the fog. "Corina, what is it?"

Unable to formulate the words, she numbly extended the bits of paper for his inspection. His sharp intake of breath only solidified her fears.

"I'm calling the police." He already had his cell phone in hand.

"Not 911. Call Officer Mike," she managed to get out.

"I need his number, then."

She pulled out her phone. Her fingers refused to cooperate, and she entered the passcode wrong twice before getting it unlocked. Her brain blanked. What was she looking for? "Here." She shoved the phone into Bryce's hands. Let him figure it out.

Her eyes returned to the newspaper clippings. Both pictures were familiar. The first, a duplicate of one in her dad's file, showed her mother's and brother's covered bodies on gurneys being rolled out the front door of her old home in Texas. The second was recent—a close-up of her standing in front of Western Outfitters at the grand opening. The sender had drawn a red bull's-eye on her forehead and a pool of blood at her feet.

The half sandwich she'd managed to get down churned uncomfortably in her stomach. Tiny specks of light intruded on her vision.

She blinked as Bryce's hand covered the disturbing image, blocking it from her view. Not sure whether to be annoyed or grateful, she ignored him and seized the moment to regain her equilibrium.

Easy. Breathe. She wrapped her hands around her nearly empty coffee cup to still their trembling.

Now she was spooked. There was no denying it. But the ease with which this guy had done it was irritating. Once, she would have taken everything in stride. Yes, she would have been concerned at the letter and taken precautions, but her confidence wouldn't have wavered. Right now, she felt like a mouse caught between a cat and a mousetrap.

And of course, Bryce had seen her reaction. It was bad enough to be confronted with her latent cowardice; why did it have to be apparent to him? She wasn't ready to unveil that part of her heart to anyone. She preferred to quash the offending emotions first.

His voice interrupted her thoughts, and she lifted her head to study his face.

"Hello, it's Bryce Jessup. I'm with Corina at her house." He glanced at her out of the corner of his eye. "We need someone out here—now."

"WHAT IS IT?" The abrupt seriousness in Officer Mike's tone mirrored his own.

"Corina just got an anonymous letter. It has some rather, uh, disturbing artwork in it along with newspaper clippings that point to—" he paused, unsure how to say it gently—"to her mom's and brother's deaths."

"What kind of artwork are we talking?"

"Violent. Threatening. You'll know when you see it."

"Anything else at all?"

"A Western Outfitters business card and a blank sheet of paper."

"Where is it postmarked from?"

Leaning over Corina, Bryce snagged the envelope from the counter. His chest constricted as he studied the upper right-hand corner. "There isn't one."

The officer went quiet, quiet enough for Bryce to detect a faint miss in his car's engine. When he finally spoke, it was with the air of having made a major decision. The commands came fast.

"I'm calling this in to dispatch. I'm off duty and not near you right now, but I'll make sure another officer gets there ASAP. I'll be there as soon as I can get back. Check that all the windows and doors are locked, and just lie low until someone gets there. Keep Corina inside and away from the windows. And don't touch that letter again. We need to see if he left any prints behind."

Bryce grimaced and dropped the envelope on top of the pictures. Both his and Corina's hands had been all over them already.

Officer Mike was still talking. "If Corina shared those files with you, then you know about as much as I do at this point, which isn't much. But this guy's dangerous."

That's an understatement. Bryce bit back the sarcastic comment.

Static sounded in the background, and there was a pause as Officer Mike listened to the scanner. "I have to go. Just got a response on the BOLO for Will's vehicle."

"Where?"

"Cincinnati. Not too far from where I am. I'm going to check that out first. Tell Corina I'll call when I know something. And, Bryce?"

"Yes?"

The officer stressed the next words. "*Do not leave her alone.*"

He dropped his eyes back to Corina's face. He identified the lingering fear before she looked away. She knew he'd read her, and she didn't like it. He set his jaw as fresh determination shot through him. "Not a chance, sir."

"WHAT DID HE SAY?" Corina asked as Bryce put his phone away and moved to double-check the locks on the back door.

"He thinks the threat is real. He's sending someone out. And they got a hit on your dad's car."

"Where?"

"Cincinnati. Officer Mike doesn't know anything yet, but he said he'd let you know when he did."

"What about Dad?"

"He didn't say. The call just came in."

They'd found the car, then, but not necessarily its occupant. Corina swallowed the lump that had risen in her throat. Yesterday's total silence had told her something was terribly wrong, but she'd held out a faint hope the situation was just some sort of mix-up. So much for that.

There was absolutely no way her dad had willingly stayed somewhere overnight that close to home. She didn't know why he would have gone there in the first place, but even in the unlikely event he'd had both car and phone trouble, he still would have gotten home somehow or found a way to contact her. Unless he was incapacitated.

The morning mail caught her eye again, and she wondered if *he* had anything to do with her dad's disappearance. If not, it was a huge coincidence.

Bryce reached for her hand and squeezed it gently. She started at his touch, and he let go, that same unreadable expression from yesterday in his eyes. She bit the side of her lip as he moved to check the window latch and left—probably to do the same in the other rooms. A slight sigh escaped her. His touch had surprised her, as had the realization that she missed it.

I miss it? She quickly dismissed the thought and rose to help him secure the house. It wouldn't take much. Her dad was a stickler about keeping everything locked up. They both were—what with the way her mom and brother had died. Another wave of anger and sorrow swept over her. She'd thought they were defending against random crime all these years, not targeted attacks.

Bryce had moved counterclockwise. She could hear him in the living room at the front of the house, so she went the other direction, starting with the main bathroom.

The window in here was tiny. Was it even possible for an adult to get in this way? She wasn't sure, but she checked the lock anyway then moved into her dad's bedroom. Although he'd been gone less than two days, the room still held an abandoned air.

Her eyes lingered on a five by seven of the two of them taken when she'd received her associate's in business. Pride shone on her dad's face, and confidence radiated from hers. That had been a mere twenty-four hours before the accident that rocked her world. Again.

Just the thought of that horrible day sent the nightmares rushing back. This time, she was powerless to stop them. It was supposed to have been a great day—had even begun well—but everything had gone so wrong.

After working her morning shift at the grocery store, she'd picked up Bryce and Allye's fifteen-year-old brother from school. The four of them were supposed to go ice skating in Cincinnati, but Derryck needed new skates, and Bryce and Allye were both working.

She had tried to get out of running that errand. She didn't mind taking Derryck somewhere, but getting to the nearest town with a sporting goods store wouldn't leave them enough time to return to Kincaid and carpool with Bryce for the evening's activities—and she really hated driving in Cincinnati.

But Derryck insisted, and Corina found it next to impossible to disappoint him. Despite the fact that Derryck had surpassed her in height the year before, she still saw him as the eight-year-old kid who had been overjoyed to show her his loose teeth. The one who'd become almost a replacement for the brother she'd lost. As usual, she'd given in.

As the past crowded the present from her awareness, she sank to a seat on the bed, clutching her now-aching left arm.

Corina turned up the car radio as the first notes of her favorite song sounded. She hummed along to the verse as the traffic light flashed from red to green, and she followed the vehicle in front of her into the intersection. Halfway through, she glanced to her right. Then did a double take.

An SUV was speeding toward the passenger side of her car. No. No! *She spun the steering wheel, but there was no time to avoid it. A scream tore from her throat. Metal crunched. Glass shattered. The car spun. Tires screeched on pavement. A second impact, this time on her side. Pain shot down her arm as the world went white. Black. Pinpricks of light danced across her vision as the airbags deflated and the car skidded to a stop.*

She couldn't think. Couldn't process the last few seconds. Burnt rubber and hot metal mingled with the coppery scent of blood and assaulted her nostrils.

The combination of smells pulled her from her confusion and filled her with horror. Her eyes shot to the passenger side of the car—Derryck's side. She saw the familiar curly red hair first. Then the blood. So much blood.

16

TEARS STREAMED DOWN her face as she remembered Derryck's lifeless form. There had been nothing she could do to save him, but she'd tried. That fact didn't make her feel any less responsible, nor did it ease the sense of loss that threatened to swallow her even now.

I have to stop this! She had struggled for years to forget that day and had been largely successful. Until the past few days. She'd had the dream again last night and had been afraid to go back to sleep when she'd awakened at four thirty. And now the memories were coming in the daytime too. The stress of her current situation was wreaking havoc on her emotional control.

She couldn't have that. Couldn't lose control. She clenched her fist, making the nails bite into her palm. The pain helped. A little.

A rustling sound preceded Bryce into the room. She turned her face away, hoping he wouldn't see her tears, but she wasn't quick enough. He sat beside her on the bed and took her hand in his, gently prying open her fist.

"Talk to me." The softly spoken words brought a new burst of tears.

She didn't want to talk about it, but her mouth betrayed her. "Why didn't I notice the SUV wasn't stopping for the light?"

Bryce didn't answer immediately. Finally, he said, "What happened that day was an accident—one you had no way to prevent. No one blames you for that. We never did."

"I still feel like it's my fault," she whispered, her eyes fixing somewhere around his chin. "I was driving. I should have seen it."

Bryce's Adam's apple bobbed. He seemed to be struggling to control his own emotions.

"Corina—" He took a deep breath and started again. "Corina, you are not responsible for his death. You were at the wrong place at the wrong time. The guy who ran the red light was the one at fault."

She couldn't stop the questions now any more than she'd been able to stop the memories. "We shouldn't have been there at all. Why did I agree to take Derryck shopping? Why didn't I tell him to just rent skates that night? We were supposed to ride with you. We never would have taken that route if we'd waited for you."

"That isn't your fault either. If anyone is to be blamed for that, it's me." He sighed. "I asked Derryck to think of something to get you out of town and keep you occupied as long as he could."

"Why?" That didn't make any sense. She finally lifted her eyes. He was the one avoiding eye contact now, but she could see the tears he was trying to hold back.

His voice was husky when he answered. "Because I was going to propose that night. I'd had the ring specially designed and everything planned out for the evening, but the ring came in several days later than they'd told me to expect. I had to pick it up after work, and I couldn't think of a way to keep you from riding with me, so I asked Derryck to think up something to get you out of town earlier."

"You were going to propose?"

HEAT ROSE IN BRYCE'S FACE as Corina stared at him. He released her hand and scrubbed the side of his face. "Yeah," he admitted.

"With you graduating college and my service obligation nearly finished, it seemed like the perfect time."

"But then you left."

"I thought that's what you wanted." And he hadn't been thinking clearly. His brother's sudden death had hit him like the speeding SUV that caused it. Between the loss, his unintentional part in it, his family's grief, and Corina shutting him out—he'd been desperate to escape. "I couldn't fix it. I couldn't bring Derryck back, couldn't repair our relationship." So he'd run. He shrugged helplessly.

Corina didn't respond except to drop her eyes. Her already flushed face gave nothing away, but she didn't deny that she'd wanted him gone.

A knock on the front door rescued him. Relieved, he rose to answer it.

He hadn't intended to tell her about his almost-proposal. But he hadn't realized she blamed herself for Derryck's death. He'd been too caught up in his own grief and self-blame at the time. Although he had eventually come to peace with his part in the events leading to the accident, she apparently hadn't. He wasn't going to let her continue down that road if he could help it. Still, maybe he should have just said he was planning a surprise for her.

He checked the peephole before disabling the alarm. Eric Thornton stood on the porch, thumbs hooked in his duty belt. Although they hadn't kept up with each other during Bryce's absence, they'd been pretty good friends in high school. Eric was thorough. A quality that would serve them well in a situation like this.

Bryce quickly took care of the alarm and unlocked the door. He glanced at his watch as he let Eric in. A little under ten minutes since he'd talked to Officer Mike. Pretty good response time, considering they didn't have an immediate emergency.

"Bryce." The officer acknowledged him as he entered, eyes already scanning the interior.

"Hey, man, glad you're here." He led the way to the kitchen, bypassing Will's room to give Corina time to hide the traces of her tears. He pointed to the table. "That stack there is what came in the mail. It could have been yesterday or today, we're not sure."

Eric pulled on a pair of gloves and slid each item into a separate plastic bag. He frowned at the edited picture but made no comment as he examined it.

"I hope we didn't mess anything up—Corina and I both touched them before we realized what was going on."

"We'll find out."

"Hello, Eric." They both looked up as Corina entered the room. Her eyes were still red and her face a little puffy. For her sake, he hoped Eric wouldn't notice. Knowing Eric, he would. But he probably wouldn't comment.

"Hi." Eric glanced back at the bags in his hand. "So it looks like you've made someone mad."

"I don't know."

He raised his eyebrows. Her eyes flicked away from him, and she didn't expound her answer.

"We think it's from the same guy who murdered her family," Bryce offered, wincing when Corina's face paled.

The officer's eyes widened marginally, then narrowed. "Mike didn't relay much over the radio. How about you guys level with me?"

Bryce glanced at Corina and received a nod. He quickly filled Eric in on what they had discovered in the files. The officer's frown deepened as he listened.

"Apparently, they never caught the guy. Will and Corina moved to get away from him." Bryce raised his hands. "Now Corina gets rammed on her way home from work, her dad disappears without a word, and this gets left in her mailbox."

"Is there any chance this could be some sort of practical joke?"

"What kind of person would make a joke out of stuff like this?" If that was the case, he'd like to get his hands on the sicko.

"You tell me." Eric's eyes were fixed on Corina. "I'm not saying it is a joke. I just want to rule out the possibility. Is there anyone who knows about this that might want to enjoy a laugh at your expense?"

She took a moment to think. Bryce could see the change in her demeanor as she set aside her fear and shifted to observation mode. The difference was almost tangible. He watched her, curious.

Finally, she shook her head. "Eric, *I* didn't even know about most of this until yesterday. I don't know how anyone would have put the pieces together. Besides"—she pointed at the evidence bags in his hand—"that newspaper clipping of my mom's and Colton's bodies is an original, not a photocopy. It's a *twelve-year-old* clipping from a regional Texas newspaper. The average person in Kentucky isn't going to randomly find a copy lying around."

Her phone rang, and she snatched it. "Hello . . . Hello?" After another moment, she pulled the device away to look at it, then ended the call.

She held the phone up where Eric could see it. "Here's something else. I keep getting hang-up or dead-air calls. The number is private."

Bryce shot her a look. "You didn't mention the phone calls. How long has that been going on?"

She pursed her lips. "A couple weeks, maybe? I didn't think anything of them until last night because they usually come through my business line. I've gotten one or two on my cell but not an abnormal amount. I guess since I have the shop's calls rerouted right now, I'm getting them all on my cell."

"So whoever this is might not have your cell number—depending on whether the personal calls and the shop calls are from the same person," Eric observed.

"That would make sense." She shrugged. "I don't really know, though."

"All right, if you don't have anything else for me, I'll take these to the station and see what we can find out on those phone calls."

Bryce slapped his forehead. "Wait, there was a note left on the front door yesterday morning." He couldn't believe they'd forgotten it. "I think it was referencing the accident from the night before. It said, 'Consider yesterday a preview.'"

Eric's eyes darkened, and he turned back to Corina. "Why didn't you report it?"

"I didn't know about any of this then. Since it was so ambiguous, I didn't see the need to. I guess I was wrong." Corina's voice dropped on the last sentence.

"Let me grab it for you." Bryce retrieved the note from the pocket of yesterday's jeans, careful to only touch the edges, and turned it over to Eric. "Sorry, but our prints will probably be all over that one too."

"You had no way of knowing, I suppose." He added it to his growing mass of evidence. "Have you checked the security video from when it was left?"

"I meant to, but I forgot about it. I can pull it up now," Corina offered.

"Please do."

They waited while she retreated to her dad's office and returned a moment later with a notebook. She entered the necessary information into her phone and located yesterday's footage. Bryce and Eric moved closer to watch it with her.

A man in a ball cap approached from the street and climbed the porch steps. He wore gloves and kept his head down. After placing the note on the door, he knocked and hurried out of sight.

"You recognize him?"

"I couldn't see enough of his face to be sure, but he doesn't look familiar," she said.

"Too bad. Send that to me." Eric gave Corina his email address, then fixed his attention on Bryce. "You're hanging around?"

"Yeah."

"Good. Keep us updated."

"Sure thing." He followed Eric to the door. "Do they know anything about Will yet?" He kept his voice low, hoping Corina wouldn't overhear.

Eric shook his head. "No, Mike was just arriving on scene when he requested that I head out here. I'm sure he'll be in touch soon."

"Okay, thanks." He watched as Eric drove away, then he scanned the area for anything suspicious before closing and bolting the door.

17

HER PHONE STARTED RINGING again almost before Eric made it outside. This time, Corina looked at the caller ID before answering. Officer Mike's name scrolled across the screen, and she almost dropped her phone trying to accept the call.

"Hello?"

"Corina? How are things out there?"

"Quiet. Nothing else has happened." That weird phone call didn't count. "Eric took the pictures to the station. What do you know about my dad?"

His sigh came through the line. "Not much. The vehicle was parked in an alley in a seedy section of the city. They went ahead and accessed the vehicle at my request since you reported Will missing and they could see his wallet lying open on the floorboard. His driver's license is still in there, but it's been emptied of any credit cards or cash."

"Did it look like it had been broken into, like maybe he left his wallet in there and someone happened to see it?" She looked up as Bryce entered the room. *Officer Mike*, she mouthed in answer to his questioning look. He nodded and leaned against the wall, arms crossed.

Officer Mike's voice continued in her ear. "There's no sign of a forced entry. The keys are still in the ignition. And if someone were going for a wallet in a random vehicle, they would have taken the whole thing, not spent time sorting through it for what they wanted." He paused and cleared his throat. "I'm going to call the local hospitals to see if he or anyone matching his description was brought in recently."

A weight settled in the pit of her stomach as the words sank in. "Was there any blood?" She had to force the words out.

"Not that we can see. There hasn't been time to have a crime scene unit look at it closely, though."

Breath whooshed from her lungs. That was some relief. Not a lot, but some. "Let me know as soon as you hear anything?" She knew he would, but she couldn't help asking.

"You'll be the first," he assured her. "I'll call you soon."

It can't be soon enough. Corina pocketed her phone, his words echoing in her head. More than anything, she wanted to look out the front door and see her dad pulling into the driveway. With this latest development, she knew he wouldn't—not in his car, anyway—and that realization had her blinking away tears again. Her hands curled back into fists. *Where are you?*

She shook her head, hoping the motion would clear it. She needed to have a level head when Officer Mike called back with an update. She could only hope his definition of *soon* fit hers. If the worry didn't kill her, the waiting might. Or the family killer.

At least I have options. She huffed a silent laugh but kept the thought to herself. Bryce wouldn't appreciate her logic. And on second thought, she wasn't sure she did either.

She shot a quick glance his direction. He hadn't asked for the particulars of Officer Mike's call, but he was still watching her with compassion and something more in his eyes. She dropped her gaze and turned away. The memory of his words before Eric's arrival sent heat rushing to her neck as she began to wash the lunch dishes and the few left over from last night. She hoped she wasn't as red as she felt.

After a moment, retreating footsteps signaled he'd left the room, but she turned to make sure. The kitchen was empty except for the corner Houston had claimed. Good. She hung her head and let her shoulders slump, thankful Bryce didn't seem to want to continue their previous conversation.

Had he really come that close to proposing?

She shouldn't be surprised. Five years ago, she wouldn't have been. She might have been surprised at the timing or the method, but not at the proposal itself. And she would have said yes. There was no doubt in her mind about that.

And if he were to pop the question now? She shook her head. They barely knew each other anymore. That wasn't even a possibility. And if it were, she'd say no, although the thought of that left an unexpected heaviness in her stomach. But saying yes wouldn't be an option. That would require a courage she no longer possessed.

Well, it wasn't something she needed to worry about. Bryce seemed to have done just fine the last five years without her. And she'd been fine too. She didn't need anyone in her life.

She scrubbed a little harder than necessary at a burnt puddle of cheese in the skillet she'd reserved for last. It finally came away, taking a bit of the nonstick coating off with it. Oh well. Her dad needed new pans anyway.

She jumped when her phone began to ring. Could it be Officer Mike already? She glanced at her watch. It hadn't been long since his last call. Scrambling to dry her hands and get to it before voice mail took over, she barely took time to confirm it was him as she snatched it from her pocket.

"Hello?"

"I may have found him." Something in his tone warned her the news wasn't good. Throat suddenly dry, she braced herself against the counter and waited for him to continue. "A John Doe fitting his description was admitted to a hospital on the east side yesterday afternoon. I'm on my way over there now to see if I can identify him."

"Did they give you any details?"

"Just that he's been unconscious since he was brought in, and they haven't been able to get an ID."

"He's been unconscious for twenty-four hours?" She slid to a seat on the floor and rested her elbows on her knees. Something had to be seriously wrong to keep him out for that long.

"It may not be him, Corina."

But what if it was? She worried her lower lip between her teeth. "How soon will you know?"

"It's not quite rush hour yet. It shouldn't take me more than fifteen minutes to get to the hospital, a few more to park and get access to his room. We'll know something soon."

Corina stared at her phone after Officer Mike cut off the call. The hospital's John Doe might not be her dad, but what were the chances of him being admitted the day her dad disappeared? And if it wasn't her dad, then where was he? At least the guy in the hospital was alive.

Her chin trembled. Tears welled, but she bit her tongue to keep them at bay. She didn't know which of the two outcomes was worse, but she wasn't going to cry until she knew what exactly she was crying for.

With effort and not a little pain—she really had to start remembering her injuries before she put herself in uncomfortable positions—she pulled herself off the floor. For the next thirty-five minutes, she paced the kitchen, sending up desperate pleas to a God she hoped was listening this time.

Her energy was almost spent when Officer Mike's call came through.

"Yes?"

"It's him."

She wilted at the defeat in his tone. "How bad is it?"

"I don't know, but he doesn't look good. You'll want to head this way."

As he gave the hospital and room details, she stumbled into her bedroom and reached for a pair of boots. With the assurance that he would stay close to her dad until she arrived, she ended the call. She grabbed a jacket and her purse and headed for the hallway.

She didn't have a vehicle. The realization struck her as she reached for the doorknob. She wanted to scream. Instead, she called for Bryce.

"In here." His voice emerged from the living room. He must have retreated there after the awkwardness in the kitchen. She rounded the corner to face him.

"Bryce, they found my dad. I need a ride to the hospital."

"How is he?" He was already in motion.

She bit her lip, stifling her emotions. "Not good."

To her relief, he left it at that as they hurried to his car. She noticed his not-so-discreet glance around as he held the passenger door open for her. He was watching for trouble. The door slammed, and she shook her head. She couldn't bring herself to care about killers or stalkers right now. The only thing that mattered was getting to her dad.

18

DRIVING NORTH ON HIGHWAY 27, Bryce cast a sideways glance Corina's direction. She hadn't spoken since passing on the name of the Cincinnati hospital, but he could feel the tension radiating from her. She was biting her lower lip again, something he'd observed her doing often the last couple of days.

He peered into his mirrors. The road was almost deserted. Oncoming traffic was sparse, and there were only a couple of vehicles behind them. They weren't close enough for him to identify the model, but one was green, the other dark blue. Assuring himself that neither was a police cruiser, he let his foot rest a bit more heavily on the gas pedal. Normally, he didn't like to speed, but today was not the day to be a stickler about it.

A thought struck him, and he broke the silence. "Hey, could you text Allye and tell her where we're going?" He'd hate for his sister to show up at an empty house. Besides, she'd probably want to come to the hospital anyway to support Corina.

A frown crossed Corina's face as she turned to him. "I'm sorry, what?" Obviously, her thoughts had been far from their present location. He repeated himself, and she nodded. The frown didn't totally disappear, but it did ease a little as she turned her attention to her phone. Message sent, she lapsed back into silence.

He made a few attempts at conversation, trying to get her mind off the unknowns of her dad's condition, but short answers were all he received in reply. Finally, he gave up and reached for the radio dial. The drive to the hospital was going to be another long one.

"HE HAS A HAIRLINE FRACTURE to his skull, some definite bruising. There is mild swelling on the brain, which is our primary concern. He was unconscious when he arrived. He tried to wake up—" the doctor consulted her dad's chart—"twice. But he was obviously agitated, and in his condition, that's more dangerous than beneficial. We had to induce a coma to help combat the swelling and prevent unwanted distress and movement."

Corina tried to process the information as it was being given, but there was too much to take in. Her attention began to drift as the doctor's words got lost somewhere between her ears and her brain.

They had been here over an hour and a half now. She had wanted to see her dad immediately, but they had arrived during a non-visitation time slot. Officer Mike and Bryce had both encouraged her to take the time to learn about her dad's injuries and take care of any paperwork the hospital might need. Everything was signed now, and only a few minutes remained until the next visitors' session.

With a start, she realized she was staring at the doctor in silence. *Focus.* She thought he had asked if she had any questions. Did she? She tried to think.

"What does recovery look like?" Bryce spoke up, and she shot him a grateful look.

"At this point, we can't say for sure. We'll know more once the swelling goes down and he wakes up. The fact that he was regaining consciousness on his own is a good sign, but brain injuries are tricky."

"Do you know what happened?" She hated the smallness of her voice.

"He was found behind a convenience store, with no wallet or other form of ID. I'm no detective"—he glanced at Officer Mike—"but his injuries match what you'd expect from a mugging. He was definitely struck on the back of the head and probably sustained another impact when he fell. The other bruises we've found are consistent with a fall and possibly some roughing up." He gave her a sympathetic look. "Unfortunately, from all indications he wasn't found immediately, and the time spent untreated and exposed to the rain and cold . . ." He lifted his shoulders and let them drop. "Well, it didn't help."

She slowly nodded, thanking the doctor as he excused himself. Bryce lightly squeezed her shoulder, and she turned to face him.

"Would you mind if I went in alone first?" she asked him.

He studied her, and she refused to flinch under his gaze. "If you're sure."

"I am." She was sure. Not sure that she would be okay, but sure that if she wasn't, she didn't want any witnesses to the breakdown.

Bryce didn't argue with her, but she could tell he knew exactly what she was thinking. With a soft "I'll be out here if you need me," he turned to find a seat in the waiting room.

It was time. Affecting a confidence she didn't feel, Corina squared her shoulders and found her way to her dad's room. Once inside, she caught her breath. Despite her efforts to prepare herself, the puffy black-and-purple bruises covering his face unnerved her, as did the number of tubes, monitors, and IV lines attached to him. Was it possible for someone to be so bruised and yet look so pale?

Her eyes traveled to his hands. No bruises there, other than a small spot surrounding the IV insertion point. That meant he likely hadn't put up a fight. Again, she blinked back tears. Whoever did this had caught him by surprise and hadn't cared how badly he'd been hurt in the process. They'd just left him there.

She sank into the chair next to his bed and reached out to touch his fingertips. They were colder than she expected. Careful not to disturb the IV, she wrapped her hand around his. A tear ran down her cheek, and she brushed it against her shoulder.

God, I know we haven't really talked much lately, but I still do believe in you. Please, please let my dad be okay. She held back a sob and leaned her head against the bedrail. *I need him, God. Please let him be okay. Please.*

BRYCE LOOKED TOWARD Officer Mike. The man had moved to stand guard near the nurses' station. He rose to join him. He had some questions that needed answers. Seeing him coming, the officer motioned him to a secluded corner where they could watch without being easily overheard.

Bryce crossed his arms. "So is this connected?"

"I can't say for sure. I called in some favors to see if we can get a profiler working on the case." He ran a hand over his balding head. "My gut is telling me no."

"Don't you think it's a huge coincidence that this would happen at the same time Corina's stalker shows up?"

"Absolutely. But it doesn't fit with anything that man has done before."

"Anything we know about," Bryce pointed out. "From the files I read, he was never identified or linked to any other crimes." And this guy was good. If these were his first and only crimes, he was a criminal genius.

Officer Mike drew in a deep breath. "Still—"

He paused as a man in jeans and a sports jacket paced close to them, phone to his ear. The man didn't slow or acknowledge them, but Bryce still followed him with his eyes until he disappeared down the hallway.

Mike cleared his throat. "Still, I can't see him bouncing between targets and leaving one with a fifty-fifty chance of survival. The previous murders were committed with precision. Each crime scene was a testament to his power and ability to outsmart law enforcement. Leaving Will's survival to fate would be taking the power out of his hands."

The analysis rang true. It sounded as if Will and Mike had discussed this case enough over the years to give him added insight.

Bryce watched the sports jacket guy reenter the waiting room and choose the seat he had just vacated—the one with a prime view of the room and its exits.

"One other thing." Officer Mike waited until Bryce turned to meet his eyes. The intensity of his gaze sent a chill through him. "Will believed he was the ultimate target—that all the other murders were simply ways of making him suffer first."

The import of that statement hit Bryce hard. But he got it. If Will's theory was correct, the killer wouldn't lay a hand on him until everyone close to him was dead. Corina was the only one left, and she was in the killer's sights. Not good.

Did the killer know what had happened to Will? If so, would this interference with his plan buy them enough time to catch him before he struck again?

19

SO. THIS LITTLE EXCURSION clarified everything. He scowled inwardly but kept his face neutral. William would pick a time like this to be injured.

His gaze flicked to the two men standing guard near the hall where Corina had disappeared. He recognized the local cop that was buddy-buddy with William, and Bryce Jessup of course. Broaddus hadn't shown any sign of recognition when he entered—thanks to the quick disguise he'd thrown on—and neither man was paying him any attention now, so he stayed where he was.

His eyes narrowed as he pondered this development. Getting to Corina had always been easy—at least since he'd found them again—and he didn't expect this new situation to change that too much. With his planning and setup, he had plenty of options to make things happen. But it would all be virtually pointless if William was unaware of it. He would have to move slowly enough to give the man time to recover.

And if William didn't?

His jaw tightened. That wasn't a possibility. William had to regain consciousness. Corina had to die first. After that, it didn't much matter if William relapsed. Either way, he would give the man time to wallow in his grief before completing his mission.

Once they were all dead and the debt paid, perhaps he would finally be at peace.

20

AT SEVEN THE NEXT MORNING, Bryce located his Camaro in the hospital parking garage. He scanned the surrounding cars, what few of them there were. Nothing out of the ordinary. Nothing that triggered his internal alarm. He slid behind the wheel and pulled forward out of his parking space.

It had been late last night when Corina remembered Houston. Not wanting to leave her dad, she'd begged for someone to go back to Kincaid this morning to take care of him. Her part-time employee had taken care of putting a sign up at Western Outfitters so customers would know the hours would be off for a few days, but Gus didn't have a key to Will's house—and Corina's father would flip if she shared the security code with a neighbor. He'd think it was bad enough that she was sharing it with Bryce and Allye while they stayed with her.

So that left Bryce to take care of Houston. He could have asked Allye to go—she'd stayed with them at the hospital last night too—but despite the uncomfortable waiting room, his sister wasn't awake enough yet to drive. But she'd be there if Corina needed her, and Officer Mike had alerted hospital security yesterday to the possible threat. They were taking the warning seriously.

And things had been quiet. They'd seen no evidence that Corina had been followed to the hospital, though there were no guarantees. But the fact the killer hadn't tried anything strengthened his belief that the man was biding his time until Will woke up. Corina would be all right for a few hours this morning.

His fingers tightened on the steering wheel. She'd better be all right.

This case with its lack of evidence was bizarre. How did four people get murdered at three different times, in their respective homes, in the same manner—without the killer leaving a single unintentional clue?

Why had no one been able to positively pin down a motive? Or identify even a possible suspect?

As a PI, Corina's dad would have had plenty of opportunity to make someone mad. Apparently, he had. But what would prompt such a deep-seated rage in an obviously brilliant individual? A common crook couldn't have pulled this off, nor one acting in the heat of the moment.

They needed to figure out the who and why. Until they did, there was little hope of putting a stop to this vendetta. And Corina would never truly be safe.

By hitting the road so early, Bryce managed to avoid rush hour traffic and made it back to Kincaid in record time. He pointed his car toward Will's house.

The street was quiet as he turned onto it. He hadn't had much of a chance to refamiliarize himself with the neighborhood, but Allye had indicated that, excepting Jamie and Collette and a guy who worked night shift, most of the current residents on this street were retired or semi-retired. Which meant most were probably still home, just not out and about yet.

He pulled into Will's driveway and shot his sister a text.

Everything going okay?

Almost immediately, a buzz signaled her reply.

Seems to be.

Good.

A school bus turned onto the street, and a boy around five or six years old darted out a front door. He made it to the end of his driveway before the bus did and transitioned to a moon walk while he waited. Could that be Jamie and Collette's boy? Bryce grinned at the kid's energy. His teachers—and parents—must have their hands full.

He pocketed his phone, just to have it buzz again. He pulled it back out and read the text.

Bring ice cream on your way back. Corina could use some chocolate.

He cocked an eyebrow and messaged her back.

Corina prefers peanut butter cup.

Fine. Then get both. 😁

He chuckled and stepped into the chilly morning air. Ice cream he could do. And if his business here took long enough, maybe he'd stop at the library when it opened and get Corina a couple of books—in case their wait was a long one.

An excited Houston almost bowled him over the instant the door was open. "Just a second, boy." He entered the code Corina had given him to shut off the alarm, then he bent to rub the German shepherd's neck. "Let's go for a walk, huh?"

He looked around. Where did Corina say the leash was?

After five minutes of searching and no luck, Bryce settled for letting Houston loose in the fenced-in backyard while he did a walk-through of the house.

Nothing seemed out of place—everything was as they'd left it yesterday afternoon. Everything down to the case files strewn about the coffee tables in the living room.

Bryce stooped to snatch a worn paper off the carpet and flipped it over. It was a list he'd been studying when Corina got the news about her dad.

He let his gaze wander to the rest of the files. He needed to go through them again. Needed to be as familiar with the killer's MO as possible so he could better identify any suspicious happenings.

Would it be safe to take them along to the hospital? If something happened to them . . .

Yeah, probably better not risk it.

But Will had a copier. Bryce had seen it the day they searched his office. Hopefully, it wasn't a temperamental one. If he had to, he could use his phone to take snapshots of the pages, but running off duplicates he could write on would be preferable.

He gathered the pages into a semi-neat stack and headed toward the office. After placing the documents in the scanning tray, he flipped the power switch on the machine and watched as *PLEASE WAIT* scrolled across the digital readout.

Great. If the machine was on the slow side, this could take a while. He blew out a breath and double-checked that Will's list was in the front of the stack. At least he could study it while waiting on the rest of the pages.

When the readout finally indicated the copier was ready, he hit the start button. About ten seconds later, the first copy appeared. He snatched it off the machine and ran a finger over the columns.

Case names and dates—everything Will and his stepbrother had worked on in the two years before the killings began. Some lines were crossed out with the letters *NI* jotted to the side. NI? Not important?

Maybe.

Then did Will consider the others possibilities?

They hadn't found any files from Will's closed cases. With how quickly he and Corina had pulled up stakes, Will might not have packed them at all.

Which would make it hard to figure out what was significant about them. Bryce might be able to do an internet search for archived news articles, but all of these cases were twelve to fourteen years old and might not have been newsworthy at the time anyway. Not to mention the fact he didn't even know if the names on the page were official designations or just Will's shorthand for them. The chances of finding the right info were slim to none.

If only he could just out-and-out ask the Houston police department. They might be able to pull up info on some of the cases, though they weren't likely to have anything on ones that didn't fall into the criminal category.

His eyebrows drew together. Maybe he could.

Ryan Jenkins, a guy who'd gotten out of the military a few years before Bryce, was from the Houston area. After going home, he'd signed on with the local PD, planning to aim for detective.

Setting the paper aside, he tugged out his phone and scrolled through his contacts. He tried to keep contact info for his buddies, but keeping track of everyone was impossible. Hopefully he still had RJ's.

Found it. As long as RJ hadn't changed it.

He pressed the call button and waited for a connection. It rang three times before someone answered with a groggy "Hello?" He couldn't tell if it was RJ or not.

"Hey, this is Bryce Jessup. This RJ?"

"Yeah, man. What you doin' calling at seven in the morning? I was on a case till almost midnight."

Bryce grimaced. He'd forgotten the time difference, and that it was still early even here. "Sorry, I wasn't thinking. What I need can wait. You want to call me back?"

"Nah, I'm awake now. Just give me a sec."

Bryce heard rustling in the background, then water running.

"There, coffee's on. I just might survive. Now, what you up to, man?"

"It's complicated."

"I don't do complicated in the morning, Jessup."

That was the RJ he remembered. Probably said it with a straight face too.

"I'll keep it as simple as I can."

Bryce ran through the basics of Corina's situation, stopping occasionally when RJ had a question.

"So we're trying to figure out who might be targeting her. I've got a list of cases her dad and his partner worked prior to the murders. I was wondering if you might be able to check some of them out for me—just so we can get a feel for the cases." And who Will might have made mad enough to kill.

"What I can share'll depend on the nature of the case and whether it's been closed." There was no mistaking RJ's tone. He wasn't going to break the rules, even for a military buddy.

"Understood. I have no clue what all Will handled, so I'll have to leave that up to your discretion. Hold on a minute, and I'll send you a pic of the list."

Bryce pulled the phone from his ear and snapped a picture. The second column with the dates was slightly blurred, but he sent it anyway. He heard a ding from RJ's side.

"That should be it."

"Lemme check." Sound muted, then RJ's voice came back. "Got it." From the sound quality, Bryce was probably on speaker now.

"I think Will ruled out the ones he marked through, but I haven't decided whether to completely discount them or—"

RJ's whistle cut him off. "He was involved in the Espinoza case? Now *that* was a big one."

His stomach tightened. "How big?"

"The guys still make references to it. That was what—ten, twelve years ago?"

"Yeah, somewhere around there." He shifted the phone to his other ear and reached for a pen. "What do you know?"

"Just what I've been told. That was long before my time here. It was a cartel-type deal, but family run. Kinda like the Mafia, know what I mean? The Espinozas had been on the radar for a while, but the PD could never nail them for anything much. Then a coupla PIs just blew the case open."

A couple of PIs. Will and Alan.

Bryce wet his lips. "So when you say they blew the case open, what do you mean?"

"They got someone talking. I dunno who or how, but they got names, locations, stuff nobody even suspected the Espinozas were involved in. By the time they verified things, there was enough evidence to call the FBI in."

His pulse sped up. The FBI got involved in Will's case? This was news. He circled *Espinoza* on the list.

"So what happened? Were arrests made?"

"Sure were. Top guys, like *top*, top. Pretty much shut them down."

"How did it play out? Were they sentenced?"

"I don't know the details of whether everyone was, but no way that case'd be touted as such a victory around here if the head guys got off."

Finding out for sure would be easy enough. "What are the names of the guys that got indicted?" He jiggled the computer mouse and waited for the screen to come to life. Password protected. Of course.

"Sorry, man. Other than Papá Espinoza himself, I don't know."

"Any way you could find out for me? Quietly, though—I don't want word getting out that I'm looking into this."

"No problem. Anything else you need to know?"

"I'll take any details on these cases that you can legally give me."

"Sure thing, man. I'll get back to you."

"Thanks. I owe you one."

RJ barked a laugh. "I'll put it on your tab."

"Do that." Bryce disconnected the call and leaned forward, tapping his pen against the wood of the desk. There was something here.

He glanced back down at the list and marked a single word next to *Espinoza*.

Motive.

21

CORINA DROPPED HER HEAD back to stare at the ceiling. Morning was nearly over, but it felt like a full day had passed since she'd woken from last night's fitful sleep. She'd never had to spend extended time at a hospital before, and she could already tell it wasn't going to improve her opinion of them. It would help if her dad were awake or in a normal room with regular visiting hours. At least then she could worry less and expend some energy by keeping him company.

She jerked when her phone started vibrating in her pocket. She'd set it on silent to avoid disturbing the other occupants of the waiting room. Pulling it out, she tilted the screen to check the caller ID: Officer Mike.

With a quick glance at Bryce, now back from Kincaid and dozing in the chair next to her, she stood and took a few steps toward a deserted corner. "Hello."

"Corina, hi. Got some updates on your dad's case if you've got a minute."

She straightened. "Of course."

"We've been tracing his credit and debit card uses from the day he disappeared. Several charges popped up. The first couple from that morning look legitimate—a significant ATM withdrawal, a

Dunkin' Donuts charge, a gas pump purchase. There's no video on the Dunkin' Donuts, but security footage confirms your dad's presence for the others.

"The gas charge is what interested us because the station is across the street from the convenience store where he was found."

Corina's fingers tightened around her phone. "Meaning, he was dragged across the street and dumped?"

"No," Officer Mike was quick to assure her. "According to the video, he pumped his gas, got back in the vehicle, and drove off. There's no sign of duress, no one approaching the vehicle. No passengers that we could see."

"And then?"

"The next charges start thirty minutes later, and according to what footage we've been able to pull, someone else had his cards at that point. We're trying to get an ID on who that someone is."

"So it's safe to say whatever happened to my dad happened in that thirty minutes."

"That's what it looks like."

"And you don't have anything yet on how he got to where he was found?"

"Working on it. It's not a friendly part of town, and the guy working the cash register at the convenience store wouldn't give access to the videos without a warrant or the store manager's okay."

"Seriously?"

"Unfortunately, yes." Officer Mike's frustration was obvious. "The manager was on vacation, and we just got ahold of him about an hour ago. A local officer is reviewing the footage now."

"Okay." Corina tried to think but couldn't come up with any other specific questions for him. "Anything else I need to know?"

"Not at the moment, but hopefully I'll hear something soon."

"Keep me posted."

"You got it."

She hung up and returned to her seat. So much they still didn't know. What exactly happened to her dad. Who was responsible. Why he was even in Cincinnati that morning to begin with. She groaned and rubbed her forehead. At least they had a time frame to work with now.

As much as she wanted to have those questions answered, she was more concerned about his recovery. The doctors' prognosis was less than encouraging. In the time since her dad had been brought in, he hadn't gotten any worse. But he wasn't showing much sign of improvement either. A tear escaped her eye, and she hurried to wipe it away before anyone noticed. She had embarrassed herself enough by bursting into tears this morning after receiving the latest report on his condition. Thankfully, Bryce hadn't been here to witness that.

She had to be strong. She didn't have a choice. But the strain of this waiting game was wearing on her. She was powerless to help her dad recover. Useless to change any of this.

At least her stalker was lying low. She bit her lip, unsure whether she was more comforted or frightened by that fact. She knew better than to think he had actually gone away. A man who appeared out of her past and traveled over a thousand miles to avenge a wrong at least twelve years old wasn't going to give up because her dad was in the hospital. That wouldn't make any sense.

But neither did his apparent inactivity. An uneasy feeling settled in her stomach, and she shifted to survey the room. Besides the nurses, there were a few people waiting—like her—for the next visitation slot, but no one looked out of place. And no one seemed to be paying the slightest attention to her.

She leaned back again, but her mind insisted on forming questions she had no answers for. How closely was she being monitored? Was the stalker here in the building? On this floor? Or biding his time elsewhere? The only thing certain was that he was too close for comfort.

A light snore snagged her attention. Bryce. The poor guy had to be exhausted. Other than his trip to Kincaid this morning, he'd barely left her side. And these weren't comfortable chairs. At least not after the first couple of hours.

She wasn't sure how she felt about his constant companionship. Or the fact he'd intended to use this week and next to finish moving before starting his new job at Bud's Auto—something Allye had let slip last night. Instead, he was spending the time sitting at the hospital ensuring nothing happened to her. And making sure she was as comfortable as possible. On his way back to the hospital, he had even taken time to stop at the library and grab her a few books. He'd remembered her favorite author. And her favorite ice cream.

He was a good guy. But that had never been in question.

The longing to allow herself to love Bryce again—or maybe to admit that she still loved him—bothered her. It warred with her need for self-preservation. No one could predict when a loved one would be ripped away. Was love, or even friendship, worth risking the very real possibility of heart-wrenching loss? Once, she would have said yes. After one-too-many of those losses, though, her answer had changed. And she was no longer sure if that was a good thing or not.

Frustration bit at her. Frustration at the unfairness of her situation. At the losses that had brought her to this self-imposed isolation. At the ability to psychoanalyze herself but inability to fix the problems she found.

Well, if there wasn't anything she could do about it, she wasn't going to dwell on it. Not now, anyway.

Heaving an irritated sigh, she straightened, winced, and reached for one of the library books Bryce had brought. She'd read it before, but it was a good one.

Although she felt a little guilty, she was able to find some escape in the story, effectively pretending her own problems didn't exist. But with the reprieve her eyelids grew heavy, and she soon found herself rereading more and comprehending less.

Someone tugged the book from her fingers. She looked up to see Bryce, a gentle smile on his face.

She yawned. "I must have dozed off."

"It's okay." He set the book aside. "Go ahead and get some sleep. I'll wake you up for the next visitors' session."

Too tired to protest, she nodded and tried to find a more comfortable position. He could keep watch for a while.

22

THE BOREDOM was getting to him.

And so was this weak coffee. He resisted the urge to spit it back into the flimsy Styrofoam cup. He swallowed a grimace—and the coffee—then tossed the remainder into a trash can.

He reached for a small mirror on the nurses' station and angled it so he could see Corina's sleeping form. She was curled up in one of the oversized chairs scattered about the room, her arms crossed protectively over her chest. She didn't sleep much and never soundly. He wasn't sure if her insomnia was due to her dad's condition or her own dormant danger. Probably both.

He felt her neighbor's eyes turning his direction, and he calmly disguised his activity by straightening the lapels on his suit jacket, then adjusting the thin wire-rimmed spectacles he wore. The goatee itched. He hoped it didn't leave a rash that would have to be covered up by tomorrow's disguise.

Today he was the nephew of an elderly Mrs. Fennel. Yesterday, he had masked his voice and struck up a conversation with one of her visitors, a friend from the woman's church. He'd learned Mrs. Fennel had only distant family and none expected to visit. She was also conveniently unconscious and in the early stages of Alzheimer's, so even if she did awaken, her lack of recognition would be expected. The perfect cover.

He settled back into his seat in a row of chairs turned away from Corina and Bryce Jessup. Although he would prefer to keep an eye on them at all times, variety kept him from being noticed. And they couldn't leave the area without passing him.

So he would sit here with his back to his prey and pretend to be interested in a book that, frankly, he didn't even remember the name of. But it contributed to his scholarly façade, and that's all that mattered.

An hour passed, then two. Words blurred before his eyes. The impulse to fidget was growing, but he tamped it down. He hated being inactive. Current circumstances gave him little choice, though. For the time being, his operation was confined to the surveillance of one floor of a hospital.

And it angered him. He wasn't even gathering information or strategizing. He was merely waiting. Ensuring they didn't elude him again.

Despite his unconventional methods of doing business, he was accustomed to industriousness, not dormancy. Even now, when most responsibilities were delegated to underlings, he was still actively involved in the planning and execution of each major venture. He thrived on challenge, on power, on accomplishment.

He would never retire from this business. Work and revenge were all he had to live for. His face contorted. That hadn't always been the case. He'd once had five other reasons to live, but because of William, all that had been stripped away.

Besides, he was wired to work, and everyone who knew him was aware of that fact. Not since his stepfather's drunken tirades had anyone dared to call him lazy.

He narrowed his eyes. If only the man could see him now.

Unfortunately—to use the word loosely—his mother's third husband had stumbled in front of a speeding vehicle one night some thirty years ago. He would never know what power his "lazy, no good, stupid stepson" wielded now. The man was lucky to have died at the hand of fate before he could be repaid for every verbal and physical assault he'd inflicted.

And he would have been repaid. With interest. Vengeance, as well as justice, demanded that debts always be repaid.

And that brought him back to William, the reason he sat in this foul-smelling room watching dust settle on cheap countertops.

He had overheard Corina talking with the Jessup siblings earlier this morning before Allye had left to run errands. There was still no change in William's condition. It could be anywhere from days to weeks before the doctors would consider bringing William out of the coma.

That possibility made him want to scream. This was the second day since Corina had discovered her father's location, and already this waiting was driving him mad. His jaw clenched. He wasn't sure how much longer he could take this.

He stilled as a thought occurred to him. Why not make use of the time he had? He wouldn't kill Corina until he knew for sure her father would survive to grieve her death. He didn't kill needlessly, and he had nothing against her personally. She was nice enough—he might even have liked her in different circumstances.

No. He couldn't kill her now. But he could antagonize her a bit more. Make her sweat. Raise the stakes high enough to get her out of this building and force her to let William wake up alone when the time came. If the man never awoke, Corina would have some additional trauma, but she'd live.

That was worst case. But the doctors expected William to survive, so he shouldn't have to worry about his plans being truly derailed. It was only a postponement. Time for him to make sure his last opportunity counted. Every action on his part would be one more thing William grieved when he remembered his daughter.

He weighed the risks. Every movement he made increased the chance of exposure, especially in a close environment like an ICU floor. It wouldn't do to get caught before he reached his goal.

But he wouldn't.

He'd never been caught before—never even suspected. He was too careful, too meticulous to be picked up by a bunch of small-town cops or hospital security. The only thing that might pose an issue was the security cameras, but they would be easy enough to work around.

His mind reeled with possibilities as he watched Corina pass by on her way to her father's room. The neighbor didn't follow, and he had a feeling the man was again scanning the area for any possible threat. A glance in the mirror confirmed it. He fought back a smirk.

Scan away, military boy. Nothing will happen to your girlfriend today.

After a moment, he stood, stretched, and made his way to Mrs. Fennel's room, pausing to inquire about his "aunt" Gwen's condition when he passed a nurse in the hallway.

He ducked into room 268. Three away from William's. Although his business here was done for today, he couldn't just leave. That would be suspicious. The charade must be maintained. After all, Bryce Jessup was watching. The young man would know soon enough of Corina's impending danger, but he mustn't be able to identify any suspects. The elusiveness of his identity was part of the thrill.

He sat by the woman's bedside and stared at her, unseeing, for ten minutes. Finally, he exited, flashed the nurse a smile, and walked purposefully toward the elevators. He had a bit of work to do this evening.

Corina wasn't going anywhere tonight. But tomorrow would be another story. After she received his note, she would distance herself from this place quicker than changing prices in a trade war. And with the new tracker he'd placed on Bryce Jessup's Camaro, he'd always know exactly where she ended up.

It was time for action.

He smiled. William could take as long as he wished to recover. The days wouldn't be wasted.

23

THE NEXT MORNING, Bryce stood and stretched as Corina disappeared in the direction of her dad's ICU room. His stomach rumbled. Allye would be here with food in a couple of hours. She had taken the evening shift for dog care, then stayed home last night. She would check on Houston again this morning, then bring Bryce and Corina something more palatable than hospital food.

He eyed the vending machine on the other side of the room and checked the time on his phone. With all the fast food and vending machine fare they'd had in the last couple of days, he ought to wait until Allye arrived. His stomach gurgled again. Okay, so maybe a snack wouldn't ruin his appetite.

He ambled to the machine and pulled his wallet out. Sour cream and onion chips for breakfast. Why not? He smoothed the corners of a bill and tried to insert it.

The machine made a whirring noise but wouldn't accept the money. He flipped it around and tried again. Still nothing. He dug a crisper one from his wallet, but it had the same result.

Funny. It was working fine last night.

He ran his fingers over the exposed part of the bill acceptor. He didn't feel anything amiss, so he leaned down to eyeball it.

There it was. Just a hint of green showed between the rollers, but it was too far in to grasp from this side. He huffed an exasperated sigh. Someone would have to take the thing apart to get to the jammed bill.

Too bad this wasn't an updated machine that accepted credit cards. He dug around in his pockets on the off chance that he had some loose change. A nickel and two pennies were all he came up with.

He hesitated, calculating the time it would take to find another vending machine. There should be one close by, and Corina had only been gone a few minutes. He'd be back well before she was.

And their stuff? He glanced toward the corner they'd claimed for the last couple of days. A few library books littered the end table, and their overnight bags were shoved underneath the chairs. Most of it would be fine for a few minutes, but Corina had left her purse too. Should he just push it back behind their other bags?

He blew out a breath. He knew better.

Walking back to their seats, he stared at the purse, trying to figure out the least conspicuous way to take it with him. At least it was small and solid black. If it had been Allye's, there would be no chance of his carrying it unnoticed. He chuckled at the image of himself holding one of Allye's supersized floral purses. Those things were more like suitcases.

Nothing for it. He grabbed the bag and headed in the probable direction of the nearest vending machine. Maybe he'd get lucky and not pass anyone. This wasn't prime visiting time. A few halls away, he found a vending area with working machines and purchased his chips and a Coke. So far so good.

Halfway back to their waiting room, he had to step into an alcove to make room for a janitor's cart. The thing was loaded so high with cleaning supplies and bulging trash bags that the man shuffling behind it was hardly visible. After he passed, Bryce continued on his way. Just before he reached a corner he heard "Nice purse."

Bryce turned and glared at the janitor's back, but the man didn't stop or say anything else. He shook his head. Oh well. He'd almost made it.

CORINA COLLAPSED into the seat next to Bryce, closing her eyes to ward off any conversation. The all-too-short visits with her dad were just as draining as the stretches of time between them. Seeing him lying there, still and helpless . . . He didn't look at all like the strong man who had taken care of her all her life.

The bruises were beginning to fade to a sickly yellowish green—not pretty, but it gave her hope that he was recovering. Once he woke up, she didn't know what they would face. The possibilities the doctors had warned her of included memory loss and personality changes, as well as other residual brain damage.

Until he regained consciousness, there was no way to accurately predict the extent of the damage done. With that in mind, she tried to ignore the frightening possibilities and concentrate instead on the next milestone. They'd deal with the rest when, or if, it happened.

A sigh escaped her, and Bryce shifted. She opened one eye to look at him. How did this man look so good after sleeping in a hospital waiting room? He had shaved while he was gone yesterday, but the stubble was returning with vigor. She liked it. The rugged, unkempt look fit him somehow.

As for herself, she'd been avoiding mirrors. Her imagination did a good enough job telling her she looked awful. She didn't need confirmation. Last night, Allye had tried to coax her into leaving long enough to take a real nap and a shower, but she was afraid to leave her dad. Just in case there was a change.

"How is he?" Bryce asked.

"The same." She let out another sigh and turned to fully face him. He offered her a potato chip, and she shook her head, resisting the urge to wrinkle her nose. Sour cream and onion at eight in the morning? That would do wonders for morning breath.

He shrugged sheepishly. "Allye will be here soon with some real food, but I couldn't wait. I should have grabbed pretzels or something for you."

"It's okay. I'm not hungry." She breathed a laugh at his disbelieving look. "Trust me, I've eaten more in the last couple days with you two standing over me than I normally do in a month." An exaggeration, but no matter how she felt about it, Bryce and Allye had been hounding her to eat every meal plus snacks in between. It was getting ridiculous.

He popped the chip into his own mouth and picked up his cell phone. "Whatever you say."

That'll be the day. She reached for the book she'd been reading and frowned. Something stuck out from between the pages. She pulled the slip of paper free and unfolded it, quickly scanning the typed message.

I've been watching you. You don't seem to be enjoying yourself. But I think hospitals are wonderful places. They bring families together and provide a nice, comfortable routine to follow. Oh, but routines can be a problem. They make it too easy to predict what a person is going to do and when.

You should watch your back a bit better. Someone with ill intent could follow you right into your father's room and take advantage of his vulnerable state. And yours. It would be easy with both of you together. Just an observation.

A picture was taped to the bottom of the page—a grainy photo of her exiting her dad's hospital room.

Corina lifted her head and shot a look about the room. There were only a few people in here, and none of them seemed to be paying any attention to her. But someone had to be.

"What's wrong?"

145

She silently passed the note to Bryce and turned her attention back to the room's few occupants. An elderly lady dozed in a chair across the room, and a middle-aged couple whose son had been in a car accident had just returned to their seats. Across the hallway, two nurses stood over a computer at the nurses' station.

"Where did this come from?" Bryce's whisper was urgent.

"It was in my book." But how did it get there? "Did anyone come over here while I was gone?" She turned her gaze on him, hoping he might have seen the guy.

"No, no one." His eyes narrowed, and he set his jaw. "I left for about five minutes to grab these chips from another vending machine. The one over here is jammed." He stood and moved in front of her. "He must have put it there while I was gone."

That meant the stalker was watching, just like the note said. And not just her, but Bryce too. Watching closely enough to take advantage of an unplanned window of time when neither of them was present.

She swallowed and closed her eyes, then opened them again when Bryce began talking. His words weren't directed to her, though. He held his phone to his ear, his tone grim.

"We've had another incident."

24

CORINA LIFTED HER HEAD from the car window as they approached her dad's house. Hospital security was cooperating with local police to review this morning's security footage, but everyone had agreed she'd be better off to relocate. If the note hadn't threatened her dad, she'd have fought the consensus, but she couldn't bring danger his way. Even if that meant she had to leave him in the hospital staff's hands.

Her conscience pricked her at that thought. Okay, so he was in God's hands too. But with the number of people he'd allowed to be taken from her already, that wasn't entirely comforting.

Her ringtone sounded as they pulled into the driveway, and she snatched her phone from her purse. Had they found something already?

But it was her landlord's number that showed on the caller ID. Not the police. She let it go to voice mail. Although she was grateful he was finally taking steps to repair last spring's flood damage to her living room, now was not the time to discuss paint or carpet. Again.

"Allye's here." Bryce pointed out the Jetta sitting in front of his house.

Corina glanced at the empty car, only now remembering that

Allye had her keys. Good thing she was here. She was probably already inside—likely taking over the kitchen.

A notification dinged on her cell as she gathered her things. She ignored it. Mr. Bright could wait.

She followed Bryce to the front door. It inched inward at his touch. He shot her a look. What was Allye thinking, leaving the door practically wide open?

Her hand slipped toward her weapon, which she'd retrieved from the lockbox Bryce had mounted in his trunk. Having the familiar weight back on her hip now that she was away from the hospital just felt right. Especially after that note and all the other revelations of the last few days.

Bryce grabbed an old wood-handled broom her dad always left on the porch and motioned her to stay back.

She raised her eyebrows. Not happening.

His shoulders rose and fell one, two, three times—then he shoved the door completely open and scanned the entry. A sharp intake of breath was his only audible reaction, but it sent her heart rate into double-time.

His body blocked her view, and she nudged him out of the way.

Allye's current collection of bags littered the floor as if they'd been abandoned in a hurry. The entryway table stood at an awkward angle, and sunlight from the doorway glittered on the shattered remains of a crystal candy dish.

The house was quiet. Too quiet.

She drew her gun and laid her other hand on Bryce's forearm. He turned slightly and leaned toward her, but his eyes never stopped scanning the area before them.

Rising to her tiptoes, she put her mouth as close to his ear as she could reach. "I'll take the rooms to the right, you go left."

His jaw tightened. He shook his head. "Stay with me."

"I'll be fine." She shoved his shoulder. "Just go."

Indecision flashed in his eyes, but she didn't wait. Allye might be in serious trouble right now.

She stepped over the broken glass and began a counterclockwise sweep of the house. No further sign of struggle met her searching gaze. Nothing out of place in her dad's room or her temporary bedroom.

Bryce met her in the hallway just outside the kitchen.

"Anything?"

He shook his head.

"She had to have been—" Scuffling from the direction of the front door cut her off midsentence.

"Stop!"

That was Allye's voice.

Bryce took off down the hallway, broom handle raised like a club. Corina raced after him. At the turn in the hallway, he stopped abruptly, nearly causing her to run into him. She braced her hand against his back.

"Just hold on. There's glass all over the place." Allye sounded more annoyed than alarmed.

Corina edged around Bryce to see her friend struggling with Houston.

"Allye?"

Allye's head shot up, and she held a hand to her heart. "Oh, you scared me!" Her eyes rounded. "What's with the . . . weapons?"

Bryce grunted and set the broom aside, and Corina holstered her revolver. "We thought something happened to you. You left the door open and with this mess . . ." He swept an arm toward the glass and scattered bags lying between them.

Allye's already flushed cheeks flamed brighter. "That wasn't supposed to happen, but when I got here, this guy"—she tightened her grip on Houston's collar as he strained toward Corina and Bryce—"decided he wanted a run through the neighborhood without a chaperone." She eyed the remains of the candy dish. "I'm sorry. I had to disarm the security system before chasing him. The table was a little closer than I thought it was when I spun back around."

"It's okay. No worries." Corina turned. "I, uh, I just need a minute." Without waiting for an answer, she made her way to her dad's office and wilted into his oversized chair.

Running down the hall hadn't been her brightest idea. Her heart was working overtime, her lungs demanding deep breaths, and her ribs . . . hurt.

She cradled her head in her hands. False alarm or real, thinking Allye was in trouble had frightened her. Images of her family and Derryck flashed through her mind, and she gripped handfuls of her hair, trying to force the memories away.

"Hey."

She lifted her head to see Bryce depositing Houston in the office. As soon as Houston's paws touched the floor, he bounded to her side. Some of the tension in her shoulders eased as he thrust his muzzle into her lap.

"Aw, did you miss me?" At her quiet words, his tail—or rather his whole hind end—wagged as forcefully as the day she'd picked him from the litter. She ruffled his neck and ears, earning herself a canine kiss on the nose.

Bryce coughed, and she looked back up at him. "All right if I close him in here with you while I get the glass cleaned up? Allye's going to work on breakfast."

"You don't have to do that. I can get it." She started to rise.

He held up a hand. "I've got it covered. Besides"—a grin lit his face as Houston pawed at her knee—"I think someone wants your undivided attention."

"Thanks." She sank back into her seat. "You're a keeper."

His grin widened, and she flushed. She hadn't meant to say those last few words.

"I'll remember that." He stepped into the hallway and winked before pulling the door shut behind him.

Really, Corina? She shook her head and forced her gaze away from where he'd stood.

Houston whined and dropped his head back in her lap, rescuing her from her embarrassed thoughts. "I'm sorry, boy." She buried her fingers in his thick fur. He seemed content enough with that.

Several minutes later, her phone dinged, reminding her of the ignored voice mail from earlier. With one hand still entangled in Houston's fur, she pulled up the message.

"Corina, this is Arnold Bright. Please call me back ASAP. It's urgent."

She bit her lip, not sure she wanted to get involved in a possibly lengthy conversation. But her landlord's tone indicated it was more than an inconsequential question this time. With a sigh, she pulled up his contact info. She stood and took a few steps away from the desk.

Mr. Bright answered on the second ring, his words rushed. "Corina, I need you to come out here. Everything's a mess."

"Come out where? What's going on?"

"I came out to let the painters in, and your place is completely trashed."

Corina sucked in a breath. A painful one. "What?"

"Trashed. *Trashed.*" He emphasized the word without elaborating on its meaning.

"Have you called the police yet?"

"Yes, they're here, but once they're done, I'm going to have to figure out the insurance claim, and I'll need your help for that."

"Oh . . . I don't have a vehicle right now. but"—she glanced at Bryce as he reentered the room—"I'll get there as soon as I can."

"Do that." He disconnected the call.

She stared at her phone. "Can this day get any—"

"Don't say it." Allye's voice sounded from behind Bryce.

She rolled her eyes. "Whatever. I've got to get to the duplex. Mr. Bright just called and said someone broke in."

Allye's jaw dropped. "What? How bad is it?"

"He didn't give me details, but it sounds pretty bad." She slipped the phone into her pocket. "He didn't say anything about your side. I'm assuming he hasn't called you?"

"No." Allye pulled out her phone and double-checked it, leaving a streak of flour across the screen. "But I was just at home—everything was fine at my place."

Bryce moved toward the door. "I can take you over there."

"Oh no, you don't." Allye frowned at him. "You two just got here, and you haven't had breakfast yet. I'll drive. You two eat on the way."

"I'm really not that hungry," Corina protested. As much as she liked Allye's cooking, food sounded terrible at the moment.

"Nonsense. You need to eat."

"Allye—"

"You. Need. To. Eat." She leveled a stare at her, then transferred it to Bryce. "Don't you say a word."

He held up his hands. "Fine. I won't turn down food. Let's get it and get going."

25

ALLYE MADE UP their plates in a hurry, and they all piled into her cherry red Jetta.

Corina picked at her breakfast on the short drive. Who ate pancakes in the car anyway? At least she didn't have to worry about making a mess since she'd passed on the syrup. If she were in the back with Bryce, she'd sneak some of the food onto his plate—a little harder to do from the front.

Bryce caught her eye in the visor mirror, and she mouthed, *Help.* His brows drew together in confusion, so she lifted a bite of pancake and stared at it pointedly before eating it. He got the drift. Either that, or he chose that moment to choke on his own food.

When he finished laughing, he tipped his head toward the space between her seat and the door. She glanced from his reflection to her plate and back, and he nodded. Worth a try. She waited until Allye was focused on a left turn, then slipped two of the three pancakes off the plate and held them behind her until she felt Bryce's tug.

"I saw that." Allye didn't turn her head.

Of course she had. But Bryce kept the pancakes.

Corina's phone began to vibrate, and she glanced hesitantly at the readout. So few of her calls had been anything but trouble lately. She wasn't sure whether to be glad or nervous to see Officer Mike's number. With a quick tap, she accepted the call.

"Hello?"

"I just got word about your house. How are you?"

Her lips pursed. "I'm fine. We're on the way over there now."

"I'm sorry, Corina. Really, I am. We'll catch this guy soon if I have anything to say about it."

"I hope so."

Officer Mike cleared his throat. "That isn't the only reason I called. I have some good news to share. Following the security footage and charges on your dad's cards paid off. The Cincinnati police have a suspect in custody."

Good news? That was the best news she'd heard all week.

"Is he talking?"

"He tried to deny everything, but he still had the credit cards when they picked him up. When he heard we had security video of him using them and that we were investigating it in connection with a murder case, he cracked. Apparently, your dad drove from the gas station to the convenience store across the road and paid cash for his purchases there. This guy was standing behind him in line and caught a glimpse of his wallet."

And her dad had just been to the ATM that morning. The contents would have been pretty enticing.

"According to him, he signaled a buddy, and they ambushed your dad when he left the store. Pulled him around back so he wouldn't be found as quickly, then grabbed his wallet, keys, and the disposable phones he'd just bought. Used his car for a quick getaway, then dumped it in an alley."

"No connection to the stalker, then?"

"None that we can see. Looks like a wrong place at the wrong time kind of deal."

"Okay. Thanks, Officer Mike. I really appreciate your keeping me updated."

She ended the call and filled Bryce and Allye in on the new

info. She shook her head. The story fit everything they knew so far, but it made her blood boil. What some people would do for a couple of bucks was sickening.

A minute later, they rounded the last corner, and her house—complete with police cruiser and landlord—came into view. She sucked in a breath, not sure she was ready to face anything else just yet. Allye reached over to give her hand a quick squeeze.

Mr. Bright made a beeline for their car before Allye had time to shift into park. His hair looked like he'd run nervous fingers through it a few too many times, and the twitch below his right eye worked overtime.

"I'm so glad you're here." He switched from wringing his hands to gripping hers in a killer handshake as soon as she exited the car. "The police aren't finished yet, but as soon as they are, we'll get you inside to assess the damage."

She tugged her hand free and casually flexed it as Allye circled the car to stand beside her. "How long have they been working on it?"

"It's been a while."

A car door sounded behind her, and Mr. Bright glanced briefly at Bryce as he joined them, then checked the time. "I'm hoping they'll have the scene cleared soon. I have a meeting in an hour that I can't miss."

Corina moved closer to the house, hoping to catch a glimpse through the open front door. The door she knew she'd locked—she hadn't set the alarm so Mr. Bright could give the painters access, but still. "Was the door open when you arrived?"

"Yes, at first I thought maybe you'd come home to pick something up, but your truck wasn't here. When I went inside . . ." Fingers in the hair again.

"How bad is it?"

He reached into his suit jacket and removed a cell. "Here. I snapped some pictures when I first arrived." He pressed it into her hand.

Anger began a slow burn in her stomach as she flipped through the photos. This was more than a break-in—it was vandalism. And she had little doubt who was responsible.

FORTY-FIVE MINUTES LATER, Mr. Bright left for his meeting, and Bryce breathed a sigh of relief. The man's nervousness had set them all on edge. More so than they already were.

Allye tipped her head toward the two officers emerging from Corina's front door. "Looks like they're about done."

Bryce hooked his thumbs in his pockets and listened as the police spoke with Corina about their report. These officers hadn't worked with them on previous incidents, but they seemed aware of her situation and assured her they would do everything they could to find the responsible party.

He hoped they would. And soon.

Finally, the police took their leave, and the trio watched the patrol car until it disappeared from sight around a corner.

Allye bumped him with her shoulder, and he followed her gaze to Corina. Her expression didn't reveal much, but hesitancy showed clearly in her eyes.

He set a hand gently on her shoulder. "You ready for this?"

"Yeah." But she swallowed hard before turning back to the house. She led the way inside, Allye close at her heels and Bryce bringing up the rear.

They all stopped just over the threshold. A verbal report and cell phone pictures didn't do justice to the damage.

Corina turned slightly, and he noted her compressed lips and the silence she lapsed into when frustrated or angry. Allye was quiet too. Shocked speechless for once?

Evidence of rage touched nearly everything in sight. Small pieces of furniture lay scattered about—many of them either splintered or embedded in the drywall, which looked like someone had taken a hammer to it. The larger upholstered items were slashed irreparably. Corina would have to start over, at least where this room was concerned. Not much of this was salvageable.

She bent to pick a framed picture off the floor. He knew the portrait—one of her as a preteen with both her parents and her brother. Gashes rendered it almost unrecognizable now. Gently, she pulled it from its smashed frame and shook off the loose glass. Her hands trembled as she hugged the defaced memento to her chest.

He clenched his fists. If he ever got his hands on the person responsible for this—

"This is awful." Allye found her voice. He looked her direction just in time to see her already wide eyes open further. "Hold on, I'll be right back."

He turned to watch as she hurried to her car, popped the trunk, and pulled out a large camera bag. Within a few seconds, she was back, snapping pictures at lightning speed. Good idea. The police had taken photos, of course, but Corina would need her own for the insurance claims.

Corina didn't respond to Allye's actions. She stood, portrait in hand, staring at the damage. Should he give her space to process or offer comfort? He reached a hand toward her, but she turned her back and headed for the hallway.

Space it was. He dropped his hand and wandered to the kitchen, choosing his steps carefully to avoid as much debris as possible.

His phone rang as he reached the doorway. A Cincinnati area code showed on his caller ID. "Hello?" He hoped this was good news.

"Hello, Mr. Jessup?"

"Yeah. Who is this?"

"Officer Samuels. I'm on the team looking into your incident at the hospital today."

"What did you find out?"

"Not much." Regret and irritation came through the phone quite clearly. "The footage from this morning was wiped from the recording before we got to it. Forensics might be able to recover it, but that's going to take time."

His chest tightened. "How much time?"

The man sighed. "It depends on how backed up our specialist is. I'm sorry, it's not something I have control over."

"Anything on the picture he left her?"

"Based on the angle, it appears to have been pulled from the security system, so he may or may not have been there himself when it was taken. We're not sure how he managed to hack in yet. Security wasn't aware of any breaches."

"Until now." Bryce muttered the words.

"Yeah." Officer Samuels paused. "That's all we have right now. The nurses didn't notice when you left the waiting room, much less who might have been there while you were gone, and they didn't get a good look at the janitor you mentioned. Please keep us posted if you recall anything else that might help."

"All right. Thanks for calling." Bryce did appreciate the update, even though the news wasn't much to speak of. He slipped the phone back into his pocket and went into the kitchen.

There was no less mess here. Table and chairs were strewn in various states of uprightness, cabinet doors ripped off their hinges, drawers emptied on the floor. The refrigerator still stood open, and slightly cooled air wafted his way. Might as well close that.

He stepped over shattered china and forced the now off-balance door shut. Turning back toward the living room, he saw something Mr. Bright's pictures hadn't caught.

Most of the wall he now faced was covered in amateur graffiti. Various clocks, all nearing midnight, surrounded a single phrase in bold red lettering.

TIME IS RUNNING OUT

26

THE ENTICING SCENT of bacon hung in the air as Corina made her way to the kitchen the next morning. Too bad she wasn't hungry. Her stomach growled a challenge.

Maybe she'd have just one piece.

She rounded the corner to see Bryce at the table, nursing a cup of coffee. He practically glared at her over the plates of food.

Maybe bacon didn't sound good after all. She bypassed the dishes on the table and filled a thermos with coffee from the full pot on the counter.

"Your going in today is not a good idea." His tone straddled a fine line between frustration and exasperation.

"We discussed this last night," she said, focusing on keeping her own tone even. More than once they'd gone over whether she should open the shop today. She'd thought the matter was settled.

"And you still aren't seeing reason."

Apparently it wasn't.

She added a healthy dose of the pumpkin spice creamer that Allye had brought and turned back to face him. "I can't stay cooped up here forever."

"I didn't say you should stay here forever. But the threats toward you haven't slowed. Your house was just ransacked yesterday." He slammed his mug down, dark liquid sloshing over the sides.

Her stomach tightened at the reminder. "Yes, *my* house. Where *he*"—she couldn't bring herself to say *stalker* or *killer*—"knew I wasn't staying." She notched her chin up. Gripped the thermos tighter. "I'll be ready to leave in ten minutes."

She stalked back to her room and set the thermos on her dresser. Ten minutes? Make that five.

She grunted her way into her vest and boots, then leaned against the dresser to catch her breath. She hoped these simple motions would become less painful soon.

Houston nudged the back of her knee, and she turned. In his mouth, he held her favorite Stetson—her only Stetson now that her stalker had bashed or shredded the others. Along with nearly everything else she owned. She tugged lightly on the brim, and Houston released his hold.

"Thanks." She scratched his ears, then twirled the hat on her index finger before placing it on her head.

"What do you think, Houston?"

Footsteps sounded behind her, and her eyes caught Allye's in the mirror.

"Oh, hey."

"Morning." Allye perched on the edge of the bed and offered Houston half a slice of bacon, which he wolfed down in point two seconds.

Allye didn't meet her eyes again, so Corina studied her. There was no mistaking the uneasiness there, and she was pretty sure she knew the cause.

"Did Bryce tell you to talk me out of going?"

Allye rolled a shoulder. A yes.

"Well?"

"My brother needs to learn to pick his battles."

"You don't think I should go, though, do you?"

"No." Allye left it at that.

Corina focused back on her own reflection and adjusted her already straight hat. "Saturdays are my busiest days. I can't expect Gus to handle things by himself—especially with how much he's already covered for me this week. And I can't afford to stay closed and lose more business." Even if she could convince herself to let Gus handle the afternoon alone, he only had about four hours to work with before he'd reach his weekly limit for his social security benefits. That left the morning and early afternoon totally up to her.

Allye didn't respond. Just broke off another piece of bacon for Houston.

"Besides, I have a delivery coming in today that needs my signature."

"I'm not arguing with you."

No, but she wasn't agreeing either. Normally, that wasn't a big deal, but today, Corina needed someone to support her decision. Bryce sure wasn't filling that role.

Maybe if she tried a different tack, Allye would understand. She spread her hands and turned to face her. "Look, I need to be doing something. I can't stand the thought of staying cooped up in this house for who knows how long when I'm probably just as safe at Western Outfitters."

"Like I said, I'm not—"

"Arguing." Corina finished her sentence. "I know." She pressed cold fingertips to her forehead and closed her eyes. "Sorry. I guess I'm the one arguing."

"Mm-hmm."

She opened one eye in a mock glare. "Sure. Agree with me about that."

Allye didn't smile. "It's too early for arguing. Besides, you're going to go regardless."

"Yes. I am." But she winced inwardly. She was being stubborn, and she knew it.

But what she'd told Allye was valid. She had a business to run, and she needed something—anything—to feel normal for just a little while.

She grabbed her purse, thermos, and jacket and headed for the front door, Houston following close behind. Should she take him along today? She'd have to convince Bryce or Allye to bring him back around lunchtime. Gus was slightly allergic to dogs, and she tried not to aggravate his symptoms by taking Houston on days he was working.

But Houston had been cooped up for several days too, and maybe having him along would help Bryce feel better. Not that there was likely to be any real danger. She pulled the leash from a small drawer in the entryway table and clipped it onto his collar.

After disarming the alarm, she led him out to the porch and looked around to assure herself no one lurked within sprinting distance.

Houston growled and strained at his leash. She tensed and searched the direction he was focused on. Several squirrels frolicked in the yard next to them. Two ran up a tree, chattering like mad while a couple of others helped themselves to the contents of a birdfeeder.

"Down, Houston."

He whimpered but obeyed, still gazing that direction. She grinned and wrapped the end of the leash around her wrist. The squirrels were safe today. Mrs. Anderson complained about their thievery, but Corina got the idea that she secretly liked the uninvited visitors.

She resumed her survey of the street. A few houses farther down, Gus knelt in his flowerbed, digging up tulip bulbs and placing them gently in a metal bucket beside him. The elderly man glanced up. A grin split his face as he caught sight of her. He pulled himself to his feet, wobbling just a bit as he got his footing, and headed her direction.

Behind Gus, a car turned onto the street, and Houston rose and let out a bark, sending the remaining squirrels running.

Corina tugged at his leash. "Hush now, or I'm going to put you back inside until we leave." Houston made a disgusted sound in his throat. "I mean it," she warned as the car pulled into the garage of the house next to Bryce's. Who lived there now? She couldn't remember.

"Morning!" Gus stopped at the end of her dad's driveway and propped his dirt-covered gardening gloves on his hips. "How you feeling today?"

She grinned back at him. "Morning, Gus. I'm doing all right."

A forty- or fifty-something man exited the still-open garage and strode to his mailbox. She didn't recognize him. A new neighbor? He looked up, caught her watching him, and gave a half nod before snatching the mail from his box and quickly returning to his garage. Friendly sort. She'd have to ask her . . .

"How's your dad?" Gus's question landed at the same time she realized she couldn't ask her dad right now.

She blinked back the threatening tears. "No change."

"I'm sorry to hear that." He eyed her. "You sure you're up to running the shop today? If you'd rather be at the hospital with him, I can pull a few extra hours as long as I shave some off another week to keep the average down."

"No." She managed a weak smile. "You've been a lifesaver this week, but I've got this morning covered. The hospital will let me know if there's any change."

"If you're sure." Gus didn't look convinced.

"I am. Enjoy your morning."

"All right. See you at one."

"See you. And thanks!" she called after him as he headed back toward his flowerbeds.

She glanced across the street. The stranger's garage was closed now, and all the window blinds were closed. The ones on the nearest window had a broken slat near eye level. The blinds swayed slightly as if someone had bumped them. Was he watching her?

Or she was being paranoid. He could have simply passed by the window. Either way, he was inside his own home—not bothering her. Refusing to be creeped out without good reason, she turned her focus to observing the neighborhood. Other than Gus, no one was in sight.

Satisfied for the moment, she lowered herself to a seat on the steps to wait for Bryce, who didn't seem in a hurry to leave. Houston sat beside her, attention again focused on the yard next door.

"You're going to have to stop scaring those squirrels away if you want to watch them," she told him, stroking his head. He accepted the attention without complaint, and she allowed herself to rest in the moment. Autumn was all around them. In the crispness of the air. The scent of woodsmoke. The flamboyance of the scarlet maple at the corner of the yard.

A few leaves fluttered to the ground—a slight breeze was all it took to loosen their clutch on the branch that had served as their lifeline for so long. Others would be more obstinate, hanging on for dear life until the last possible moment. But they would eventually fall too.

She could relate.

The wind kicked up, sending a chill through her. She tightened her jacket, longing for the warm Novembers of her childhood. She shoved her free hand into her pocket. Kentucky might have been home for half her life now, but she would never get used to the cold.

Houston crowded her right side, his warmth providing some comfort. The rest of her body felt like it was turning to ice already. *Come on, Bryce.* She should have grabbed his keys so she could wait in the car. Not having her own vehicle stank.

She made a mental note to call Bud's and see if they'd been able to start on her truck yet. Insurance had chosen not to total it, but the auto shop hadn't known how long it would take for the needed parts to arrive. They probably wouldn't be open this early, but she'd have to call before noon if she wanted to catch them before they closed.

The door opened behind her, and she turned her head halfway to catch a glimpse of Bryce's combat-style boots.

Without a word, he offered her a hand up. She took it and stood, but her foot slipped on the edge of the second step. He tightened his grip and grabbed her elbow in his other hand to keep her upright. Her hat jolted askew.

"Um, thanks." She swallowed. His face was close. Really close. Something in his expression changed—the scowl he'd worn all morning softened, and the concern in his eyes gave way to longing. He leaned closer.

"You two all right over there?" Gus's voice and a sharp bark from Houston shattered the moment and sent heat rushing up her neck.

Bryce immediately let her go and stepped back, head swiveling in Gus's direction. "Doing just fine. Yourself?" There was a slight tremor to his words. Not enough for Gus to notice, perhaps, but she did.

Gus grinned at them for a second too long before replying with a "Same as always. Same as always" as he turned back to his garden.

Corina let out a breath she hadn't realized she was holding and righted her Stetson. What was it with her almost falling off the porch when Bryce was around?

"You sure you want to do this?" He spoke softly.

"Yeah." She cringed at the breathless quality of her voice. She cleared her throat but didn't meet his eyes. "I—I guess we should get going." She readjusted her grip on Houston's leash.

"Can you make it down the steps by yourself?"

"Excuse me?" Her head jerked up just in time to catch the twinkle in his eye before he sidestepped her and again offered his hand.

She let out an exaggerated and totally fake-sounding huff and reached for the railing instead. Bryce just raised an eyebrow and let her and Houston lead the way to his Camaro.

As they pulled out of the driveway, disquiet reared its head. Was her stalker watching nearby? Her gut said yes.

She let her eyes roam, taking in every detail of the street, the houses, what she could see of the backyards. Everything looked . . . normal.

And that bothered her more than anything.

BRYCE PULLED into Western Outfitters' lot and eyed the building. This was the last place Corina should be right now. The building was too exposed. Too open.

"I don't like this at all." He tried to temper the scowl on his face. Judging by the tightness at the corners of his mouth, he was failing badly.

Corina blew off his concern. "I'm as much a sitting duck at my dad's as anywhere else."

"But this place is a security nightmare." He waved a hand toward the picture windows that covered most of the shop's front. The rolling bars were down now, but he had no doubt she would change that once they got inside. Even if he could convince her to leave them in place, they didn't offer any additional privacy. Anyone driving by could see nearly the entire front room.

"It's just for the day, Bryce. I'll be fine."

Fine.

He snapped his mouth shut and backed into the parking space closest to the door.

Now it was Corina's turn to frown. "I usually leave this spot open for customers."

"Not today." If they had to make a hasty exit, he didn't want to have to cross a lot of open space. He'd prefer to park near the back door, but the alley butting up to it wasn't quite wide enough for the Camaro.

Actually, he'd rather turn around and head back to her dad's house. That's exactly what he would do if she hadn't threatened to walk here if she had to. And she would—bruised ribs or not. The best he could do was keep an escape option close and Corina even closer.

He stalked around the car to open her door, but she didn't wait for him. Well, he'd get Houston, then. The dog was more appreciative of his assistance.

He turned to see Corina at the shop entrance, struggling with the lock. "Something wrong?"

"It doesn't like the cold any more than I do," she muttered as she drew back, shaking her hand. Before he could try, she kicked the door and jerked at the key again. This time, the bolt slid back. She rushed inside to the sound of a pulsing alarm.

Following her, he closed the door behind them and bent to release Houston from his leash. The dog immediately disappeared into the back room.

Bryce chuckled and shook his head, but it was only when he straightened that he registered the inside temperature.

The room was cold. Too cold.

"You forget to leave the heat on?" He turned his attention back to Corina.

"With this weather?" She grunted. "It's been midforties for the last week and a half. I'm from Texas, not Michigan." She stepped inside the back room. Bryce followed her as far as the doorway as she fiddled with the thermostat.

The furnace kicked on, and air shot out a vent above him. "Hey! You running the AC or the furnace?" That definitely wasn't warm air he felt.

The artificial breeze died with a click as she shut the system off.

"Great. Just great." She stalked past Houston's monstrous doggie bed and yanked the front off the old-fashioned looking unit, revealing a reset button. She held it down for a few seconds, then returned to the thermostat and turned it on again.

More cold air.

Bryce leaned against the doorjamb and crossed his arms. "And you're sure you want to open the shop today?"

"Shut up." She may have muttered the words, but he still heard them. He didn't bother to hide his smirk.

She pushed past him to the front room and pulled a space heater from beneath the checkout counter. "Not as good as central heat, but it's better than nothing. Hopefully it'll warm up before any customers get here."

And before they got hypothermia.

She moved from the light switch to the door and flipped the sign to *Open*. A tremor passed through her body.

He shook his head. They'd only been here a few minutes, and she was already shivering. No way she was going to get comfortable with that tiny space heater. He sighed and slipped out of his jacket. "Here." He draped it over her shoulders.

She tensed at his touch, then jerked the jacket off and turned to face him. "I've already got a jacket. You need this as much as I do."

"Keep it." He headed back to the other room. "I'm going to take a look at your furnace. The jacket'll just be in my way." Sort of true, depending on what was wrong with it.

Bryce double-checked the thermostat settings, then moved to the unit itself. The front panel was still off, and he scanned the unit. His specialty was engines, not HVAC. But if it was something simple, he might be able to figure it out.

Here's hoping. As much as he'd prefer Corina to return to the safety of her dad's house, he understood her need to be here—to be doing something. He rolled up his sleeves. *Help me fix this, God. Corina could really use a break.*

27

NOT LONG AFTER BRYCE began work on the furnace, Corina's expected delivery arrived. As soon as the driver was gone, she knelt beside the packages. She'd already given them a quick perusal to verify everything was there before she signed the invoice, but she hadn't taken the time to look closely. Excitement made her fingers tingle. Or was it the cold?

She set aside the smaller package—Bryce's order from earlier in the week. He'd be glad to get it, she was sure, but she was more interested in the contents of the other crate. Pushing the too-long sleeves of Bryce's jacket up higher on her wrists, she dug in.

The case of specialty sporting rifles had been on backorder for over a month. She lifted one from the case and tugged the plastic off.

These were beauties. She ran a hand over the stock, admiring again the new camouflage that blended in so well with the woods around Kincaid. Imprinted foliage reminiscent of cedar, buckeye, and sycamore twined together in a pleasing display. No wonder they sold so quickly.

She stood with a grunt and placed two of them on the shelf. Much better than the *Out of Stock* sign she'd been staring at the last few weeks. She ran a finger over the top of the glass case, and it came away coated in dust. Already? Business was slow the last day she'd been at the shop, so she'd given everything a good cleaning. That was only this past Monday. She frowned and put dusting on her mental list of things that had to be done this morning.

She turned her attention to the rest of the delivery. The remaining rifles needed to be stowed for now. The safe was in the back room, but if they moved as quickly as the last shipment, keeping them close would make more sense—at least for the hours she was here. Gus didn't work with the firearms side of the shop. She pursed her lips and tapped a fingernail against the crate. Behind the counter would do for now. Any overstock could be moved to the safe later.

She moved the small package to the counter first, then returned to the larger crate and tugged. She let out a grunt. It was heavier than she'd expected. Not as bad as some she'd moved, but still heavy. Gritting her teeth, she half carried, half dragged the crate across the floor and dropped it into position behind the counter.

There. Not so bad.

She recognized her mistake as soon as she straightened. Her chest muscles spasmed, and she bit back a gasp. She held her breath until she made it to a chair, then doubled over to get her bearings.

One. Two. Three. She counted silently. Straightened her posture just slightly. Counted again. The last thing she needed was for Bryce to come in and see her acting like an out-of-shape gym newbie who'd started off her routine with a run.

Breathe.

Houston emerged from the back room, clutching a stuffed armadillo between his jaws. He approached her, dropped the toy at her feet, then snatched it up. Dropped it, jumped backward, and half crouched—daring her to attempt a rescue of the armadillo—then snatched it again. His favorite game.

And one she couldn't play right now.

Keeping one hand firmly across her middle, she reached out the other to ruffle the fur around his ears, but he dodged her and repeated his armadillo dance.

"Houston, I can't play right now." She kept her voice low and shot a glance in Bryce's direction. He didn't look up from his phone.

The dog's tail drooped. He picked up the stuffed animal and stared at her. She could almost see the word *traitor* in his eyes. He padded into the back room and looked at Bryce. Looked back at her. Dropped the armadillo at Bryce's feet.

Now who was the traitor?

But she couldn't stop a grin as Bryce pocketed his phone and joined in the game. Soon the two were involved in a full-out tug-of-war that lasted several minutes.

She'd played enough with Houston to know when he began to tire. His wagging tail moved a fraction of a beat slower, and he let Bryce have just a little slack. She laughed silently. There it was.

With a renewed burst of energy, the dog backed up and shook his head, making Bryce fight for it. Without warning, Houston released his grip.

Bryce landed on his rear with a thump.

Mouth twitching, Corina stood and slowly straightened to her full height. *Ouch.* She pasted on a smile and joined Bryce and Houston in the back.

"Good show."

Bryce gave a low chuckle and rubbed his sore spot. "I won, but I think I lost."

"I know." She smirked. "The only way to beat Houston at that game is to let go before he does."

"Noted." He stood and tossed the armadillo in Houston's direction.

Corina pulled a can of Dr Pepper and a water bottle from her mini fridge and held them up. "You want something to drink?"

"Water would be great."

She tossed him the bottle and slid the soda back into the fridge. Until they got it warmed up in here, she'd stick with her coffee.

Bryce took a long swig of his water and recapped the bottle. "I figured out your problem." He reached for something leaning against the wall behind him. "Your filter."

She grimaced. There was enough lint caked on the thing to stuff a new armadillo for Houston. She had no idea how long it took for that much lint to accumulate, but just the thought of all that floating around in her air supply was gross.

"I'm assuming since you pulled it out that replacing it is pretty easy?" she asked hopefully.

"Yeah, you just slide it in. Do you have a new one already?"

"Uh, no." She shook her head. "First winter here. I haven't had to replace it before."

"That's fine. Allye texted a few minutes ago and said she was going to pick up some groceries, so I'll see if she can stop and get one on her way." He pulled out his phone and snapped a picture of the filter's label. "If she can't find the right one, the hardware store employees can find it for her." He grinned.

Likely, that was exactly what would happen. When Corina settled on this location for Western Outfitters at the beginning of the year, there had been a lot of fixing up to do before she could open shop, and Allye had insisted on helping her with the work. Purchasing hardware and the like wasn't her specialty, though, as they'd quickly learned. Food—yes. Nuts, bolts, and screws—not so much.

"Thanks." She grabbed a bottle of glass cleaner and some paper towels. "I'm going to try to get some stuff done until then." That's what she was here for. Besides, the front room, where the space heater was set up, would be at least a tad bit warmer than in here. She started for the front but paused at the doorway. "Oh, your Sig came in. When you're ready, we can get the paperwork filled out and the background check run, then it's all yours."

"Great! I'll be in after I call Allye."

A couple of minutes later, Bryce emerged from the back, and she looked up from the display case she was working on.

"Guess I didn't catch her in time. She's already at the grocery and will have to drop the food at your dad's house when she's done. It'll be a bit before she can get the filter here."

"That works." They'd have to deal with the cold a bit longer, but the delay was that much more time she'd have until Bryce was after her again to head to a "safer" location.

She'd take what she could get.

A couple of hours and several customers later, Allye pushed sideways through the front door, arms loaded with bags and the new filter.

"Hey, you." Allye eyed the case of steel thermoses she was pulling from to restock the displays. "I hope you didn't lift that by yourself."

She made a face. "Bryce wouldn't let me."

"Good for him." Allye headed toward the back room, and Corina followed.

"About time you got here," Bryce called from a corner, where he was putting up some storage shelves she hadn't gotten around to yet. He set down his drill and took the filter from Allye.

"I brought you lunch. Be nice." Allye glanced at the used filter. "Wow. Is that dust-bunny heaven?"

Bryce grunted. "Something like that. Let me get this in and see if we can get some heat in here."

Corina crossed her fingers as he slid it into place.

"That should do it." Bryce replaced the cover and pointed to the thermostat. "Try turning it on now."

She did, and air—warm this time—started flowing from the vents.

"I guess that did it." Bryce rose with a grin on his face. "This filter should last you about three months."

"Thanks." She felt her cheeks flushing. "I can't believe I didn't think to check it sooner."

He shrugged. "It's an easy thing to forget." He moved to the sink to wash his hands.

"Well, now that's done." Allye pushed her glasses up higher and turned to open her bags. "Let's eat." She set a couple of takeout boxes on the counter.

Houston perked his ears but didn't move from his place in the doggie bed. *Good boy.* He might stare at them while they ate, but he knew better than to try to snatch anything—a behavior Corina always made sure to reward.

Her stomach rumbled at the tantalizing smells coming from the boxes. Maybe skipping breakfast this morning hadn't been the greatest idea. Less than a week with Bryce and Allye, and her body was already readjusting to a normal eating schedule. Not a bad thing, but she'd gotten out of the habit of bothering. Eating regular meals alone was a hassle.

She grabbed a box of plastic forks and some disposable plates from a cabinet and set them next to Allye's boxes. "That smells good. Chinese?"

"You got it." Allye opened the lids to reveal lo mein, fried rice, and broccoli-beef. "Thank goodness they're still warm. I was afraid everything would be cold by the time I got the filter and got back here."

"I'm sure it'll be fine." Corina surveyed the counter to see if anything else was missing. "What do you want to drink? I have water and Dr Pepper."

"You also have peach Snapple hidden in the back of the fridge," Allye said with a wink. "I put it in there the last time I was here."

Corina rolled her eyes in mock disgust. "I'm assuming that's what you want, then?" She opened the mini fridge and located the bottles of tea.

"Yup."

"Bryce?" She glanced over her shoulder.

"I'll take a pop, thanks."

She pulled out two Dr Peppers. "Why don't we take all this to the front? It's going to take a while for this place to heat up, and it's a little warmer in there."

"Sounds good." Bryce grabbed two folding chairs and a box of food and led the way.

Once they had everything transferred to the area behind the checkout counter, they each grabbed a plate and started in on the food.

"Chopsticks?" Bryce offered her a set.

She shook her head and grabbed a fork. "Never got the hang of those. Besides, this is faster." She speared a large bite of noodles and lifted them triumphantly.

"Suit yourself." He wielded his chopsticks with ease, lifting a bite just as big as hers to his mouth.

Show-off.

She chewed slowly, savoring the taste as she glanced about the room. The shop already looked cleaner than when they'd arrived. Except for the case of thermoses she'd left in the middle of the floor. Better get that before a customer came in and tripped.

She set her plate on the counter and circled the barrier.

"What's wrong?" Allye asked.

"Just need to move this out of the way."

Bryce stood, but she motioned him back to his seat. "It's almost empty. I've got it."

She hefted the box to her shoulder and turned to face them. "See? Not heavy at all."

A sharp crack sounded.

Glass exploded around her.

28

BRYCE'S HEART LURCHED as Corina hit the floor, thermoses flying from the case she'd been holding.

He dove to the ground, then realized Allye still sat frozen, chopsticks midair. He yanked her out of her chair. The hollow counter wouldn't be enough to stop a bullet, but it would break the shooter's line of sight.

Shots continued to pepper the wall near where Corina had been standing. Was she hit? *God, please, no!* He needed to get her back here.

He glanced at his sister. "Keep your head down and find cover in the back room." He gave Allye's shoulder a shove when she didn't move. "Go! Once you're in a safe spot, call 911."

He watched only long enough to see her start that direction before he pulled his new pistol from its holster and stuck his head around the corner to assess the situation.

Corina was crawling toward him, her progress agonizingly slow. But she was moving. That was a good sign. He looked toward the windows but couldn't see anything from this angle. Which meant the shooter probably couldn't see him. Or Corina.

But they were still sitting ducks.

The shots paused. He waited, listening for clues to the shooter's next move. Between the ringing in his ears and Houston's frantic barking, he couldn't make out anything else. Was the shooter reloading? Or waiting for one of them to expose themselves?

One way to find out.

He reholstered his weapon and rushed out from behind the counter, staying as low as possible. Another volley of shots erupted. He grabbed Corina's wrists.

A bullet whizzed by his head and shattered the display case behind him. Way too close. With a burst of speed, he pulled Corina behind the counter and dropped beside her. He looked her over, hardly daring to believe she'd managed to escape without a bullet hole. She had several cuts from the glass and was struggling to catch her breath, but he saw no significant blood.

He touched her shoulder. "You okay?"

She nodded, but there was no mistaking the look on her face. Corina was livid.

Good. As long as she was mad, she wouldn't freeze. His girl would fight.

His girl?

He shook his head. No time to untangle that thought.

"Let's get out of here." Anything beat sitting and waiting to get shot—even if it was just as dangerous somewhere else. What he wouldn't give to have left his car anywhere but in front of the building. So much for a quick escape.

They crouch-crawled into the back room, and he kicked the door closed behind them. He caught a glimpse of Allye wedged into a corner behind the safe, holding a straining Houston by the collar with one hand, her phone in the other. Good choice. Most likely bulletproof, it was probably the safest spot in the room.

Three more shots sounded, then the bullets stopped. At this point, he had no idea if that was a good thing or not, but he'd take what he could get.

"Is that the police?" Bryce indicated the phone Allye held to her ear. His sister nodded.

"We're all in the back room now," she said into the phone. She surveyed the two of them. "No, no one was hit."

Thank you, God. He squeezed Corina's hand. Felt her return squeeze.

"No—no, I won't hang up." Allye turned the phone slightly away from her mouth. "The police are on their way." Her voice shook. She clutched her phone tightly, knuckles whitening around it.

Finally. They just needed to stay out of the line of fire until backup got here. "What's their ETA?"

Allye spoke softly into the phone, never taking her eyes off him as she waited for a response. "Three or four minutes."

He looked at his watch and counted off thirty seconds to ground himself back in real time. Three to four minutes. He kept watching the second hand. If the shooter continued to hold off, they would be fine. But if he started shooting again, how many bullets would he be able to get off in the time he had left?

As if in answer, two more shots rang out in quick succession. Bryce spun around. Those shots had come from behind the store.

He darted a look at the back door. Bolted, but the locks didn't appear to be the type to withstand a bullet if the shooter decided to blast his way in. How long did they have now? Two and a half minutes? Three?

A shadowed figure darted into view outside the room's single window. Bryce caught a glimpse of an outstretched gun before the figure was again out of sight. But his trajectory would take him right to the door. In those two or three minutes, the shooter would either be inside or gone.

An overwhelming urge to end this came over Bryce. This was the first time they'd glimpsed Corina's stalker. He was close. So close.

"Stay put," Bryce hissed as he sidled up to the window.

"What are you doing?" Corina rose and started toward him.

"Shh." He motioned her back before refocusing on the window. Keeping to the side, he peered out. His range of vision was small, but he could just make out a person standing outside the door. If the shooter stayed there for a few seconds longer, it was the perfect spot.

Bryce dashed to the door and turned the bolt back, tossing a thanks heavenward when no click gave him away.

One. Two. He threw the door open and was rewarded with a thunk and the sound of a firearm skittering across gravel. He charged around the open door and slammed it behind him, fixing his sights on the man before him.

"Freeze."

The guy's hand stopped inches from the dropped weapon.

"Don't even think about it." Bryce took a half step closer. The man was young—much younger than he'd been expecting.

"No, behind you." Something in his wide-eyed expression overrode Bryce's good sense. He half turned his head.

But not in time to avoid the masked figure barreling toward him.

He didn't have time to brace himself, much less get a bead on this new threat. The impact was anything but gentle. He released a grunt but let the forward motion carry him into a roll.

As Bryce regained his feet, the first man—the one he had been holding at gunpoint—rose quickly and threw a punch, not at Bryce, but at the second attacker. Mask Face ducked, but still caught the fist on his cheekbone. He countered with a glancing blow to the other man's jaw.

Bryce took a few steps back and tried to assess the situation. Should he jump in? His gun wavered between the two men as they traded blocks and strikes. They appeared pretty evenly matched. Mask Face seemed to be the real threat, but Bryce had no idea who the nonmasked fighter was. Friend? Foe? Neither?

As long as Corina was safe, better to stand back and let them duke it out until he could answer that question.

Approaching sirens broke the almost-rhythmic pounding,

momentarily distracting Mask Face. His opponent took the opportunity for an uppercut. It didn't land squarely, but it pushed the edge of his mask up enough to reveal a slightly pointed chin.

With a cry that sounded more animal than human, Mask Face feinted left, then drove hard into the other man's right side—forcing him backward into Bryce. The collision threw them both off-balance, and Bryce landed hard on the ground, the younger man on top of him.

It only took a few seconds for both to regain their feet, but by that time, Mask Face had vaulted the privacy fence lining the back of the alley. Bryce gripped the top of the fence and drew himself up. An empty back parking lot met his eyes.

Mask Face was gone.

He dropped back into the alley and aimed a vicious kick at the fence. Everything in him screamed to give chase, but without any idea which direction to go, the chance of Mask Face circling back for Corina before his return was too great.

He turned toward the other stranger, who was now scaling the fence. "Oh no, you don't." Bryce grabbed his collar and yanked him back to the ground.

The man shot to his feet, eyes blazing. "What's your problem?"

"Who are you, and what are you doing here?" It wasn't until the words were out of his own mouth that the guy's accent hit him. British?

The back door opened, and Corina stepped outside, gun drawn but lowered. Bryce didn't miss the relief that flashed across the stranger's face. *Wait. What?*

"Bryce, what's going on?"

He gritted his teeth. "I thought I told you to stay put."

She ignored that statement and came closer. "Who is that?"

Bryce positioned himself between them in case the guy tried something. He tightened his jaw and stared the man down. "Well, answer the lady. Who. Are. You?"

The man met his gaze squarely, apparently unperturbed by

the challenge. "Peter Lewis, certified and slightly mortified body-guard." He extended a hand, but Bryce didn't take it.

"Bodyguard for whom?" Corina echoed his thoughts, her voice drawing the man's attention back to her.

Peter looked mildly confused at the question. He glanced from her to Bryce and back again.

"For you, of course."

29

CORINA NARROWED HER EYES and closed the distance between her and the men. "I didn't hire a bodyguard."

"Your father did."

The explanation hit like a linebacker. Her blood went cold, and all she could do was stare.

"Didn't he tell you?" Peter's words lacked his earlier confidence. That was a loaded question. She shook her head.

"You've got to be kidding me," he muttered, running his fingers through dark blond hair. "I've never dealt with this situation before."

She wished she could say the same. Her whole life seemed to be nothing but secrets, threats, and half-truths. Oh, and random but not-so-random attacks. She forced her gun hand to relax, but the other curled itself into a fist. "How long?"

His head jerked up. "Pardon me?"

"How long since he hired you?" If he'd been guarding her, he hadn't been doing a very good job of it.

"He signed the papers with my agency on the twelfth. Normally, I would have begun immediately, but I was out of the country until this morning. I couldn't get ahold of him by phone when I landed, but he had made it clear that I was to begin as soon as possible and could either find you here or at home. It appears I didn't show up a minute too soon."

Her mind reeled with this new information. Her dad had hired a bodyguard for her on the twelfth? That was four days ago. The day he went missing.

"Not to be rude," Bryce said, his tone indicating he couldn't care less how his words came across, "but we've just been shot at, and my trust factor is a bit on the low side. How do we verify your identity?"

Peter slowly reached for his wallet and offered his credentials. Corina glanced at the cards—photo ID, concealed weapons license, certification. They looked legitimate, but that didn't mean much. Bryce scrutinized them more closely before returning them. She couldn't read his expression, but he didn't look convinced.

"Where's your agency located?"

He rattled off an address, sparking her recognition. She'd seen the street name on one of the online maps she'd studied in the hospital. Her dad had been found near there. So this was what he'd been doing in Cincinnati when he should have been at work. Hiring a bodyguard to protect her from the killer he hadn't told her about. If Peter was telling the truth.

Her jaw clenched so tightly her teeth hurt. Obviously, her dad hadn't planned to get himself mugged, but when was he intending to break the news? When Peter showed up?

She turned her back on them to find Allye in the doorway, holding Houston back and simply watching—the color beginning to return to her cheeks.

Did you hear all that? Corina didn't say the words, but Allye nodded slightly as if she understood exactly what she'd been thinking.

This whole situation was ludicrous. In less than a week, she'd gone from an admittedly reclusive small-business owner to the grand prize winner of a mysterious stalker avenging an unknown wrong, a comatose father, an overprotective ex-boyfriend, and a tardy bodyguard.

She didn't know if laughter or tears were more appropriate. Either would draw unwanted attention. Instead, she holstered her revolver and leaned her forehead against the back wall of her shop, letting the cool brick soothe her developing headache. Why had she insisted on coming today?

Bryce returned to his interrogation. "Remind me again how you managed to get here at exactly the same time someone was shooting up the place?" His skepticism was apparent in his voice, although she had no doubt his face remained impassive.

Peter sighed. "Like I said, I couldn't reach Mr. Roberts by phone or at home, and this was the second address he had listed in the paperwork. When I arrived, I heard the gunshots and pulled into a parking lot a bit up the road so I could approach more discreetly. The shooting paused, and I saw a masked figure dart across the road and toward this alley. I assumed he was going to attempt to cut off your escape, so I followed from the opposite end of the building."

Corina looked over her shoulder to gauge Peter's reaction as deafening sirens announced the arrival of the police. He showed none. The close proximity of law enforcement didn't seem to bother him.

He continued his explanation. "I circled the corner and drew my gun on him when he discharged his magazine to reload, but you shot that advantage in the foot." He rubbed his swelling jaw. "You saw the rest."

She bit back the urge to defend Bryce. It wasn't his fault Peter looked less like a choir boy and more like an active shooter prowling the back alley. If she'd been the one to see him, she would have come to the same conclusion.

Allye spoke up before Bryce could continue his interrogation. "Corina, Bryce, the police are coming through the front door. You want me to send them out here?"

Bryce shook his head. "No, we'll go inside." He looked at Peter and lifted his chin. "After you."

Corina let the two men go in first, then started after them but stopped at the doorway, her brain finally catching up to Peter's story. If he had surprised the gunman while he was reloading . . .

"Hold on a minute."

Bryce turned around. "What?"

"I need to check something out." She headed for the end of the alley where the shooter would have entered. The police would be processing this area in addition to the interior of her shop, but if what she suspected was there, she didn't want to desert the area until they sent someone out here. If she was wrong, then it wouldn't matter.

An object caught her eye, and she stopped, letting her gaze travel until it rested on a larger object.

"Bryce, look."

She pointed out her finds as he dashed to her side, Peter a few steps behind. There was the empty magazine, and a pistol lay a few feet away as if it had been dropped and kicked out of reach.

Bryce inhaled sharply. "We need to get the police out here to log these."

"What is it?" Peter skidded to a stop and smacked his forehead when he saw what they were looking at. He muttered something about jet lag and sloppy work, but she didn't catch all of it. He snapped his mouth shut when Bryce shot a glare his direction.

Without touching either piece, she bent to examine what the shooter had left behind. The pistol was a .45mm and a high-end brand. She glanced at the magazine and did a double take. It looked almost new and exactly like some she'd had in stock a couple of months ago.

Was it possible her stalker was a customer? She shivered, not even wanting to consider the possibility that if her stalker had succeeded in taking her life, he might very well have used ammunition she had supplied.

She stood and took a deep breath. *Ouch.* But she didn't flinch. Her chest already ached from crawling and being dragged across the floor. The bit of additional pain almost felt good. It grounded her emotions at least. She chewed on her lower lip. The magazine was a popular brand, likely carried by many sporting goods stores. There was no reason to believe the shooter had ever visited *her* shop.

But he'd had one of her cards. She froze for a second, remembering the mail from a few days ago.

No, that still meant nothing. The business card could have been picked up elsewhere. Besides, she recognized most of her customers—by face if not by name. Had any strangers been in recently?

Her headache was progressing toward migraine level now. She closed her eyes and massaged her forehead.

"Hey. You okay?"

Her eyes flew open at Bryce's touch. Concern rested in his eyes and in the lines across his forehead.

"Yeah." Her voice scratched on the word. She cleared her throat. "Let's help the police figure out who's doing this."

He nodded and tucked her under his arm in a protective gesture, much as he had the night her truck was rear-ended. He turned his gaze to Peter. "Get an officer out here. We'll wait to make sure nothing is disturbed."

Peter stared at them for a moment, and she could almost see his gears turning. Was he wondering if she was safe enough out here without his presence? She had no idea how close bodyguards were supposed to stay to their clients, but if he thought he was going to shadow her every move, he had another think coming.

His lips firmed as he seemed to make a decision. He spun on his heel and strode inside.

She sighed as he disappeared. "I think he's telling the truth."

Bryce frowned. "Maybe, but I want to do some digging on him

before I trust him enough to leave him alone with evidence." His muscles tensed. "Or with you."

She didn't respond to that. He was right. And although she was already convinced, asking Officer Mike to check into his background or whatever Bryce had in mind wouldn't hurt.

It only took a minute for an officer to join them in the alley. She pointed out what she'd found, then let Bryce lead her to the front of the shop, where several cops, including Eric and Officer Mike, were congregated.

"—one thing about him now." Officer Mike was saying. "He's obviously not a trained sniper. No way in the world he would've missed such an easy shot."

"Unless he wanted to," Eric pointed out.

Officer Mike lifted his eyebrows. "What're you thinking, Thornton?"

"Look at the line the bullets cut across the wall."

Corina turned around to see what he was talking about. One bullet hole—probably from the shot that ripped through the case of thermoses she'd been holding—was right at her shoulder level. All the others were lower, which made sense because she'd thrown herself to the floor after that first shot.

But they weren't low enough. Even if the shooter couldn't see her, he could have guessed roughly where she was. These shots had been taken through the window, where he could see he wasn't hitting anyone. If his goal had been to harm her, he would have attempted to shoot through the wall or saved his shots for when he had her in his sights again.

So this whole incident was just another part of his scheme? Another event to set her on edge and mess with her mind?

She sank into a chair and buried her face in her hands. As much as she'd like to deny it, he was succeeding.

30

A COUPLE OF HOURS LATER, Bryce stationed himself at Will's front door and scanned the neighborhood. Other than Corina and Allye, who were waiting with Houston in Allye's car, the street seemed deserted. Odd for a beautiful, though still slightly cool, Saturday afternoon, but he'd take it.

After they'd finished giving their statements and the police released the scene, Eric, Officer Mike, and Peter had helped him board up the windows while Allye busied herself cleaning up the worst of the glass. They'd told Corina to sit, and for once, she'd listened—only coming out of the back room when it was time to set the alarm and lock up.

He drummed his fingers against his pant leg. The day was clear and quiet, but he could still hear the pop of gunfire and shattering glass. See Corina collapsing to the floor.

Older memories crowded behind. A scorching sun. Dust plumes shooting into the air. The heat of a too-near explosion.

With effort, he forced his attention on the present, on their surroundings. Everything was fine at the moment. But they were exposed, and he didn't like being out in the open. Didn't like Corina and Allye being out in the open. But Peter had insisted on clearing the house before the ladies went inside. Not a bad idea, but Bryce preferred to do the clearing—and he would have if that hadn't meant leaving the ladies outside alone or, worse, alone with Peter. Instead he'd disabled the alarm and allowed the man to do what he claimed was his job.

He trusted the so-called bodyguard about as much as one of Afghanistan's carpet vipers. Officer Mike was running a check on him, but until the report came back—

The door opened, and Peter stepped outside. "Clear." He looked up and down the street as Bryce had a few moments earlier, then motioned for the ladies.

Allye emerged with her ever-present bundle of bags and joined them on the porch. Corina followed slowly with Houston, her movements stiff. She had to be hurting right now. She'd refused to go to the ER again, insisting that her cuts were superficial and any bruises would have to heal on their own. She was probably right, but he hated seeing her in pain.

He stood aside so she could enter first. "You okay?" he whispered as she passed him.

"Peachy." She didn't stop or make eye contact. Not okay. But he already knew that. He'd just hoped—what? That she'd open up a little? Ha.

Allye followed Corina inside, and Bryce motioned Peter ahead of him. Once they were all inside, he closed the door and flipped the locks. When he turned back to the others, Allye was edging around Corina, who had paused to release Houston from his leash. As Houston ambled toward the kitchen, Allye made her way to the guest bedroom she'd laid claim to.

And that left Peter standing awkwardly between Bryce and Corina. Bryce crossed his arms. The guy shouldn't be here. Not until they were certain he was who he claimed to be. But Corina had made the decision to bring him along. And it was her decision to make, not his.

Peter broke the silence. "Could we talk?"

Corina's shoulders sagged, but she motioned toward the living room. "Sure." They started that direction, Bryce again bringing up the lead. She directed Peter to a seat angled toward the fireplace on the far wall. She settled at the far end of the couch, then looked up at Bryce. "Oh, we didn't set the alarm. Do you mind?"

"No problem." He returned to the hall, smirking as he activated the system. He'd be willing to bet she hadn't forgotten the alarm before and that the chair she'd chosen for Peter hadn't been an accident. From that spot, there was no way the man could inconspicuously observe him entering the code.

Good. Despite her earlier statement about believing Peter, Corina didn't fully trust him. And no matter how tired or shaken up she was, she wasn't letting down her guard.

"Where are you from?" Corina was asking as he reentered the living room. Bryce joined her on the couch, again positioning himself between her and Peter.

"Southampton, England, but I've lived here for several years." Peter grinned.

"What brought you to the US?" Bryce asked.

He shrugged. "My father was from the Cincinnati area, and I visited my grandparents there nearly every summer growing up. I liked it."

"So you have dual citizenship?"

"I do."

"What made you choose to become a bodyguard?"

"It interested me." He didn't elaborate further. Evasion or nothing more to tell?

Corina's ringtone interrupted them. She glanced at it. Her face crumpled, but she answered quickly.

"Oh, Gus, I'm so sorry. I should have called you. . . . Yes, I'm fine. Everyone's fine, but the shop is a disaster. I don't know when we'll be able to reopen." She reddened as if trying to hold back tears as she listened to his response. "Thank you. You don't know how much I appreciate you. . . . Yes, I'll let you know as soon as I figure things out."

After hanging up, she dropped her head in her hands and groaned. "I totally forgot Gus was coming in this afternoon."

"Who is Gus?" Peter asked.

"My employee. He was scheduled for an afternoon shift. It didn't even cross my mind to let him know about the shooting."

"How long has he been working for you?"

"Almost since Western Outfitters opened."

"You trust him?"

"Of course I trust him," she snapped, leveling a glare at him.

Peter held his hands up. "No offense. I'm only trying to feel out the territory here."

She deflated. "I'm sorry."

"It's all right. But it does lead into what I wanted to talk about." He leaned forward in his chair. "There are things I need to know. Who you spend time with, who you trust and distrust, who might be a threat, what your routine is."

Corina groaned again.

"This isn't a good time," Bryce objected. "She's been through a lot today." Not to mention the last several.

"I understand that, and I respect it. However, waiting for a good time could have disastrous consequences." Peter kept his voice level but firm as he pulled a pen and small notepad from his pocket.

"Waiting until tonight or tomorrow morning isn't going to—"

"It's okay, Bryce. I'd rather have it over with." She fixed an unarguably tired gaze on Peter. "I spend time with my dad, Allye, and Gus. And Bryce." She glanced at him.

"Anyone else?"

She returned her attention to Peter. "Not really."

That was it? Her circle was down to four people? And he hardly counted since they hadn't been in contact for years until this week. Corina had always been somewhat of an introvert, but she'd been active in the community and involved in church before Derryck's death.

He shouldn't have left when he did. Should have stayed to work things out between them. He wouldn't make that mistake again.

"Water, anyone?" Allye bustled into the room with a bag over her shoulder and several bottles tucked under her arm. After passing the waters out, she chose an empty seat and pulled a knitting project from her bag.

Peter thanked her, then returned his focus to Corina. "Who do you trust?"

She sighed. "The people I just named, the police officers you met today, and Bryce and Allye's mom. I don't distrust anyone else specifically, but I can't say there's anyone else I implicitly trust."

"Anyone you suspect?"

She shook her head.

"Anyone that's shown up recently that you don't know? Anyone who's acted suspiciously?" he prodded.

She spread her hands in a helpless gesture. "I don't know. There's a new neighbor across the street that I don't recognize. But I don't have any reason to suspect him."

"Which house?" He wrote down the number she gave him.

"James Johnson?" Allye asked.

Corina lifted one shoulder in a shrug. "I have no idea."

"The house next door to Bryce?"

"Yes."

She nodded. "That's James."

"What do you know about him?" Peter asked.

Allye's knitting needles continued to click as she answered. "Not much. He lives alone. Works overnights in IT or something like that. Paid cash for his house." Leave it to Allye to know details like that on someone she didn't know much about. But then again, with their mom in real estate, she could have overheard some of that from her.

Peter pressed for more. "He's a new neighbor? How long has he been around?"

Allye frowned as she thought. "A couple months. I don't re-member exactly. Sorry."

"No, that helps." Peter flashed her a smile and focused back on Corina. "We're almost done. How about your routine? We may need to switch things up so it's harder to predict where you'll be."

"My routine is running Western Outfitters—which I can't do right now."

Again, she didn't mention church. Was it truly no longer a part of her life? Bryce pressed his lips shut against the question. Now and in front of Peter wasn't the time.

The bodyguard noted her answer. "I'm sorry, but that may work in your favor. We don't want your stalker able to anticipate your moves."

"No, he just has me worked into a box," she mumbled.

"But you have a good setup here. That's an advantage. If I'd been here this morning, I would have recommended you stay here."

Even though Bryce had said the same thing, it grated coming from Peter. Especially when Corina seemed to shrink into her seat.

Bryce balled his fists. "She didn't have any way of knowing something like that would happen today."

"Not saying she did. But there are precautions that we'll have to take now."

"Obviously."

Peter quirked an eyebrow but didn't respond to that. Instead, he turned back to Corina. "I'm going to work up a security plan. Your friends are welcome to stay, but they needn't feel obligated to."

"We're staying," Bryce cut in.

"Fine by me. I just need to be aware of any comings and go-ings."

"Is that all?" Corina's voice sounded small.

Peter nodded. "For now."

"Okay." She stood, swaying slightly, but waved Bryce away when he reached for her. "I'm fine. Just tired."

"Can I get you anything?" Allye asked, her knitting needles stilling.

"No, I think I'm going to lie down for a few minutes." She glanced at her clothes and grimaced. "Or maybe take a shower. Call me if anything comes up."

Bryce watched as she slowly left the room. That conversation had drained her—well, more than she already was.

"You shouldn't have pushed her."

"It was necessary." Peter flipped his notebook shut and returned it to his pocket. "The situation is bad. Surely you can see that."

"We were managing it long before you showed up."

"Yes, it looked well managed when I arrived," Peter said dryly.

Bryce launched to his feet. "Do you have a problem?"

Peter stood, his movements more deliberate, controlled. "I do not. However, it appears you do."

Bryce tried to tamp his anger. Where had it come from? With effort, he lowered his voice. "I don't trust you," he bit out. "You show up out of the blue, asking questions, taking charge. We haven't even cleared you yet."

"You will. This is my job. I was hired to keep Corina safe, and that's what I intend to do."

"So you say. But I will protect her, even from you if necessary."

"Likewise."

"Boys!" Allye inserted herself between them, the top of her head barely coming above their chins. "We're all on edge, and your arguing isn't helping anything. Sit."

Neither of them moved.

She pushed herself up on her toes, making herself just tall enough to force him and Peter to break eye contact. Bryce stepped sideways, but she moved with him.

"Allye."

She ignored his growl. "I know today shook you up, but you're being ridiculous. You"—she tapped his chest—"and he are on the same side. You want Corina safe, and that is what he's here for. To *help*." She half turned toward Peter. "*Not* to take over. But Corina needs all the protection she can get right now, so I suggest you learn to work together." She took a step back, allowing them to face each other again.

Peter seemed to be sizing him up. Finally, he inclined his head. "I'm game if you are."

Bryce held his gaze another few seconds. When the bodyguard didn't flinch, he jerked a nod. "Deal." As long as that background check came back clear.

31

SUNDAY MORNING POSSESSED none of the previous day's sunshine. Corina let Houston in from the fenced-in backyard and shut the door against the gray chill. As the German shepherd headed for his water bowl, she dragged herself to the coffee machine. *Stiff* and *sore* didn't begin to describe how she felt after yesterday. Caffeine wouldn't do much for that, but maybe it would give her the energy to push past it.

Mug in hand, she sank into a chair and texted Peter to let him know the alarm was off and the back door unlocked. He ought to be returning to the house soon—he'd spent the night outside, keeping watch from his car and taking random walks around the property. She should probably give him a key and the code so he could let himself in and out. After all, Officer Mike had verified last night that he was who he claimed to be. She had a bodyguard. Unreal.

Rustling sounded from the living room, then the bathroom door closed. Bryce was up. Which meant he'd be joining her soon. Great. She'd likely be dealing with Bryce and Peter together before the coffee kicked in. And Allye wasn't up yet, so there'd be no help in refereeing if they got into another male-dominance match.

She drained her mug and poured another.

A few minutes later, Bryce emerged from the hall. He smiled when he saw her. "Good morning."

"Morning." She indicated the coffeepot. "Help yourself."

He poured a cup and sat across from her. "How are you feeling?"

"Like I got shot at and dragged through glass."

He cringed, and she instantly regretted her flippant words. "Sorry."

"Sorry about that," he said at the same time. They shared uneasy smiles.

Bryce looked around. "Heard anything from your bodyguard today?"

She glanced at her phone and saw the return text. "He's making one more quick round before coming inside."

He stared into his mug. "I think I owe him an apology."

"Probably." She studied him. He was apparently not at all comfortable with the thought. "I've never heard you angry like that."

"You heard?"

"Part of it, anyway."

"Getting shot at—seeing you get shot at—rattled me." His fingers flexed around the mug.

"Yeah." Her too.

Silence fell between them, then Bryce said, "I was looking forward to being back in our church this morning."

Our church. Could she even call it that anymore? She probably hadn't attended a service since Easter—and that was more to appease her dad than anything. Not something Bryce would know unless Allye or his mom had kept him informed. She decided against a correction. "It's early. You could still go. Allye probably will."

"I don't think I'm ready to leave you alone—with or without Peter." Bryce gave her a lopsided grin, but his gaze dropped to his coffee. "I noticed you didn't mention church when he asked about your routine yesterday."

She stifled a sigh. So much for not addressing that topic. "I don't attend very often anymore."

"Why?" A simple question. Too bad she didn't have a simple answer.

She shrugged. "I just got away from it, I guess."

"That surprises me. You were always so passionate about your faith."

"God left when you did."

Bryce winced at her words. Oh, why had she said that? But she wasn't sure how to backtrack. Before she could figure out a way to fix it, he spoke.

"I may have left, but I can guarantee you God didn't."

She managed a weak smile. "Unfortunately, that wasn't my experience. I haven't felt him in years."

"Feelings can be deceptive. 'We walk by faith, not by sight,' remember?" They'd memorized that verse together. Too bad it was easier to quote than to do.

The door opened, and Peter stepped inside. Thankful for the interruption, Corina pointed him toward the coffee and stood. "I'm going to call the hospital. See if there's any update."

Bryce reached for her mug. "I can bring this for you."

"Thanks, but I can carry my own coffee." She might be sore, but she wasn't an invalid. And the men needed to clear things between them. Taking her mug, she gave him a pointed look.

He sighed. "I'll be in in a minute."

She started toward the hallway. "Take your time."

BRYCE WATCHED CORINA until she disappeared from view, then turned his attention to Peter. "Everything quiet last night?"

"No problems." Peter took a sip of his coffee and leaned against the counter.

"You plan to stay outside every night?"

"For the first couple. If things still aren't resolved, then I'll reevaluate."

"Makes sense. Especially if the weather really turns cold."

"True." He glanced toward the window. "This weather reminds me of home—just add a cold drizzle. Can't say I miss that part of England."

"I wouldn't either." And they were into small talk. *Just say it.* He set his mug aside. "Look, I'm sorry about yesterday."

Peter's eyebrows shot up. "No apology necessary."

"Yes, there is. My attitude was uncalled for."

The bodyguard studied him then slowly nodded. "All right. Apology accepted." They were silent a moment. "I looked you up too, you know."

Bryce chuckled. "Can't say I'm shocked."

"You were army. Saw action?"

"Yes." As a mechanic, he hadn't seen as much as some of his buddies had, but there had been moments. Ambushes.

Peter cocked his head. "I imagine yesterday triggered some rough memories."

"I don't—"

He waved a hand. "Not suggesting you have PTSD or that there'd be something wrong with you if you did. But you experienced things most people haven't. A day like yesterday?" His eyes got a far-off look to them. "I'd be surprised if it didn't affect you."

Bryce stilled. Peter was right. He'd been fine during the heat of the action yesterday. But once the adrenaline wore off, he'd had to fight off the flashbacks. He eyed the bodyguard.

"You sound like you have experience. Did you serve?"

Peter refocused on him and shook his head. "My older brother did. Had a pretty rough time of it. But he's home and leading a normal life. One of the best men I know." He clapped a hand on Bryce's shoulder. "I'm glad you're here. Corina needs you, and together, we'll keep her safe."

32

THE CASE FILES LANDED on her father's desk with a thump. Corina stared at them, unmoving. She didn't want to do this, and yet, she needed to.

Alone.

After everything that had happened the past few days, she needed time. Time to process. Time away from the hovering. Morning had passed into afternoon, and there had been no moves from her stalker. And although Peter had excused himself to grab some sleep, Bryce and Allye had stuck to her like glue—asking if she was okay, feeding her, trying to distract her from the situation. It was starting to get to her.

It wasn't so much the company she minded—it was the fact that everyone was focused on her and on keeping her safe. The fact she could no longer run the business she'd poured her heart into. That she could go nowhere alone. That she'd lost her independence.

Bryce meant well, so did Allye. And Peter . . .

She didn't know what to think of the bodyguard. He seemed nice enough. Capable. But she didn't know him, and he was yet another secret her dad shouldn't have kept from her.

A muscle twitched in her cheek. Perhaps she didn't want to process anything right now.

She turned her attention back to the case files. Files she had read before. Fine, skimmed was more like it. The images were burned into her memory, but the words hadn't stuck. Shock had blurred all but the basic facts when they'd first found them, and she'd avoided them after that day. Now she needed details.

Acid burned in her stomach at the thought of what she'd find, and she almost gave in to the lure of procrastination.

She bit her lip. She *had* to do something, and it needed to be done now. Waiting around for the stalker to make his next move wasn't an option. With her dad in the hospital, running wasn't an option. The only thing that was an option was to go on the offensive, and these files were the best place she knew to start. It was time to turn the tables—for her sake and her dad's.

Pulling in a breath to fortify herself, she took a seat. The rolling desk chair had been purchased to fit her dad's muscular frame. It swallowed her, so she attempted to adjust it to a more comfortable position. Only partially successful, she gave up and turned her attention to the task at hand.

She grabbed a pen and notepad and began mentally reviewing what she remembered from that time frame. The murders had happened so long ago, many of her memories were fuzzy. Still, she jotted down anything she could think of. Snippets of her parents' conversations that hadn't made sense at the time. Odd actions or reactions.

All things she'd gone over before. She tapped the pen against the desk. What else did she know about the night her mom and brother died?

Her dad had been working late, not an uncommon occurrence, but something he'd been doing more often. Likely trying to track down Alan and Miriam's killer. If only he'd succeeded.

She squeezed her eyes shut. And while her dad was tracking down criminals and her mom and brother were dying, she had been at a birthday party. A *party*.

She'd felt guilty that the party had likely kept her from being killed that night. Or kept her from being able to help her mom fight back. But now that she knew it hadn't been an armed robbery but rather a carefully planned attack, she didn't know if that was true. The killer had chosen to murder Alan and Miriam on separate nights. Nights when each was alone and he could pick them off one by one.

Was that a pattern? And if so, why had he broken that pattern by murdering her mom and Colton together?

She sucked in a jagged breath as a realization hit her. Her mom was supposed to be home alone that night. Colton had been invited to the birthday party too but had gotten sick at the last minute and stayed home. Had the killer known that? Or had he been surprised by her brother's presence?

Fidgeting with the clip on the pen, she sighed. There was no way for anyone but the killer to know that. And it didn't change the facts. Her little brother had been there.

And some monster had murdered him.

The clip snapped under the pressure of her thumb. She stared at it, then slowly set the pen aside. Her gaze snagged on the stack of files, and she firmed her jaw. It was time.

She lifted the topmost file and pulled it toward her, briefly scanning the name scrawled across the top of the page: *Miriam White.*

Alan's wife. The first of the victims.

Corina fingered the file open and allowed determination to seep into her. Somewhere in these three files was a clue, a detail, some lead that hadn't been fully explored. And she was going to find it. The stalker after them was good—too good—but he was still human.

And all humans made mistakes.

OR DID THEY? An hour later, she wasn't so sure.

Corina closed Alan's file and leaned back in her chair, rubbing her burning eyes. There was plenty of evidence in the files. Plenty, but nothing substantive. It gave her the odd feeling of being acquainted with their invisible enemy without knowing anything about him. Almost like a pen pal who ended his letter with a simple "Yours truly."

Without straightening her posture, she reached for the notes she'd taken during her perusal. Tension had made her writing smaller than usual, and the script blurred in her already-strained vision. It took a few blinks to bring the words into focus.

She had separated her notes into three groups—one for each of the Whites' files to record anything outstanding, and another to note the similarities between them. She would add a new group for each of the other files as well. It was her dad's preferred method of analysis when working on connected cases.

Before her mother's and brother's deaths, Corina had been fascinated with her dad's work. Of course, he never allowed her to look at the actual cases, but seeing her interest, he sometimes designed mock crimes for her to solve. At first, he would walk her through it, showing her how he would perform an investigation, but it didn't take her long to catch on. Soon she was solving the cases on her own.

Easy enough to do when all the information was provided and nothing was at stake. Unlike now.

This case was no game, but she could still use things her dad had taught her.

If only she could see the crime scenes. The passing of over a decade made that impossible. Not that the police would have let her study them anyway. No, she was stuck working with photographs and the recorded observations of CSIs—evidence she wasn't so sure her dad, much less she, was supposed to have access to in the first place.

She skimmed the notes she'd just made, then tossed them aside. The investigation had been thorough. Both her father and the police had desperately wanted to find the murderer.

But neither had uncovered enough evidence to keep the case from going cold.

If Corina's already slouched posture could have slumped more, it would have. Maybe they hadn't found the needed information because it just wasn't there.

She pushed the thought away and reached instead for the crime scene photos, forcing herself to flip slowly through them again. There had to be something they'd all missed.

When she came to one showing the back of the chair where Miriam's body was tied, she stopped. Something was off in this one. She'd felt it earlier but hadn't been able to pin it down.

She cocked her head to the side.

Utilizing another of her dad's tricks, she turned the picture upside down, covered all but a small portion with her hand, studied it, then moved to another section.

When she got to the center, her eyes widened.

It was the watch. Miriam was wearing a watch, the face turned to the underside of her bound wrist so the time was visible to the camera. That in itself could be a coincidence, just a loose band, but Corina knew better.

Miriam didn't wear watches. Didn't like them; didn't wear them. Ever. She'd gone on and on one Christmas about how Alan should have known better than to buy her one. Poor guy hadn't deserved the rant.

Squinting, Corina struggled to make out the time on the watch. *11:43.* Her eyes dropped to the time and date stamp in the bottom corner of the picture. *9:12 p.m.*

She snatched the official report off the desk and began searching for the estimated time of death. There it was. According to the medical examiner, Miriam had died around six or six thirty. Nowhere near the watch's recorded time.

She frowned. So Miriam had been wearing a randomly stopped watch. What did that mean? Anything?

On a hunch, she picked up the next set of photos—Alan's—and located the corresponding view. No watch.

A disappointed sigh escaped her. So much for that.

But that watch meant something—she knew it. Could there be one somewhere else in Alan's file?

The theory ignited a spark of hope inside her, and she began to repeat the cover-and-search method.

A few minutes later, Corina lined up a series of photos across the desk. One. Two. Three. Four.

Miriam wore a watch stopped at 11:43. There was a wall clock behind Alan, stopped at 11:44. The last crime scene—her mother and brother's—held two. A digital kitchen timer sat on the counter, and at the edge of one of the pictures was her mother's treasured cuckoo clock. 11:45 and 11:46.

Corina leaned back in her seat. What significance did time hold to the killer?

Time is running out.

He'd painted that message on her wall. She'd assumed he was referring to her time to live. Was there something more to it?

She skimmed back over the case notes but found no mention of the timepieces. This piece of the message the killer had been sending was completely overlooked in the initial investigation. She'd found it.

But what did it mean?

33

SHE WAS STILL PUZZLING over the photos when Allye poked her head in the door. "Hey, pizza's here."

The heady aroma of Parmesan and roasted garlic filtered through the opening, and Corina's stomach rumbled despite her anxiety.

"Just a minute." She used her phone to snap a picture of the photo lineup, then grabbed her notes before following Allye to the kitchen, where Bryce was already sampling a cheesy bite.

Allye put her hands on her hips. "Thanks for waiting."

He swallowed and shot them an apologetic look. "Sorry, I haven't had Zhan's in years. Forgot how good it was until I smelled it." He passed them the stack of paper plates, then added another couple of slices to his.

"After you." Allye motioned her ahead while she poured four glasses of tea from the gallon jug delivered with their meal. Corina envied her ease at the whole hostessing thing. It wasn't even her house. Allye would probably make a terrible mother-in-law to someone one day. Her mouth twitched at the thought.

Bryce whistled, and she turned to him. He tilted his head toward the food and grinned. "Eat."

She rolled her eyes and went for a breadstick and the smallest slice of pizza in the open box. Her appetite wasn't likely to hold out, but she'd give it a shot.

Peter emerged from the hallway and went straight for the pizza. "Time to see if this stuff lives up to its reputation."

"Oh, it does," Allye said, handing him a full glass.

His hair was tousled as if he'd just woken up. He must have managed to sleep all afternoon. Probably needed it since he planned to keep watch outside again tonight.

Corina slid into the chair across from Bryce and toasted him with the breadstick. "Cheers." She took a bite and closed her eyes. Savored the taste. Bryce was right. Zhan's Pizza, with its signature Parmesan-covered everything, was the best. Maybe she could eat a second piece after all.

Peter slid into one of the open seats and took a bite of pizza. His eyes lit up. "This is good."

Allye laughed. "Told you." She claimed the remaining seat and turned to Corina. "So what'd you find in there? You looked pretty intent when I came in."

"I was studying my dad's files." Corina glanced at Peter, but he didn't look surprised or confused. Right. Her dad had briefed the agency about everything when he filed out the paperwork. Again, she bit back her irritation at the whole situation. She took a long drink of tea and forced calmness into her tone.

"When I was going through the photos, I happened to notice a detail the reports hadn't mentioned." She wiped her fingers on a napkin before pulling out her phone. While she opened the snapshot, she explained what she'd found. "Here. Look at these." She zoomed in on Miriam's picture and handed it to Allye.

Rather than wait his turn, Bryce stood and leaned over his sister's shoulder. He studied the photos, his forehead furrowed. "Any idea what his point was?"

Corina blew out a breath. "No, that's where I got stuck. I was trying to make sense of it when Allye came to get me."

She blinked as a thought came to her. If her dad had briefed

Peter on the situation, maybe he'd shared some detail with him that hadn't made it into the official files. Or something new he'd learned recently.

She turned to the bodyguard. "I need to know everything my dad said when he hired you."

Peter finished chewing his bite of pizza. "I'm happy to share what I have. Officer Broaddus had the same request." He frowned. "But remember, I never actually spoke with your father. I received an emailed briefing from my agency with a copy of the contract he signed."

She sighed and glanced down at her plate. "We'll take whatever you know."

Bryce's ringtone cut off his reply.

RJ. FINALLY. He'd texted yesterday to let Bryce know he hadn't forgotten them—things had just gotten busy around the station. Maybe he had something on Will's list.

"Excuse me." Bryce stepped back from Allye and lifted the phone to his ear.

"Hey, RJ. Please tell me you have good news."

Pause. A sigh.

Bryce's stomach tightened. "What?"

"I got the names you wanted, but they won't do you any good. Papá Espinoza and his top three?" RJ blew a frustrated breath into the receiver.

"Just say it, Jenkins."

"They're all dead."

"*All* of them?"

Corina's and Allye's heads jerked up at his sharp tone. Peter started to stand, but Bryce waved him back to his seat and stepped into the hallway.

"Sorry, man. I know it wasn't what you wanted to hear."

He rubbed his forehead. "When did they die?"

"About a month after they were sentenced. A fight broke out in the prison. Half a dozen dead, including those four."

"Isn't that suspicious?"

"Sure. But there wasn't an obvious reason for anyone to target 'em at that point—unless it was a revenge killing or a rival. I mean, the trial was done—it wasn't like someone was afraid they'd be ratted out if Espinoza tried to cut a plea deal or something. And the other prisoners killed didn't have any ties to them." RJ sighed again. "It was investigated, of course, but nobody could find a motive or anything that pointed to it being premeditated."

"But what if it was a revenge killing? The guy we're looking for seems to thrive on that motive. Who would Espinoza have made mad?"

RJ snorted. "He was organized crime. I doubt either of us has enough paper to list everyone with a reason to be mad at him. But again, he was behind bars. That would've been enough for most people."

He was right. Tracking down everyone that Espinoza had hurt would be far out of their league. And what good would it do? Even if Espinoza's death had been orchestrated, what were the chances his killer would also be after Will and Corina?

Not much. Anyone that considered Espinoza an enemy should be glad Will had exposed him. So much for their most promising lead.

"Did you find anything out about any of the other cases?"

"I've only managed to track down a few of 'em so far. Nothing's really standing out to me, but I'll shoot you an email if you wanna go over what I got."

"Yeah, that would be great." He gave RJ his email address.

"Sorry I didn't have anything better for you."

"Not your fault. Hey, one more thing." Bryce relayed Corina's clock discovery. "We don't know what it means, but there was also a graffiti message left in her house that had to do with clocks. If you come across any cases with that kind of link to them . . ."

"Sure thing."

"I really appreciate you doing this, RJ."

"No problem. Tell your girl to keep her head up."

"Will do." Bryce ended the call and headed back to the kitchen.

Everyone stopped talking and stared at him as he reentered the room.

He took his place at the table. "RJ got a dead end on the Espinoza case, and nothing to speak of on the others so far."

Disappointment washed across Allye's face, and Peter muttered what sounded like a curse, then glanced at the ladies and apologized.

Corina's reaction was more subtle, but Bryce noticed the marginal slump of her shoulders and slight firming of her lips. The desire to smooth away that tension rose in him. He took another bite of pizza instead.

It wasn't nearly as good as it had been five minutes ago.

He looked at Peter. "So did you have anything to add?"

"Not much. Mr. Roberts indicated he wasn't positive the stalker had found them. He hired me as a precaution—so he could take the time to investigate without worrying that someone would harm his daughter in his absence."

"That's why he bought the phones," Corina said, her words thoughtful.

"What phones?" Bryce turned his attention to her.

"Officer Mike said the guy who mugged him at the convenience store took his wallet and some disposable phones Dad had just bought. I didn't have time to think about it then, but it's been bugging me why he'd go to a convenience store across the street from where he'd just fueled up and buy not just one but multiple phones he didn't need." She pushed the remains of her pizza across her plate. "He wanted to make calls that couldn't easily be traced."

"He wasn't taking any chances." Just in case he was wrong, and the stalker hadn't actually found them yet. Bryce rubbed his forehead. The knowledge helped explain Will's actions, but it wasn't helpful information.

Everyone was quiet as Allye moved to refill the glasses. She slid his in front of him and sat down, propping her elbows on the table. "So where does that leave us?"

"Back at square one, I guess." An unexpected tiredness washed over him. *It's not that late.* He glanced at the oven clock. Well, it wasn't that early either. He stifled a yawn and saw Corina mirror the action from across the table.

He drained his glass and stood. "Why don't we call it a night? We've dealt with a lot today. We can start fresh in the morning, and maybe with the four of us, we can make some headway."

Peter pushed his chair back. "Mind if I make a pot of coffee before I head out? Despite my nap this afternoon, all these carbs are sitting rather heavy."

"I'll get it." Allye motioned him back to his seat.

"You know you don't have to spend the night outside," Corina said. "You're welcome to keep watch from here or the living room."

Peter grinned. "I appreciate the offer, but I'll have a better view out there. Don't worry, my vehicle is plenty comfortable."

Hopefully not too comfortable.

211

34

DISABLING THE SECURITY GRID was ridiculously easy. Since he'd been accessing William's account for months, it only required one extra step to shut everything down. The man would be horrified at how easily his careful precautions were neutralized.

He clipped a body camera to his chest and pulled on gloves and a black ski mask before quietly exiting his makeshift home. Keeping a close watch for approaching vehicles, he crept toward William's home for the second time that night, detouring only to borrow a bicycle from a neighbor's open garage.

The pizza delivery had provided the perfect cover for his earlier visit. No one had questioned the dog's barking or noticed him tossing a sedative-laced treat over the fence. Judging by the lack of protest coming from the backyard now, it had been effective.

As had his other scheme. He'd had to act fast, but paying the delivery driver to let him slip a bit of "vodka"—actually a Mickey Finn—into their tea was genius. A little quick-drying nail polish applied around the cap to provide the expected snap of a breaking seal, and the happy group inside would be none the wiser and all the sleepier. The kid had been impressed and glad to pocket the hundred bucks for helping to "prank his friends."

Not that he'd lived to spend it.

Within forty minutes, the bodyguard had settled into his car across the road, and lights began to go out in the house soon afterward. He'd waited a bit to be sure the drug had time to fully kick in, but now it was time to take care of a would-be hiccup in his plan.

He resisted the urge to rub his cheek. A sizable bruise had formed from the run-in yesterday morning. For the next couple of days, he'd have to hide it with extra makeup or come up with a good story in case someone happened to see him. What had he been thinking to pursue them around the back of the building? He'd never intended to shoot anyone, and he should have backed off as soon as they were out of sight.

He clenched a fist. He knew the answer. The adrenaline had gotten to him—fed into the ever-present rage in his soul. It wouldn't happen again.

All in all, everything had turned out well. He'd frightened them. Made his point and got away.

But the bodyguard had to go.

He'd spent the better part of last night and today working out a plan to dispose of the newcomer. He could have just shot him on one of the man's rounds last night, but it would have been risky. And messy. Drugging him first was the best option—and he'd come prepared for his dealings with Corina, so he had multiple drugs on hand.

And from the looks of the figure slumped in the front seat, it had worked perfectly. This problem wouldn't be one much longer.

The doors were locked, but that was quickly remedied. With the locks disengaged, he pulled down the back seat to make extra room and shoved the bicycle inside the trunk. Then he dragged the unconscious bodyguard across to the passenger side and took his place at the wheel.

Less than five minutes later, he reached the crest of a steep hill just out of town. He turned the car around and put it in park but left it running. This wouldn't take long.

He removed the bicycle, replaced the backrest, and tugged his passenger back into the driver's seat.

It took a bit of finagling, but he soon had the car and its occupant speeding downhill toward a sharp turn in the road they'd taken only a few moments before. Slowly, he mounted the bicycle and waited.

It took less than a minute for the sounds to reach his ears—the clang of metal on metal as the guardrail met its match, and the thunk-thunk of the vehicle struggling to find a resting place.

Satisfaction flooded his veins, and he set out on the return trip to Kincaid. The brisk autumn air was invigorating. As was the sweetness of accomplishment.

He drew in a deep, refreshing breath. It had been a long time since he'd taken an evening bike ride, over twelve years, in fact. They used to go all the time, just him and Raquel.

Raquel.

He was in the lead, but not for long. He glanced over his shoulder at Raquel and tapped his brakes. She passed him then, hair trailing behind her—soft waves turned to midnight by the shadows surrounding them.

"Come on, slowpoke." She laughed, the sound gentle, almost musical—like a fairy in the last theater production she volunteered with. If he didn't know better, he would be tempted to believe their daughters' favorite imaginary creatures were real after all.

He didn't speed up. Just let himself glide behind her, absorbing her beauty, until she turned to wait for him at the corner. He caught his breath at the look of love in her eyes. So different from anything he'd known before.

A few days later, she was gone.

His satisfaction soured, and he tightened his grip on the handlebars. Getting rid of the bodyguard was a minor accomplishment. Only a step toward the ultimate goal. He pedaled faster, no longer enjoying the night air.

With no other major hills between him and the city limits, it didn't take long to get back to where he'd started. He replaced the neighbor's bicycle, then made his way toward William's property.

He was nearly to the backyard when a patrol car turned onto the street, its headlights sweeping over him for a brief instant. As soon as he was out of range of the beams, he dropped to the ground. He lay still, muttering silent curses as the car inched by. It seemed to slow as it neared his position, but it didn't stop. He ground his teeth until it rounded the corner at the end of the road.

Slowly, he rose to his feet and stared in the direction the cop had gone. That had been close. Too close.

He turned back around. He needed to get moving. He crossed the last few feet to the backyard and, with a glance over his shoulder, vaulted over the gate.

Once inside the fence, he pulled a flashlight from his jacket pocket. Careful to keep the beam low, he swept the light across the lawn. There. As he'd hoped, Corina hadn't brought her dog in. Whether that was intentional to add a layer of protection or an oversight caused by the Mickey Finn, he wasn't sure. But it made his job easier.

As long as the sedative hadn't worn off.

Houston lay about ten feet from the porch. He waited a moment before approaching the still form, hand over his gun just in case. He shouldn't need it. Truthfully, he didn't want to shoot the dog again. Hadn't really meant to shoot him last week—only to scare him off his trail—but the animal had moved at the last second.

He prodded him gently with the toe of his boot.

No response.

He pocketed the flashlight, then reached for Houston's collar.

His fingers searched its length, quickly locating the overlapped section near the buckle. A tiny tracking device—much smaller than the ones he'd left on the vehicles—slid invisibly into the small space. He didn't expect to lose sight of his prey again, but he believed in insurance. She might have left the animal here while at the hospital, but she wouldn't do that for a permanent relocation.

Straightening, he turned toward the house, aiming for Corina's bedroom. The doors and their motion-detecting lights were off limits. He'd considered disabling the lighting during the day but hadn't wanted to arouse suspicion if anyone came out after dark.

The window he'd tampered with Friday morning would do just as well if no one had rechecked the locks since then. After setting this phase of his plan in motion, he'd rushed back from the hospital—only to find the redhead already here and in his way. Taking her out of the picture would have been easy, but she reminded him too much of his Brenna.

He couldn't do it. Not directly, anyway.

While he'd debated his options, the dog escaped, providing all the opportunity he needed to slip inside and take care of things unnoticed.

As he neared the window, music from inside reached his ear. He stilled. Everyone should be in bed.

So why wasn't the night silent?

Sweat seeped into his mask and chilled in the November breeze. He waited, but no foreign sounds marred the melody emerging from the room. The curtains were drawn, but neither light nor shadow played in the window.

She had to be asleep.

He slipped a jimmy into the window casing. And froze when a twig snapped behind him.

"Put your hands up. Nice and easy." A flashlight clicked on behind him.

His mind raced. Fingers tightened on the jimmy. He hadn't come this far to get caught by a small-town cop.

"I said hands up. Now." He recognized that voice. Mike Broaddus, the cop who'd been heading the investigation. His jaw tightened.

Slowly, deliberately, he peeled his fingers from the jimmy and raised his hands above his head.

Footsteps approached. His muscles tensed.

"You have the right to remain—"

As soon as he sensed the cop directly behind him, he sprang into action. He spun, elbow connecting solidly with the man's throat. The cop gagged and doubled over. And gave him the perfect opening. One blow with the jimmy, and the large man crumpled to the ground.

He stood still, breathing hard. This was a complication he hadn't counted on. He bent to retrieve the cop's flashlight.

"Everything all right, Mike?" He almost didn't hear the words come across the radio. Wouldn't have if his ear hadn't been right next to the cop's shoulder. A curse rose to his lips, but he bit it back. Of course the cop had radioed in before setting out on foot to investigate.

"Mike?"

Thinking fast, he reached for the radio and huffed out, "False alarm. It was just a deer."

A beat of silence, then "You sure?"

He chuckled. "Yeah, I'm headed back to the car now."

"Man, you need to get your eyes checked."

"Yeah, yeah."

He waited a moment, then rose, looking from Corina's window to the fallen cop. His eyes narrowed. He'd finish with him later. No one, not even a cop, was going to derail his plans for tonight. Lifting the jimmy once again, he inserted it into the window casing and silently lifted the pane. With one final glare at the crumpled figure at his feet, he climbed through the opening and slid the window shut behind him.

After making sure the curtains had fallen back into place, he flicked the flashlight on, illuminating the room and his target. Corina lay on the full-size bed, facing away from him, comforter pulled snugly over her shoulders. Her breaths were shallow but even.

Without taking his eyes from her, he activated the body cam and slipped a pair of scissors from his pocket. As if on cue, the music changed. A haunting melody filled the night as he closed the distance between them.

35

CORINA BLINKED AWAKE, resisting the urge to turn over. Her ribs had begun to show some signs of improvement—until Saturday. Between the lifting, crawling, and being dragged behind the counter, she felt like she'd been kicked by a horse. Yesterday had been rough. Today was worse.

And her mouth was so dry. She glanced at her bedside table to see if she'd left a water bottle there. No luck. But the digital alarm clock caught her attention.

Seven o'clock?

She pressed the glow option on her watch to double-check. The time was correct. She couldn't remember the last time she'd slept past six, and without waking up to a nightmare either. The stress must be getting to her. Still, she didn't move. It wasn't like she could go anywhere.

The predawn darkness permeating the room was strangely comforting, as was the hymn currently exiting her small Bluetooth speaker. "How Great Thou Art" had always been one of her favorites, but it had been a while since she had thought about the meaning of the words. With everything going on, she was finding it harder to deny that she needed to lean on someone greater than herself. But she hadn't figured out how to do that yet or whether she had the courage to try. Or if he would welcome her if she did.

She tried to push the thought aside, but her practiced avoidance wasn't working so well these days. And it would likely get worse now that she was basically a prisoner in her dad's home. There was going to be too much time to think.

With effort, she turned her thoughts toward her father to drown out her niggling conscience. As of the last update she'd gotten, the doctors were hoping to bring him out of the coma by the twentieth or twenty-first if no more complications occurred. Today was the eighteenth. A few more days wasn't that long.

The eighteenth. It was her birthday. A light groan escaped her lips. If she weren't afraid to move, she would have pulled the pillow over her head.

Birthdays since her mom and Colton died had been bittersweet, but her dad always tried his best to make them special. This year, she wouldn't even get to see her dad, much less celebrate with him. She wished she could just ignore the significance of the day, but chances were slim that Bryce would forget, and she knew Allye wouldn't.

Her playlist flipped to an annoying song Allye had added when they were teenagers. Why she hadn't deleted it long ago was a mystery. With a sigh, she decided to brave the morning and shut the music off. She slowly sat up and dropped her legs over the side of the bed, taking care to move no more than necessary. Despite her caution, the spasms were excruciating. She bit her lip and sat as still as possible until the pain settled into a manageable throbbing.

She turned on a lamp and rose to her feet. A stray hair tickled her face as she moved toward the speaker, and she absently reached to tuck it behind her ear. The movement brought her up short.

Horror began to fall over her as her probing fingers corroborated a fact her mind desperately wanted to deny. Slowly, she turned to look at her reflection in the mirror. Something between a scream and a sob caught in her throat and stuck there.

Her waist-length hair had been chopped off in an uneven bob that fell just above her shoulders. She combed her fingers through it in disbelief, trying to come up with an explanation. Had her nightmares transformed into sleepwalking?

Her gaze swept the room, but everything appeared to be just as she had left it the night before. Moving to the desk, she glanced in the small trash can, half expecting to see a wad of discarded hair. The can was empty. She pulled open a drawer and confirmed the office supplies she'd tucked away—including her scissors—were in their proper places.

She sank into the desk chair and forced herself to think. *What did I do?* Try as she might, she could remember nothing between entering her room last night and waking a few moments ago. She couldn't even recall dreaming—a fact for which she was no longer thankful.

Finally, she stood and began to dress. She wanted to investigate the rest of the house, or at least as much of it as she could without waking Bryce or Allye.

As she stepped into the hallway, she noticed a light on in the kitchen. Cautiously, she approached the doorway and peered around the corner.

"Allye, what are you doing?"

"Making you a birthday cake." She spoke without turning around as she spooned batter into a couple of cake pans. "I wanted to wake up early enough to have it done before you got up, but"—she shrugged—"that didn't happen."

"Thanks." Despite her best effort, the word still came out flat. She grimaced. She really was grateful. Allye didn't get up before dawn because she enjoyed the sunrise.

"Come on—we're going to have fun today." Allye slid the pans into the oven and turned around. Confusion crossed her face. She took a few steps closer and cocked her head to the side.

Corina felt the tears rising. Allye must have seen her vulnerability because her expression softened, and she pulled her to a chair.

"You want a cup of tea?"

Corina nodded, swallowing back her emotion. Her eyes followed Allye to a teapot sitting on a warmer. "I'm surprised you didn't drink it all, getting up this early," she managed with a half smile.

Her friend chuckled. "This is the second pot." She winked and handed her a steaming cup.

Corina took it gratefully, reaching for the sugar already on the table. As she took her first sip, their eyes met, and she prepared herself for the question she knew was coming.

Allye spoke in a low tone, her words gentle. "So what's with the . . . ?" She twirled a strand of her own hair around her finger.

"I don't know." Her words were barely audible even to her own ears.

"What do you mean?"

"I woke up like this. I must have done it in my sleep." Heat shimmied up her neck, and she ducked her chin. "I don't even know where I did it. There's no evidence of it in my room."

Allye's eyebrows shot up. "None?"

She shook her head. "I was about to search the house when I noticed you in here. Not that it really matters." She sighed. "I guess I'm just curious—and a little scared that I was using something sharp in my sleep." She shuddered inwardly at the thought.

"I see," Allye said slowly. "Well, we'll figure it out. At least you're not hurt."

"No, but I look awful."

"It is going to need some help." Allye reached out to touch her hand. "Let's have some breakfast, then we'll see what a little trimming will do."

Corina bit her lip, wondering if they would have time to fix it before Bryce got up. The last thing she wanted was for him to see her like this. She opened her mouth to suggest they wait on breakfast, but a noise from the hallway interrupted her.

Too late.

36

CORINA GRITTED HER TEETH. The soft click of the scissors was setting her on edge, despite Bryce's attempts to distract her.

"Hey, take it easy. Allye's not going to cut you."

"Easy for you to say—you're over there," she muttered.

"Thanks for the confidence," Allye piped up from behind her.

Bryce raised his hands in an exaggerated shrug, and she allowed a tight smile to lift her lips. She had to give him credit. He'd been extra gentle this morning, saying very little about her horrible haircut, although he hadn't been able to immediately mask his surprise. He'd listened to her sleepwalking theory, then promptly changed the subject. She could hug him for that, if she weren't already so embarrassed.

A loud knock sounded at the front door, startling her. She looked up at Bryce. Officer Mike had called just before they all retired last night and had promised to come by this morning before he went off duty. Still, it was a bit early for that or for Peter to be coming in.

"I've got it." Bryce stood.

"Thanks." She watched him leave the kitchen, then shifted uncomfortably in her seat.

"Be still," Allye murmured. "I don't want to make this any worse."

She tried to comply, despite the urge to hide in her room until whoever it was had gone. She wasn't ready for anyone else to see her new look yet.

The hinges on the front door creaked—the sound reaching all the way down the hall—but she didn't hear any voices. After a few seconds of silence, the door creaked closed again.

Bryce returned alone, frowning. "Did Peter say anything about leaving? His car is gone."

She shook her head, earning another reprimand from Allye. "I haven't talked to him since last night. Allye, you were up before me. Did he talk to you?"

"Uh-uh. I came straight to the kitchen, and it was quiet in here until you got up."

Bryce opened a drawer. "Well, he isn't out there. No one was. Just a box on the doorstep."

"Did you get it?" Corina asked.

"Not yet. It's got your name on it. Nothing else. Figured I should grab gloves before moving it." He pulled a pair from the drawer, then left again.

The implication of personally delivered mail—a package this time—made her shiver. Little doubt who had left it.

A moment later, Bryce was back with a cardboard box. He set it on the table. "I don't like this showing up while Peter's away from his post. He shouldn't have gone anywhere without letting us know."

"Maybe he needed a restroom break or something and didn't want to wake us," Allye suggested.

"Maybe. If so, he picked a lousy time to do it."

Or her stalker was watching for an opportunity. He seemed to be good at that.

Corina eyed the package. "Let me see it." She held out her hands, but Bryce moved it out of her reach.

"It's probably from your stalker. We should have the police open it."

He was right, but she didn't know if she could stand staring at it until someone arrived. She blew out a breath. "If you want to call Officer Mike, go ahead, but if he's not here by the time Allye's done, I'm going to open it."

He opened his mouth, then shut it without voicing the protest written on his face. He stripped off the gloves and pulled out his phone. A minute later, he set it down. "He didn't answer."

"He'll call back." A band seemed to tighten around her chest as she eyed the box. "Are you almost finished?"

"Just about." Finally, Allye laid the scissors on the table and left to retrieve a mirror. She handed it to Corina with an uncertain look. "This isn't my normal line of work, so I hope it's okay. I did my best."

Corina swallowed back tears. Allye had done fine with what she had to work with, but she wanted her long hair back. She tilted her head and tried to hide her emotion as she examined the cut. At least she no longer looked like a five-year-old left unsupervised with scissors. The A-line bob looked intentional.

She looked up at Allye and tried to smile. "Thanks." Her voice cracked. "I don't know what I would have done if you weren't here."

"You definitely wouldn't have wanted me to fix it." Bryce's attempt to lighten the mood won him a punch in the shoulder from his sister as she began to clean up.

Corina smiled for real this time, but it faded quickly. Back when they dated, Bryce had loved her hair. What did he think of it now?

As if reading her thoughts, he ran his fingers through it, letting his hand rest on her cheek. "It's still beautiful—you're beautiful," he whispered. "The length of your hair doesn't change that."

She drew in a shaky breath as he withdrew his hand. Denying she still had feelings for him was becoming as difficult as ignoring her spiritual state. And with every passing day, the desire to do so was fading.

Her eyes fell on the mysterious box, and she pulled herself back to reality. Now wasn't the time to even think of a relationship. She had a killer to escape.

With that thought uppermost in her mind, she retrieved her own pair of gloves and reached for the package. For its size, it was really light. Her heartbeat quickened as she slit the tape holding the flaps in place. She paused to work up her courage, and her eyes met Bryce's.

"Are you sure you don't want to wait and let the police do that?"

She shook her head. "I need to know." Before he could talk her out of it, she raised the flaps and looked inside.

She caught her breath. The contents were unmistakable. Her missing hair lay neatly in the bottom of the box. She could barely process the message painted in bold red letters on the inside of the top flap.

Happy birthday. Enjoy it. There won't be another.

She pushed the package away as if it had burned her. Bryce managed to snatch it before it dumped onto the floor. His eyes widened as he caught sight of her "present."

Involuntarily, she reached up to touch the ends of her newly cut hair. Nausea roiled in her stomach. She almost didn't make it to the garbage can by the back door.

As she lost her breakfast, she faintly heard Bryce on the phone. Probably with the police. She couldn't make out any of the conversation. Shock and adrenaline blocked out any sound but the thundering of her own pulse.

She straightened to find Allye standing next to her, offering a wet paper towel. Her friend's concerned face was even more pale than usual, but she said nothing as Corina wiped her mouth. She nodded a wordless thanks and turned toward the window.

There was no stopping the man after her. Not with a bodyguard or an alarm system. She couldn't stay here—couldn't sleep another night in this house. She had to—

Her eyes focused on the toolshed a few yards from the back porch. Houston was pawing frantically at the shed's door, his tail swinging in a stiff, horizontal movement he only displayed when agitated. She let her gaze trail upward, and her breath hitched as she caught sight of an unfamiliar dark streak staining the pale gray paint. Something was terribly wrong.

And something in her broke. Without pausing to assess the situation, she threw back the dead bolt on the kitchen door and rushed outside, nearly tripping down the stairs.

Allye's voice rang from behind her. "Corina. Corina, stop! Bryce!"

But she couldn't stop. Couldn't even if she wanted to. A few steps brought her to her destination. She didn't have the words to command Houston aside, so she reached past him. Yanked open the shed's door.

And found herself eye to eye with Officer Mike. Dried rivulets of blood marked his forehead and cheeks, but it was his glazed eyes that stole her breath. Only the dead had that utterly void stare.

She might have screamed. She wasn't sure. The next thing she knew, Bryce's arms were wrapped around her, turning her from the gruesome sight. She let him lead her inside. Let him hold her as the shakes set in.

Muffled noise swirled around her—Bryce's voice. Allye's. Houston's whine. It was too much. Her stomach heaved again, and she pulled away. Dry retched. Bryce reached to steady her, but she shook her head. She needed space.

Stumbling to the living room, she collapsed on the couch and buried her face in her hands. Silent sobs racked her body. The dull pain in her chest intensified exponentially with the movement, but she couldn't stop.

God, where are you? She lowered her arms to clutch her chest, trying to lessen the impact of her sobbing. *He was a good man. And now he's dead!* As she would soon be if God didn't intervene. She grabbed a pillow and flung it across the room. "Why are you letting this happen?"

Silence met her accusations, and as her anger subsided, despair took its place.

37

BRYCE'S STOMACH CLENCHED as he paced the living room. He knew he was hovering, but he couldn't bear to have Corina out of his sight. And he couldn't banish the memory of her strangled scream when she'd found Officer Mike.

So she sat and he paced, trying to process what had happened and trying to come up with a plan of action.

Eric and another officer had responded to his call, followed soon after by the medical examiner. They'd stayed quite a while—gathering evidence, taking statements, forcing themselves to do their jobs while grieving a friend.

With Officer Mike gone, Eric was taking the lead on the investigation, and there was a new hardness in his face when he left. Mike had mentored Eric even back in high school—almost taking the place of the father figure his own had never filled. Bryce had no doubt he and the rest of the department would be doubling their efforts to catch this guy now. He just wondered how much good it would do. The killer was like a phantom whose presence—with the exception of the run-in at Western Outfitters—was only discovered post-fact.

And Eric had indicated that today's investigation had uncovered little. Records from the alarm service showed the security system had been shut off from 11:29 p.m. to 12:45 a.m. Corina's bedroom window was the point of entry. It had been jimmied but with minimal damage. The police had almost missed it, probably would have except for the crushed grass underneath it. And the drag marks leading to the shed.

And Peter was still missing. Bryce didn't know whether to be worried about the guy or concerned he'd been involved somehow and given them the slip.

It also bothered him that Houston hadn't alerted them to the danger. Did that mean the killer was someone he recognized and was comfortable with? Bryce shook off that idea. Houston wouldn't have stood quietly by while an officer was killed and stowed in the backyard—wouldn't have let someone break into Corina's room, even if it was someone he recognized. No, the killer had to have done something to him.

But the dog wasn't acting like he'd been injured in any way. His behavior had been off, but no more than would be expected with the scent of death in the area. They were missing something, but he had no idea what.

And he was afraid they were running out of time to figure it out. Last night had been a major power play. The guy had gotten close to Corina—close enough to cut her hair. And then he'd left?

Bryce shook his head, frustration rising. This guy really didn't make sense. He jumped from ransacking her house to shooting up her shop with them in it to murdering a cop to . . . cutting her hair? The last was less violent but far more personal. An escalation of a different kind. And Bryce was afraid it indicated a soon-coming climax—one he felt powerless to stop.

But he had to, because if he didn't . . . Well, that wasn't an option. He *had* to keep Corina safe. That's all there was to it.

You didn't keep Derryck safe. Your plans sent him directly into harm's way. The condemning thought rose within him like it had many times in the past.

But he set his jaw, thrusting the pain and guilt away. No, he hadn't kept Derryck safe, but he hadn't caused his death either. It was an accident no one could have seen coming.

This situation was different. He knew the danger, and he had a chance to prepare, to divert.

His phone rang. Eric—hopefully with an update.

"Hello?"

"We've located Mr. Lewis." His tone warned of bad news.

He stopped his pacing and leaned against the fireplace.

"His car went through a guardrail just outside of town. Someone called it in about a half hour ago. Mr. Lewis is alive. Barely. He was thrown clear of the vehicle. Probably a good thing since it ended up on its top with a large branch through the windshield. He's being rushed to the hospital now."

Oh, God! Bryce threw up a silent prayer on Peter's behalf. What had he been doing out of town? Following a lead? That didn't sound right. He was a bodyguard, not a detective. And why hadn't he been wearing a seat belt? Not wearing one may have saved his life, but it didn't ring true to what Bryce knew of his personality. He didn't seem like the kind of guy to neglect stuff like that, even if he was in a hurry.

"Looks like an accident—guy fell asleep at the wheel, lost control, whatever—but with everything going on around here, we're not trusting appearances," Eric said. "We're taking extra care in processing, and we've requested a toxicology report from the hospital."

"Thanks." He rested his forehead in his free hand. A thorough investigation was the best they could do, but he didn't believe for an instant that Peter's crash came out of nowhere. Not with the break-in and Officer Mike's murder.

"One more thing, Bryce." Eric's voice went taut. "The gun and magazine left behind in Western Outfitters' alley were clean. No fingerprints."

Wonderful.

He managed to finish the call but didn't resume pacing. He

rubbed at the knots in the back of his neck. Things were just getting worse. In twelve hours, their best lead had tanked, a good man was dead, and now someone else was in the hospital.

"What is it?" Allye asked. Leather creaked as she dropped into a recliner behind him.

He didn't look up as he relayed his and Eric's conversation. Corina didn't respond, but Allye gasped at the news about Peter.

"They're doing everything they can for him." He could only pray it was enough. He slammed a fist against the stone of the fireplace.

The women stayed silent.

"We've got to get Corina out of here." It was the only option. He'd known it since this morning's package arrived. Everything in him screamed she was no longer even marginally safe in this town.

Despite all Will's precautions, the stalker had no trouble penetrating his home, murdering an experienced cop in the backyard, and possibly disposing of Corina's bodyguard. All without waking any of them. His experience and stealth were uncanny. It was no wonder Corina's father had chosen to disappear so many years ago.

Could they do it again? And could he convince Corina to leave when her father's condition was still up in the air?

"The farm." His head whipped around at Allye's calm voice. She straightened and fixed him with a knowing look. "We could take her there."

He rolled that possibility around in his mind. If they could get there without being followed, there was almost a hundred acres' worth of hiding places to choose from. And it wasn't too far to travel back if something went wrong with Will.

He nodded slowly. "I think you're right."

Allye rose and headed for the hall. He'd be willing to bet she was going to start packing. She paused just inside the doorway, turned back to look at him, then glanced pointedly in Corina's direction before exiting the room.

He let his gaze trail to where Corina sat on an end seat of the leather couch, knees pulled up against her chest. Her eyes were glazed, and she didn't seem to have heard them.

She'd barely spoken to the police while they were here, answering their questions with as few words as possible. She had lapsed into complete silence after their departure.

She was nearing her breaking point. Even he could see that much. If she didn't get a reprieve soon . . .

The last five years had changed her. Yes, she'd matured. But no matter how hard she tried to hide it, Derryck's death had seriously damaged the sense of security she'd rebuilt after losing half her family. This time she'd compensated by pushing everyone away and leaning solely on herself. And now that staff had been knocked out from under her as well.

With this most recent assault, control had been ripped from her grasp. And her already fragile emotional state was threatening to shatter under the pressure.

He continued to study her. She hadn't moved in at least ten minutes. Houston was curled up at her feet, but she seemed oblivious to his presence. Her posture exuded defeat. She was losing hope, giving up.

Anger surged through him at the man responsible for stripping away her independence, her strength. It wasn't enough to take her mother and little brother away, to effectively force her to leave behind her home in Texas. Not enough for her dad to be hospitalized, her home wrecked, her business damaged. Now she couldn't even sleep safely and would probably have nightmares of Officer Mike's body for weeks, if not much longer.

He resisted the urge to pull her into a hug and promise everything would be okay. Perhaps later he could say that with confidence.

He took the seat beside her, lightly grasping her shoulders to turn her to face him.

"Hey," he said softly. "We're in this together. You, me, Allye, and God." She dropped her eyes at the conclusion of his sentence. He thumbed her chin back up. "What is it?"

"Where has he been?" He had to strain to catch her words.

"Who?"

She closed her eyes. "God," she choked out, chin trembling with emotion. "I know he promised never to leave, but where is he? Everything is falling apart, and I feel like he's just left us here." A tear slipped down her cheek. She sniffed but made no move to brush it away.

He could feel his own eyes filling. *Jesus, give me wisdom here.* He found her hand and held it, collecting his thoughts before offering an answer.

"I don't know why he's letting all this happen," he said carefully. "But I do know, positively, that God has not left us—no matter how it looks or how we feel. Try to believe that."

She nodded but didn't look convinced. Another tear escaped from beneath her lashes. He gave her hand a gentle squeeze, then thumbed the wetness from her face.

"Come on." He stood and offered her a hand up. "Let's see what Allye's up to."

38

"YOU WANT TO WHAT?" Bryce wasn't sure he had heard his sister correctly.

"I think it'll work."

"There's absolutely no way that guy's gonna think Corina is you."

"And what about you? You can't stay here by yourself if he thinks it's me here alone," Corina put in. She dropped the shirt she'd been absently unfolding and refolding. At least Allye's harebrained scheme was distracting her from the hopelessness she'd fallen into. Bryce would give her credit for that, even if the idea was less than realistic.

"I've already thought of that. Eric or someone can come over to stay with 'you,' while Bryce takes 'me' out somewhere. It would look too suspicious if we all left you alone in a house that obviously can't keep out an intruder."

"And then what? You can't stay holed up here forever."

"I won't have to," Allye insisted. "All I have to do is give you enough time to disappear. Once you're safe, it won't matter if he finds out he's been had. He won't go after me unless he thinks I'm leading him to you, and I'll be sure not to do that."

"You don't know that," Corina murmured. "If you make him

angry, he might retaliate. Look at Officer Mike—and Peter." So she had been listening earlier.

Allye's voice softened. "*If* your stalker was responsible for Peter, I don't think retaliation had anything to do with it. Peter was an active threat to his plan." She paused, emotion clearly showing on her face. "Same thing with Officer Mike. Getting them out of the way wasn't about getting even—in his eyes, it was smart. His focus is on you and your dad. I don't think he cares about anyone else."

Corina's eyes shuttered. Bryce shot his sister a look. Reminding Corina of the stalker's intensity probably wasn't the best thing to do right now—even though she was right. Allye gave him a helpless shrug but didn't apologize.

He shook his head. "I don't like it."

"Do you have a better idea? Because last time I checked, we were a bit short on options." Allye's eyes flashed defiance. She crossed her arms and glared at him.

He mirrored her movements and returned her stare. She refused to back down. "Okay, say you're right and it doesn't put you in danger. That still leaves us with the fact that you and Corina don't look anything alike," he challenged.

She snorted and dropped her arms. "You have no imagination."

"Excuse me?"

An irritated sigh escaped her lips. "What are the first things you notice when you look at Corina?"

"Allye." A sideward glance showed Corina watching him with mild interest.

"Humor me. If she's walking toward you from a distance, what do you see?"

"A small, beautiful lady."

The hint of a smile appeared on his sister's face, but she shook her head. She wasn't going to let him off the hook that easily. "Be descriptive."

"Okay." If she wanted descriptive, he could be descriptive.

"How about hair the color of late-afternoon sunshine, clothes and boots fit for a rodeo, and inherent poise in every movement?" From the corner of his eye, he saw a flush creep into Corina's cheeks.

Allye gave him an approving grin. "If he's been watching her for any length of time, he's going to have associated those things with her identification. So we replace her characteristics with mine. I'm a little taller, but not by much, so that shouldn't be an issue. If she wears my clothes, ditches the boots, and walks a little more—"

"Clumsily?"

"I was going to say *freely*," she corrected with a smirk. "And if we make our move in the evening, we should be able to pull it off."

"What about the hair?" Corina's was the wrong color, and now the length and style were totally incompatible too.

Satisfaction bloomed on Allye's face, like she knew she'd sunk the hook. She turned and walked from the room. He exchanged a confused look with Corina, then lifted one shoulder in a shrug. A moment later, Allye returned, holding the answer to his question.

"A wig? Where'd you get that?"

His sister grinned. "A leftover prop from the time I talked Corina into participating in one of the local plays. I found it in the guest bedroom the other night."

He studied the hairpiece as she held it next to her head. The color wasn't exact, but it could pass if a person didn't look too closely. Maybe her idea could work after all. "When Eric calls back, we'll run it by him. See what he thinks."

"No."

He turned his head to see determination on Corina's face. The earlier forlorn expression was gone. Mostly.

"I'm not putting Allye on this guy's radar." Without waiting for an answer, she stood and left the room.

His eyes shot to see Allye's reaction. His sister was facing the doorway, eyebrows raised, mouth slightly open. As he watched, her jaw firmed in a stubbornness that could rival Corina's—and had on occasion. She set the wig aside and followed Corina.

Bryce sank into the leather chair at Corina's desk. He didn't know what to think, what to do. No, he knew what to do—he just didn't know how to do it. He needed to get the woman he loved to a safe place without putting his sister in danger.

He banged a fist on the desktop in frustration. He shouldn't have to choose one over the other. Those two things shouldn't be mutually exclusive. And yet, he was unable to think of an option that would keep them both safe.

Sighing, he dropped his head in his hands and started praying. He needed wisdom beyond his own. And they all needed protection beyond what he had to offer.

CORINA RAN A HAND through her hair. Her fingers came to the end far too quickly. She shuddered and dropped her arm to her side.

"Corina—"

"I'm not discussing this." She turned to face Allye. "I appreciate what you're trying to do, but it's too much of a risk."

"Why?"

"Do you think this guy is going to just shrug it off if we pull something like this on him? We still don't know why he's targeted my family, just that he considers it payment of some sort. If I disappear and you're still here, he could do something in a rage or add you to the list of people who owe him." Her eyes sought the floor as Derryck's mischievous face jumped into her memory. "Your mom can't lose another child," she murmured, hoping Allye would listen to that.

Allye's arms encircled her. Corina stiffened, then returned the hug. When Allye drew back, there was a renewed gentleness in her eyes, but the determination was still there.

"Nobody's going to lose anybody else. We'll be careful and do this right. But we have to do something. He's not going to stop on his own. As long as he knows where you are, anyone around you is in danger anyway."

Corina closed her eyes. She didn't know what to think. Finally, she sighed. "Give me some time, okay?"

"All right." Allye said it like everything was settled. "We can't do anything until this evening anyway. But if we're going to do this right, we need to bring the police in on it soon so someone can arrange to be here in time."

She didn't answer. There had to be a better way. There had to.

From somewhere else in the house, glass shattered, and Houston let out a series of sharp barks. She glanced at Allye's wide eyes, then peeked around the corner into the hallway, where she had a clear view to the kitchen at the back of the house.

A flickering of light and shadow caught her attention.

"Fire!"

39

A SCREECHING SMOKE ALARM and the scent of fuel assaulted Corina before she burst into the kitchen. Bryce was already there, beating the flames with a towel. He had slowed the spread, but it didn't look like he was having much success actually putting it out.

She circled him and retrieved the fire extinguisher from under the sink. "Step back!" She pulled the pin and sprayed the area with foam.

Once the flames subsided, she dropped the extinguisher and stared at the mess. She couldn't see beneath the layer of foam, but she knew there would be a hole seared into the hardwood. Smoke streaks and what she hoped was just surface damage marred a section of one wall. The fire had been concentrated just below a window. A now-busted window.

"What happened?" She turned to look at Bryce.

His expression was grim. "I ran in when I heard the window break. The fire was already going when I got here." His gaze settled on a cylindrical object. "I think that's what started it." He pointed but didn't touch it.

Great. Her dad's house was a crime scene. Again. She raised a shaky hand to her forehead. Tylenol would be welcome right now.

"The police are on their way," Allye said, flipping on the fan over the stovetop. There was a lot of smoke in proportion to the size of the flames.

"Good. You smell that?" Bryce asked.

Corina inhaled and choked back a cough. She pulled the collar of her shirt up to cover her mouth and nose.

"Diesel. Not as explosive as gasoline but still effective."

He moved, and she caught a glimpse of his hands.

"You're burned." At her words, Bryce looked down. He seemed surprised at the redness of his right hand.

He shook his head. "It's not bad. A little cool water, and I'll be fine."

She wanted to argue with him, but Allye caught her attention.

"Hey, look over here." She was kneeling next to a softball-size object on the floor near the stove.

"What is it?"

Allye reached into a drawer and pulled out a pair of gloves before carefully picking up the object. There was a sheet of paper rubber-banded around it. "Think I should unwrap it?" she asked.

"I don't know." Corina wanted to see what was there, but she knew better. The other letters and packages had been different—he hadn't committed a crime to get them to her. Well, he had, but the crime was only evident after she'd opened them. This time, the stalker had blatantly committed both vandalism and arson. Even wearing gloves, they could compromise evidence if they opened it themselves. Probably shouldn't have even picked it up. She sighed and shook her head. "We need to wait."

Reluctantly, Allye set it back where she'd found it. Approaching sirens filled the air, and she headed for the front door.

BRYCE FOUND HIMSELF AGAIN pacing the living room on the other end of the house. Corina and Allye waited on the couch, but he couldn't sit. The police hadn't given them an update yet. He'd had to put up a fight just to keep the fire department from forcing them all outside while they confirmed the cylinder in the kitchen wasn't going to burst into flames again or explode. Normally, that would make sense, but he didn't want them outside and exposed when the killer was likely still within bullet range.

Eric finally entered the room, holding up a plastic bag with a paper inside. "We're done in there. I nailed plywood over the broken pane."

"Thank you," Corina said, joining them at the door.

"No chance of the fire reigniting?" Bryce asked.

"I don't think so—you had that part pretty well taken care of. There was diesel in the cylinder. Enough to ensure ignition, not enough to feed a large fire."

"So he's still sending messages."

Eric held up the bag. "It would appear so."

"What does it say?" Corina's voice was quiet, as if she already knew she wouldn't like the answer.

He offered her the bag, and Bryce leaned in as she read. The same red lettering from this morning's package stared back at them.

> *Did you enjoy the present?*
> *It was my pleasure.*
> *Oh, and by the by, your friends might want to find a safer place to stay. It would be a shame for them to become collateral damage. Like your cop friend.*

A sharply indrawn breath from Corina's other side indicated that Allye had read it too.

This wasn't good. He looked at Eric, then at Corina. "We've got to do something, and we've got to do it fast."

He wasn't prepared for the sharpness of the words Corina threw back at him.

"No, *I've* got to do something. It's time for you and Allye to go." She spun on her heel and strode out of the room. "I'll help you get your stuff together."

Eric raised his eyebrows at the outburst, but he didn't say anything, just bent down for the bag Corina had dropped.

Allye started to follow, and Bryce held out a hand to stop her. "Let me." She frowned but acquiesced.

He walked down the hall to the spare bedroom, where Corina was heaping Allye's things on the center of the bed.

"Hey, slow down."

She dumped another load onto the comforter. *How does Allye gather so much junk in just a few days?* He shook his head. Not important.

"It's time, Bryce. The sooner you're out of here, the better." Corina put her hands on her hips and attempted to stare him down, much like Allye had a little while ago.

And as before, he stared right back. "And what are you going to do with us gone? Sit here and hope your stalker forgets you exist?"

"That's my problem, isn't it?"

"No, it's our problem. Like I told you earlier, we're in this with you, whether you like it or not. We're not going to leave you alone."

"I'm telling you to get out!" Her voice rose to a dangerously high level.

"No." He stepped forward and gripped her shoulders. "Corina, think about this—"

She pushed his hands away. "I'm done thinking about it! This is *my* dad's house. If I have to throw you out with a police escort, I will."

"Can't you see he's manipulating you?" Bryce almost shouted the question, and Corina took a step back, then turned quickly toward the wall so he couldn't see her face. But she couldn't hide the heaving of her shoulders. He took a deep breath and lowered his voice. "Look at what he's doing. He got you out of the hospital, away from a public place. He got rid of your bodyguard. Now he's threatening us to get you alone. This guy wants to kill you. Isolating yourself is just going to make his job easier."

She didn't answer him, and he wasn't sure she was going to.

"Corina—"

"I might be an easy target, but at least I'll be the only one." She choked on the words. "I already don't know if my dad and Peter are going to pull through. And Officer Mike . . ." Her voice trailed off, and she crossed her arms protectively over her chest. "I—I couldn't take it if I lost you guys too." She turned back toward him but didn't meet his eyes. Her tears ripped at his heart. "Bryce, it wouldn't matter if he killed me after that. I'd probably want to die."

He drew her close to him. She didn't return his embrace, but she also didn't pull away. "I can't lose you either. I love you."

She tensed and shook her head. "Don't."

His heart sank a little, but he didn't push it. Her safety was all that was important right now. He drew in a breath. "Regardless, we have to get you somewhere safe and give the police a chance to figure out what's going on without having to come over here and play catch-up every five minutes."

Silence fell between them while he waited for her response. Her tears soaked into his T-shirt, but he didn't care.

"What about Allye?" she finally asked.

"You mean if we swap you two?" he said quietly. She nodded. "What if she goes away for a while too? Not with us—when we disappear, we have to stay gone and alone until they catch this creep—but I have a cousin in Montana. It's not exactly a hot spot this time of year, so chances are, I'll be able to get Allye a last-minute ticket tonight or tomorrow. Whichever officer stays here with her can take her to the airport to catch her flight."

The idea had hit him right before the fire. It wasn't foolproof, but it should work for a while. It would buy them time, and maybe give everyone some peace of mind. Best of all, it would get his sister far away from the danger, and he could focus on keeping Corina safe.

"And Houston?"

He had forgotten the German shepherd. What would they do with him? "We can't take him with us. He'd give you away." He thought about that. "Does your vet offer boarding services?"

She nodded slowly.

"Allye can see that he gets dropped off."

"We don't have much choice, do we?" Her voice emerged subdued, defeated. It about broke his heart. His arms tightened protectively around her. No, they didn't have much choice about any of this. Not really.

40

THEY ONLY HAD A SMALL SLICE of time to pull off the switch. The killer—if he was watching—needed to be able to see just well enough to be fooled by the disguise. Too much light, and he would be able to see through their charade. Too little, and he might not have enough information to reach the conclusion they were hoping for. The last thing they needed was for him to follow, trying to get a better look and confirm identities.

Sunset was just a few minutes away.

Bryce turned his attention to Corina. She had already changed into one of Allye's outfits, black leggings under a pink knee-length skirt with a zebra-striped blouse. A sparkling neon green scarf and matching shoes completed the ensemble. It was a color explosion—just the way Allye liked it, and nothing Corina would ever think of wearing.

After they'd chosen the outfit, Allye had put it on and requested one of the officers escort her to Bryce's house for a few moments, making sure if anyone was watching they'd know what she was wearing today. When she got back, she'd passed the clothing on to Corina.

With the red wig, an old pair of Allye's glasses, and the green flats instead of boots, she wouldn't look a thing like herself from a distance. They'd even added . . . freckles?

He did a double take. Oh boy. If the stalker was close enough to see the freckles, he would be way too close to be fooled by a disguise. He shook his head but kept his mouth shut.

Just as the sun began to dip below the horizon, Corina slipped the wig over her hair and let Allye adjust it until it looked believable.

Eric joined them in the hallway, and Bryce wrapped his sister in a bear hug. "Stay out of trouble."

She laughed, but it sounded forced. "I was about to say the same to you." She squeezed a bit tighter. "Keep her safe," she whispered.

"That's the plan."

When she released him, she turned to Corina and gave her a farewell hug. He wasn't sure what Allye whispered to her, but Corina swiped away a tear before she grabbed the cluster of bags that would further cement her role. Instead of Allye's junk, however, they contained Corina's and Bryce's clothing and personal items and copies of Will's files. Some of the bags were heavy, and she struggled to grip them all, so he reached for one of the larger ones, his hand brushing hers in the process.

"You ready to do this?"

She didn't meet his eyes, just lifted a shoulder and let it drop.

"Hey, if you're going to be Allye, you need a lot more energy than that." He got an eyeroll in response, but she loosened up and rolled her shoulders.

Allye and Eric moved into the living room, where they would be nearby but still out of sight of the front door. Bryce took one final glance through the peephole. All clear. But hopefully not too clear.

"Let's go."

NERVOUSNESS COURSED through her, but as they'd planned, Corina led the way to Allye's car, doing her best to imitate her friend's walk—an odd combination of grace interspersed with the awkwardness of a newborn colt. Not so hard with the ballet flats throwing her off-kilter. Halfway across the street, one shoe started sliding off, and she lost her balance. Instantly, Bryce's hand was on her arm, steadying her. She shot him a grateful look before continuing to the car.

When they reached the Jetta, she tossed the bags into the rear seat and floorboard—wherever there was room—then took her place up front and started the engine. Bryce climbed in on the passenger side.

"You really think he'll buy it?" she asked when both doors were safely shut.

"With a performance like that, I think we've got a pretty good chance."

She grimaced and decided not to tell him the stumble had been purely accidental. She firmed her lips and backed out of the driveway. At the end of the road, she screeched to a halt for the stop sign, then executed a wider than necessary turn onto the main road.

"I'm impressed."

She spared a second's glance at Bryce and saw amusement on his face. Her shoulders relaxed slightly, and she released a tight smile. "I hope Allye doesn't take offense at my imitation of her driving."

"If she found a way to watch you, she probably gave a whoop at the noise you made back there."

"Probably." Her gaze flicked to the rearview. So far, so good. "So now what? I don't know the way to your uncle's farm."

"That's fine. We're not going there yet."

"We're not?"

"Nope. Keep going north. I need to pick up something from a friend who lives on a side road near the high school."

Before she could ask which one, an unfamiliar blue suburban pulled onto the road behind them. Corina's fingers tightened on the steering wheel. From the corner of her eye, she saw Bryce lean forward slightly.

"Just keep driving," he said.

Like she planned to stop.

For the next couple of minutes, she split her attention between the road in front of them and the vehicle trailing just far enough behind to conceal the driver's identity. Sweat seeped into her shirt. Had their plan failed already? Or was this merely someone going the same direction they were?

As they neared the traffic light in the center of town, Corina flipped on her turn signal.

"What are you doing?"

"Trying to see if this guy's really following us." She hung a left at the light and watched her rearview.

The suburban sped straight through the intersection.

She blew out a breath.

"Nice," Bryce murmured.

Corina glanced at him, but his eyes stayed glued to the mirror. Just because the driver hadn't followed didn't mean he couldn't circle back if he really was tailing them.

She made a right turn into a small subdivision that connected back to the main road at the other end. This would slow them down but would give the suburban plenty of time to be on its way. And if it showed again . . .

But as they resumed their previous route a few minutes later, it was nowhere in sight.

She forced her fingers to relax their death grip on the steering wheel. No suburban meant no tail.

Not one she could see, anyway.

She glanced at Bryce. "Everything clear?"

"I think so."

Okay. Good.

She was so ready to be done with this drive.

The school lay only a few minutes outside the neighboring city of Falmouth, but the drive from Kincaid felt ten times longer than normal. Although she knew Bryce was keeping a close watch for tails, she couldn't keep her eyes from straying to the mirrors every couple of seconds. The wig started to itch, but Corina refused to scratch her scalp, afraid she might dislodge the hairpiece too soon. Hopefully this detour wouldn't take too long.

Finally, the high school came into view, and Corina turned onto the street Bryce indicated. Her headlights bounced off a small car with a *For Sale* sign in the window. Bryce directed her to an empty driveway, and she pulled in, leaving the engine running.

He smiled. "Might as well turn it off. We're ditching the car."

"What are we going to do?" There was no way she was taking a hike in these shoes. She still couldn't believe Allye had talked her out of packing her boots—said they'd take up too much space in the few bags they had. She was stuck with these ridiculously flimsy flats and a pair of sneakers she hadn't worn in years.

"Leave the car here. Eric will be by to get it in a little while. We're going to take Jimmy's old beater. My Camaro is too recognizable, and this thing isn't much better." She had to admit he was right about that. The Jetta was a bright cherry red, and if anyone had any doubts, the Allye's Photography logo would quickly give them away.

He started collecting their bags, taking a larger share of them this time, and she followed suit with what he left. She held up the keys and jingled them, not sure if he could see them in the darkness.

"Just leave them under the mat."

After they'd loaded everything into the trunk of his friend's car, they climbed in, Bryce opting for the driver's seat this time. "You're probably safe to get rid of the wig," he said as he pulled back onto Highway 27.

Gladly. She tugged the irritating thing off, hoping her hair wasn't too much of a mess underneath. She couldn't see it, but it felt frizzy. She ran her fingers through it, hoping to minimize the chances of looking like a pom-pom.

She'd never liked wearing the wig, even in the play several years ago. But she and Allye had auditioned for a minor role as a set of twins, and her dad had pushed for them to go red instead of blond.

So she wouldn't be as recognizable in pictures.

The realization hit hard. How many of her dad's actions and words were directly linked to this horrible situation he'd kept secret?

She dug her fingers into the mass of fake hair, squeezing it like a stress ball.

Better than throwing it out the window like she wanted.

"You okay?" Green dash lights illuminated Bryce's face enough for her to see the concern in his sidelong glance.

"I'm fine." But she wouldn't be if she heard that question one more time. She closed her eyes and squeezed the wig again. "Just wishing my dad had trusted me enough to tell me the truth." She jerked as his hand closed over hers.

"We'll get you through this."

"Yeah." She changed the subject. "How long a drive is it to your uncle's house?"

Bryce released her hand. "Normally around ten minutes from here, but I'm going to go the long way."

Another precaution against the possibility of a tail.

She focused her attention on the side-view mirror—much safer than looking at him—and searched the road behind them. No headlights. That didn't mean they hadn't been followed, but it was some comfort nonetheless.

Corina leaned her head back against the seat. *God, I don't know what your plan is.* If he even had one for her. But the prayer kept coming, and she let it. *Please, I'm asking you to help us. Keep my dad safe, and Bryce, Allye, Eric, and Peter. Don't let anything else happen to them for trying to protect me.*

Guilt and grief assailed her as she thought of Officer Mike. She swallowed hard. *Let this guy mess up—something—and get caught before he ruins anyone else's life.*

41

THE BACK ROADS north of the high school were narrow and winding. It wasn't wise to go too fast here, especially in the dark, but Bryce had driven this area enough to push it. If they had a tail who was unfamiliar with the area, he'd have to be more than a little reckless to keep up. Of course, Corina's stalker just might fit that bill.

A light sigh came from the other side of the car. Corina had fallen asleep, although Bryce wasn't sure how she managed to stay that way with all the bumps and curves they were taking. It had been a long day, though. She had to be exhausted.

Bryce stifled a yawn and flexed his fingers on the steering wheel, once again checking all the mirrors. Only darkness surrounded them. Confident they hadn't been followed, he turned off onto a connecting road that would lead them to the farm.

Moonlight filtered through the clouds as they pulled into the long curving driveway of his uncle's house. Corina stirred at the crunch of gravel beneath their tires.

"We almost there?"

"Yeah, we're here," he said as the house came into view. A feeling of security washed over him at the sight.

Nestled against a stretch of woods and out of sight of the road, his uncle Jesse's home was the perfect place for them to hide out for a while. The old farmhouse dated back to the pre–Civil War days, and it held a few surprises he and his cousins had enjoyed exploring on rainy days. Those surprises might come in handy.

They wouldn't be putting anyone in danger by staying here either, one of the most compelling reasons to choose this as their hiding spot. All of Uncle Jesse's kids were married now, and only the youngest lived nearby. With his aunt and uncle on their anniversary trip, the house would be empty, which meant none of them would be put at risk, and no one would accidentally betray his and Corina's presence.

They gathered the bags in silence. It seemed like they had brought a lot with them, but the files took up much of the space. At least his uncle was a stock-piler. Food wouldn't be an issue.

Corina made it onto the porch before him. She jiggled the doorknob. "Locked."

Dropping their bags on the porch beside him, Bryce fished around in his pocket for the keys. If he'd been thinking, he would have kept them out, but it was late, and he was tired.

With only a little trouble locating the correct key in the darkness, he eventually got the door open. He motioned Corina to go ahead of him while he collected the dropped bags.

Corina stepped in but stopped just inside the entryway.

"Something wrong?"

"Where am I headed?"

"Sorry. Forgot you haven't been here." He turned sideways to avoid hitting her with the bags as he passed. "This way." He led her to the bedrooms at the back of the house. "I'll be in this room." He indicated the second door on their right. "Bathroom is the next door. And you'll be there at the end in Hailey's old room."

The end room was perfect for Corina. Farthest from the door, it would take the longest to get to. More importantly, it had a built-in escape route—a hidden one.

Using his elbow, Bryce flipped on the bedroom light and set the bags on the bed.

"Before we separate your stuff from mine, I need to show you something." A glance at Corina's face left him no doubt that she would rather he didn't, but it wouldn't take long. He knelt in front of the room's massive antique dresser and removed the bottom drawer, revealing a hole in the floor.

Corina crouched next to him to peer into the darkness. "What in the world?"

"It's a tunnel. If anything happens and your stalker gets into the house, take this way out. There's a small shelf at the bottom with flashlights, so you don't have to find your way in the dark."

The farmhouse had been built less than a decade before the Civil War broke out, and the owners had specially designed it to accommodate escaped slaves on the last leg of their journey to freedom. Among other amenities, they'd equipped the back bedroom with a tunnel entrance to hide any suspicious coming and goings.

When Jesse had bought the house back in the 1990s, he'd been enamored with the idea of a historical tunnel and arranged to have it restored to a safely usable condition. It had become a favorite play area for the cousins. Bryce had never dreamed it would ever serve a useful purpose again. He still hoped it wouldn't be needed, but he wasn't sure of anything anymore.

"What about you?"

"If I can, I'll join you."

"And if you can't?"

"I'll get out another way." He cupped her chin in his hand and tried to dislodge the skeptical look from her face. "I *will* get out. If something happens, don't you dare stay in danger because you're worried about me."

"But—"

"No. No buts. Now listen. The tunnel's pretty long. You can gauge your distance by counting the support beams. Five to the magnolia, fifteen to the halfway point, thirty to the barn. The tunnel comes up inside the barn. All you have to do from there is slip out the back door. You'll be right next to the woods, and there's a nearby deer stand that I'll point out to you tomorrow. If you have to use this and I'm not with you, I'll meet you there."

She looked away, but he turned her face back toward him.

"Promise me you'll go if there's danger." She still didn't answer, and he could see the mist in her eyes. He hated to push the issue, but he couldn't risk something happening and her being afraid to leave without him. "Please, Corina. Promise me."

She stood and walked toward the bed, opening the bags to sort their things.

"Corina—"

Her hands stilled. "I can't make that promise, Bryce. The best I can offer you is that I'll evaluate the situation and try to make the right decision." He started to protest, but she cut him off, her voice strained. "That's the best I can give you. Take it or leave it."

That wasn't much of a choice.

GONE. CORINA TRIED TO SLEEP, but the word echoed in her head. *Gone. Gone. Gone.* Derryck was gone. Colton. Mama. Officer Mike. She'd been forced out of her home twice now—three times if she counted the temporary housing with her dad. Whether she would get her dad back was questionable. All she had left with her was Bryce. And he was in danger just by being near her.

The fear of losing him too nearly suffocated her.

Gone. She took a deep breath, held it, then tried to will her mind to quiet as she slowly exhaled. *Gone.* The word seemed almost audible, taunting her like a playground bully.

Frustrated, she tossed off the covers, slid into a robe, and padded into the kitchen. Maybe a cup of hot chocolate would help, if she could find some. She stopped just inside the doorway. The kitchen was empty, but the doorway to the den area was visible from where she stood. And Bryce was still up, case files spread around the recliner he'd claimed. She clenched her teeth.

Never mind the hot chocolate.

She couldn't risk getting caught in conversation. She couldn't handle it tonight. She turned on her heel and hurried back to her bedroom.

Maybe music would help. She glanced through the collection on her outdated MP3 player. She would have preferred her phone, but she'd been afraid to pack anything remotely trackable. Sighing, she chose a Celtic album, one rich with haunting melodies. The songs were lovely, yet lonely, conjuring up images of waves beating against rocky cliffs or a solitary bagpiper traversing Scotland's heather-filled moors. Just the thing she needed.

She lay back in bed, letting the music roll over her, bathing away her troublesome thoughts, soothing her toward a restless sleep.

A blue SUV sped toward the passenger side of her car. Corina spun the steering wheel, but there was no time to avoid it. A scream tore from her throat as metal crunched and glass shattered. The car spun. Tires screeched. A second impact. Pain shot down her arm. The world went white. Black. The airbags deflated, and the car skidded to a stop.

She tried to catch her breath. Her nostrils itched with the smell of burnt rubber and hot metal mingled with . . . blood?

There was no mistaking that combination of scents, and as soon as she recognized it, Corina knew what was coming. God, no. Please. She fought to forget, to focus straight ahead, to avoid the scene she'd viewed so many times before, but it was no use. Her head swiveled as if turned by an invisible hand. She was powerless to stop it. Please, God. She fought the bile rising in the back of her throat. Tried to prepare herself.

She saw the familiar curly red hair first. Then the blood. So much blood.

Mama's. Colton's. Derryck's. Officer Mike's.

An anguished cry spilled from her lips.

Corina jerked awake to the sound of her own whimpering. *So much for sleep.* The music had stopped, and the night was eerily silent. She was sweating, and she'd pulled the sheet over her head as her dreams forced her to relive the day Derryck died, this time with more excruciating accuracy than usual. Well, until the end anyway. She shoved the bedding away.

She bit her lip to muffle her sobs. "I'm so tired of hurting, God. What's the point of loving, just to have it all taken away? What's the point of being a Christian if you leave me to deal with life alone? I can't do this."

But I can. The question is, Will you trust me? The words weren't audible, but she heard them just the same.

"I don't know how."

Trust me.

"But—" She was weeping now, pain ripping her soul as hope and fear fought for mastery. If he was speaking to her, then maybe he hadn't left her. Maybe he did care.

Trust me.

And in that moment, she knew in her heart that he was trustworthy. She let herself latch onto that truth. The issue wasn't with God; it was with her own response to the hurt. She'd allowed it to mask his goodness. Hadn't been able or willing to accept the comfort he offered. But her feelings didn't change the fact of his goodness or his love. She had reveled in her hurt far too long.

"I'm so sorry," she whispered. She wiped her tears, but they kept coming. "All right, Jesus, I choose to trust you—whether I feel you or not, whether you . . . protect my loved ones or not." Those last words were hard, but they were freeing too, and saying them aloud gave her the courage to continue. "I don't know how much more I can take, but if you'll help me, I'll cling to you. I believe you can see me through this."

She felt nothing for a long time, but she remained still until a peace she hadn't felt in years began to seep into her soul.

42

BRYCE CRADLED A CUP OF COFFEE the next morning as he mulled over the phone conversation he'd just had with Eric. Peter was doing better after a transfusion, although he was so drugged up on painkillers, they hadn't been able to question him about anything.

Toxicology had come back, though. They'd found chloral hydrate in his system. He'd been drugged, confirming his accident was no accident. And when the police went over Will's home with that in mind, they'd found traces of it in the nearly empty gallon of tea from Zhan's. The police would be questioning both the kitchen staff and delivery driver when they pinpointed who'd been working that night.

His fingers tightened on his mug. They'd all drunk that tea, which explained why none of them had woken up when the stalker broke in.

He looked up as Corina entered the kitchen. "Coffee's on the counter."

He opened his mouth to relay the news about Peter, but instead of helping herself to the coffee, she took the seat across from him. "We need to talk."

His gaze slid quickly past her bobbed hair. He was already

starting to get used to the change. As he studied her face, he noticed a light in her eyes he hadn't seen since he'd arrived home. A hesitant smile lit her face.

"I'm done hiding."

Alarm pulsed through him. "Corina, this guy's too dangerous and unpredictable—"

She shook her head and reached out a hand to shush him. "Sorry, poor choice of words. I'm not talking about the stalker."

His brow puckered. Okay, he was lost.

"I'm done hiding from God, and I'm done hiding from us." She bit her lip. Tears shimmered in her eyes. "Derryck reminded me so much of Colton, it almost felt like I had a little brother again. When he died, it brought back all the loss from before. It nearly broke me." She lifted one shoulder. "Or maybe it did break me. I blamed God. And I—I pushed you away. Not because I didn't care about you but because I did." Her voice cracked. "I was afraid to lose you too. Then when I heard you reenlisted for active duty and the chances of something happening to you were so much higher, I couldn't handle it. I guess I thought if I could stop caring, pretend you didn't exist, maybe I could keep my heart from shattering again."

Bryce reached across the table and wrapped his fingers around hers. She didn't pull away. "I'm sorry for leaving like I did—with things unresolved between us." He had zero regrets over giving the extra years of service to his country. He'd grown up a lot and done his mechanic's job well. But the reason he'd re-upped, the choice to go into active duty so he'd have an excuse to leave town and not have to face his losses head on . . . No, he wasn't proud of that.

"You had every right to go. It's not like I was talking to you—or anyone else—after it all happened."

He shook his head. "You were hurting. We both were." Yes, she'd refused to talk back then, but he could have pressed harder for a conversation or waited until she was ready. Instead, he'd run. Run from the fact that he'd set the events into play that led to his little brother's death.

Run from the belief that he'd lost his brother and Corina on the same day.

She hid. He ran.

Never again.

"It's been a miserable five years." Corina's voice broke again, and a tear escaped her lashes.

"Yeah. Yeah, it has." His own voice sounded like he'd just swallowed a handful of gravel, but he didn't care.

"I decided last night that I can't keep living like this. I've got to be open to whatever God has for me—including his comfort. And I want you to know I'm not going to push you away anymore."

"I'm . . . glad." So glad.

"Me too." She gave his hand a final squeeze before pulling away and swiping the tears from her face. Then the right side of her mouth quirked upward in a shaky smile. "*Now* I'll have some of that coffee."

43

WHERE IS SHE?

The unanswered question gnawed at him. He'd broken back in last night after the *second* time the redhead left.

And found a deserted house. The thermostat was set low, no perishables left in the refrigerator. They'd escaped and obviously weren't planning to return anytime soon.

He wasn't worried. Not yet, anyway. Corina wasn't likely to go far while her father remained in critical condition. He'd kept tabs on William's condition, and despite the milestone the man had reached this morning, he was nowhere near well enough to attempt travel.

The fact that Corina had given him the slip was what really galled him. He hadn't meant to send her running. Isolate her, yes, but losing her was not in the plan. They thought they were clever, sneaking her out right in front of him.

Unfortunately, she hadn't taken the dog with her. Or the sports car.

He would find her, though. Backup was on the way now. His men would serve as extra eyes and ears, ensuring that when Corina showed up again or William was eventually released, he would instantly be made aware.

Calling them in was a concession, and he hated it. This project was personal, and he had fully intended to finish it alone. But sometimes, one had to use the available resources. This was one of those times.

The knowledge that his men wouldn't interfere with the climax he had planned was only a small consolation. Needle points raced up and down his arms, and he sucked in a breath to calm the rage threatening to erupt.

Ms. Mathis would soon be located and in his custody. And he would finish this long-overdue business. There would be no more games. No more taunts. No more waiting.

The next time he and Corina met would be the last.

44

"YOU READY?"

Corina wrapped her arms around Bryce's waist and squeezed. With a chuckle, he gunned the four-wheeler's engine.

"Let's go, then."

The wind whistled in her ears as they crossed the few feet of open area between the barn and the tree line. When they reached the woods, Bryce slowed a bit to navigate the curvy trail. He took a right at the first fork. That made the river the most likely destination.

Any other day, Corina would have watched the scenery, but today, she closed her eyes and nestled her face into Bryce's back. For the moment, she felt safe, and she would bask in the reprieve for as long as she could.

The local PD was keeping an eye on her house and her dad's. There had been no notes, pictures, or packages sent since she and Bryce had relocated. It had only been a day, but at the rate the killer had been escalating, it was something. According to Eric, records showed the security system had been deactivated again a couple of hours after he and Allye had left, but if the stalker had been inside, he'd already left by the time the breach was discovered.

Since then, there had been no visible activity, which meant the stalker was probably aware she'd escaped. But since nothing had shown up here either, she figured they could safely assume he hadn't followed them.

For now, that was enough.

A phone call after breakfast had eased her tension on another front. They'd chosen to bring her dad out of the coma early. He didn't remember what happened the morning he disappeared, but he was conscious and talking. The doctors cautioned he might never regain that particular memory, but their prognosis for recovery was hopeful.

She desperately wished she could see him. Of course, that wasn't an option right now. But she had gotten to talk to him for a few moments on one of the burner phones Eric had sent with them. Her dad hadn't mentioned the stalker or Peter, and she wasn't sure how much he knew or remembered, so she had skirted around the reason for her absence, focusing instead on his condition. He was weak enough that he didn't seem to notice her evasion.

That wouldn't last long, but Eric would have to handle that situation. At least with the posted security, she shouldn't have to worry about any outside interference with his recovery. They'd have to reevaluate things when he was well enough to be discharged.

If the man after her still hadn't been exposed, they couldn't go home. They'd have to relocate. Change their identities again. Leave everything and everyone behind.

Unless someone decided to come with them. She tightened her grip on Bryce.

His muscles shifted as he glanced over his shoulder. "Doing okay?" he yelled over the engine.

"Fine." She tried to assure him with a smile, and he turned his attention back to his driving. She pulled in a breath and thrust her unease away. This was a time to celebrate, and she wouldn't ruin it.

They quickly reached their destination—a clearing that overlooked the Licking River. She drew in a breath of pleasure. Autumn still held its color, and the reds and yellows interspersed with the green of native cedar made for a striking backdrop on the opposite bank.

They dismounted, comfortable silence enveloping them. Bryce released the straps securing their supplies and handed the picnic basket to her, then set about spreading a blanket.

Corina noted his choice of location. He'd placed the blanket in close proximity to the ATV. The machine would be at their backs as they ate, providing some protection should anyone have followed them. Not that either of them believed that to be the case. If they did, a clearing would be the last place they'd be right now.

A gust of wind hit her face. She shivered and drew her borrowed jacket more tightly around her. The day was a bit chilly to eat outdoors, but the sun was shining, and a thermos of hot chocolate awaited them.

A grin pulled at her lips, and she struggled to hide it before Bryce turned back around. Hot chocolate wasn't all that waited in the basket. They'd decided to celebrate her dad's improvement with a picnic and agreed that Bryce would choose a surprise destination and she'd surprise him with the menu.

She approved of his choice. It remained to be seen whether he would feel the same about hers.

"Ready?"

She pulled out two mugs and some napkins, then plopped onto the blanket. "Ready."

He hesitated before reaching for her hands like they always used to before sharing a meal.

She swallowed.

"Dear Lord, we thank you for this day and the food we are about to receive. We especially want to give you thanks for Will's improvement." He squeezed her hands. "We don't know where we're going from here, but we trust you. In Jesus's name, amen."

"Amen," she echoed, returning the squeeze.

Their eyes met, and he held her gaze. "We're going to make it through this."

She allowed a half smile to lift the corner of her mouth. "Yes, I think I'm finally starting to believe that."

Reluctantly, she withdrew her hand from his and popped a couple of marshmallows into each of their cups before pouring still-steaming hot chocolate over them. She handed Bryce his, then set out a few starters—some apple slices, celery sticks with peanut butter, and Cajun popcorn.

It didn't take the snacks long to disappear.

Corina closed her eyes and tipped her face to the sun, reveling in the feel and sound of nature around her. She thought she could hear a squirrel chattering from somewhere in the trees behind them. The animal had already dismissed their presence.

A light splash caught her attention, and she opened one eye to see a trio of kayakers paddling down the river. The front kayak was a single, but the one in back held an adult and a child. Jamie and Collette? She shaded her eyes to get a better look.

It was them. She smiled and waved. They'd managed to get out with their new kayaks after all. It was a beautiful day for it as long as none of them fell in. The river would be plenty cold, despite the weather's surprising shift to the lower sixties.

Bryce's stomach rumbled, distracting her from the kayakers as they disappeared around a bend. He gave her a sheepish look and shrugged.

"Main course?" she asked, refilling their mugs.

"Sounds good to me."

She produced a sleeve of crackers, then reached back into the basket. Her fingers closed around a small rectangular can. With a fluid movement, she pulled it from the basket and tossed it into Bryce's lap.

A mixture of shock and dread crossed his face as he saw the picture. Sardines.

When she'd found the can in his uncle's kitchen, she hadn't been able to resist sliding them into the basket. With effort, she suppressed her laughter as he turned the label to check the nutrition facts. He was stalling. By the look on his face, he couldn't decide whether to man-up or try to get out of it.

"You gave thanks for that, you know. You can't refuse it now."

It took a second for her sarcasm to register. He blinked, then shot her a mock glare.

She shrugged. "I know they're your favorite, but I did bring a few other things if you're not in the mood." She leaned back toward the basket. A chocolatey marshmallow splatted on her cheek. "Hey!" She swiped at the stickiness. "Now, that was uncalled for."

"Really?"

"Really." She finally let loose the giggle that had been threatening its escape. The giggle grew into full-blown laughter, and Bryce joined in. Before long, she was holding her sides. It hurt, but the emotional release was worth it. How long had it been since she'd truly laughed? Months? Years?

It felt good.

Finally, she wiped her eyes and tried, once again, to serve their real lunch. "So would you prefer black bean or chicken quesadillas?"

"Yes, please."

45

HIS MEN HAD FINALLY ARRIVED. They wouldn't come here. He didn't want any association with his cover, so he was headed to meet them in an out-of-the-way location. He stepped outside into a rapidly cooling afternoon. Curse this fickle Kentucky weather.

"Mom, can we have a picnic tomorrow?"

He glanced down the street at the young family unloading their vehicle. All three of them were half-soaked, and both parents looked exhausted. Judging by the way the boy bounced from one foot to the other, he was anything but.

"I don't think so, Jake." The mom sounded even more tired than she looked.

His lips tightened. He remembered those days with Tommy. Good days, but all too short. The parents should enjoy them while they could.

He turned his back on them and reached for his car door. He needed to head out.

But he was unable to keep himself from stealing another glance at the kid. Jake's lip stuck out in a theatrical pout. "But Ms. Corina and her friend had one today. It looked fun."

His hand froze on the handle. They'd seen them? He turned fully toward the family.

"The weather's turning cold already. They're predicting we could even have snow flurries tomorrow." A breeze kicked up, and the young mother shivered in her wet clothes, despite her heavy sweater. She grabbed a cooler and headed for their front door.

He had to find out where they'd seen Jessup and Corina. He released his hold on the door handle and summoned an easy grin. He doubted the smile reached his eyes. Hopefully, the parents were too tired to pay much attention.

"Where y'all been?" he called. "You look like you got caught in a cloud burst or something."

The man laughed. "Not quite. We decided to get in one last kayaking trip before winter hit."

"How was it?"

"Fun!" Jake's eyes lit up, his pouting forgotten.

"And a tad too cold," the mom said, aiming a pointed glare at her husband, who shrugged.

He settled into his role and nodded agreement. Then he jerked his head toward William's place, his mouth puckering in a concerned expression.

"I heard you mention Bryce and Ms. M—" He bit his tongue. *Mathis* had almost slipped out. "Roberts. I ain't seen 'em around since yesterday, and I was up pretty early this morning." He shook his head slowly. "Was starting to worry about them, what with her dad in the hospital and all the craziness around here lately."

The mom—why couldn't he remember her name?—coughed. "Well, they looked fine enough to me. Maybe Bryce thought she needed a distraction and took her up to his uncle's farm near Butler for a few days." She glanced at her husband.

The man shrugged. "Yeah, we were probably around there when we passed them. Didn't stop to talk, though, they looked kind of cozy."

I'll bet they did. He barely resisted the urge to clench his fists.

"Well, I'm glad to know everything's all right. I gotta get going."
He turned back to his car and climbed in.

An uncle's farm. He smacked the steering wheel. Why hadn't
he thought to check the public records for other properties they
might have ties to?

A tight smile spread across his face as he pulled out of the
driveway.

He'd have that information by tonight.

46

BRYCE TAPPED A PENCIL against his notes. Other than a brief break for dinner, he'd been scouring Will's files and racking his brain to come up with a lead since they'd returned from their picnic. So far, researching the man's last cases was the best thing he could come up with, but none of them were turning up any leads. With Will's shorthand, they couldn't be positive, but RJ thought he'd identified each of the cases on the list Bryce had found. And he'd confirmed that all the guilty parties had been sighted in Texas within the last couple of days or were still in prison. Or dead, like Espinoza.

Corina entered the room, bringing the aroma of fresh popcorn with her. She set the bowl on the table between the twin recliners in his uncle's den before moving to the console to study the DVD collection.

"Something's been bothering me," Bryce said.

She looked over her shoulder at him. "Yeah?"

"That prison riot RJ told us about. I know things like that happen, but for it to be connected to one of your dad's last big cases . . ." He tapped his thumb on the armrest. "I don't know. I just keep wondering if it was truly a coincidence that Espinoza and his men were among the dead or if they were targeted. And if so, why?"

Corina pursed her lips and turned back to the shelf. She ran her fingers over the cases, then pulled one out and popped the disk into the player.

She looked thoughtful as she turned back toward him. "If they were targeted, I think the important question isn't why. It's who."

Bryce scooped out a handful of popcorn and stuck a piece in his mouth. "Either would be helpful in identifying the other," he said. "And it may have nothing to do with your family."

"But the timing is odd," she agreed. She settled into one of the oversized chairs. "The case breaking, the conviction, the riot—all of it happened within months of the first murder."

"That's what has me concerned. It could be coincidence, yes, but if it is connected somehow, finding out who was responsible may tell us who's after you."

"Yeah." She sighed, and he echoed the sentiment. That was easier said than done.

Bryce set the notepad aside. He'd work on the case later. Maybe a break would give him a fresh outlook when he picked it up again.

The opening credits of *Eyes of Texas* began, and Bryce grinned at Corina. "I should have known you'd pick a Western."

Corina smiled and pulled a single kernel from the popcorn bowl. "Can't go wrong with Roy Rogers."

"Still your favorite, huh?" He chuckled at her sheepish shrug. When they were teenagers, she'd roped Bryce and Allye into watching more Westerns featuring the King of the Cowboys than he could count. Not that he'd minded. They were a great excuse for spending time with her and much better than the chick flicks his sister preferred.

Those were good times.

They watched the beginning of the movie in silence, Bryce's mind less on the movie and more on the woman beside him.

Corina's openness this morning had shocked him, as had her changed demeanor since. Grief still lingered in her eyes, especially when things got quiet, but the cloud that had hung over her since his return had lifted, replaced by a sense of peace he'd always appreciated in the old Corina.

Absently, he reached for the popcorn, and her hand brushed his. Their eyes met, and when she smiled, Bryce's gaze fell to her lips. His breath hitched.

Before he could act on his impulse to kiss her, she drew her hand back and turned to face the TV again, oblivious to the feelings she'd just evoked in him.

He swallowed, watching as her contented smile faded into a focused expression. He mentally kicked himself. Now was not the time to even consider kissing her. No matter how much he wanted to. But when this was all over—

"Who profited from his death?" Corina asked, hand frozen midway to her mouth.

Bryce blinked and glanced from her to the screen and realized Francis Ford's character had just been killed. His shoulders relaxed until he realized Corina wasn't watching the movie anymore.

"I think I missed something," he said slowly.

She grabbed the remote and stopped the movie, then turned to stare at him. "Espinoza. If his death was planned, who had something to gain by it?"

His mind raced with that possibility. When RJ had told him about the riot, his first thought was to assume revenge would be the obvious motive for foul play. That would fit the guy after Corina's family. But what if there was more to it? Something that might be easier to trace.

He grabbed his burner phone and texted Corina's question to RJ. While he waited for the answer, he thought out loud.

"The most likely person to profit from Espinoza's death would be a family member or someone high in the organization, right?"

"Yes, but I'd vote for someone in the organization. A family member might profit if there was an inheritance at stake, but most of his assets were likely frozen by the feds when he was arrested," Corina said.

"True." He thought back to his previous conversations with RJ. "But his top guys died with him in that riot, and the organization essentially imploded once the head was gone."

Something gleamed in Corina's eyes. "Law enforcement *thought* the organization shut down. But I can guarantee you crime in the area didn't."

He caught on to her line of thought. "Someone could have capitalized on the void left by Espinoza's arrest and death."

"Exactly."

He shot another text to RJ even though he hadn't responded to the first yet.

> You said Espinoza's conviction shut down his organization. Did a similar crime ring pop up soon after?

RJ texted back a minute later.

Bryce read the message, then leaned back in his chair. "RJ says he doesn't think so but he'll check."

Corina frowned and chewed on her lower lip.

Was this another dead end? *God, could you give us a little help here? We need to figure this out. And soon.*

When Corina restarted the movie, he tried to focus on it but had a feeling the attempt would be futile. From the look on Corina's face, she wasn't having much luck either.

Their popcorn ran out before the film did, and Bryce volunteered to refill it. Corina shifted to reach for the remote, but he waved her off.

"Leave it going. I won't be long." He'd seen the movie before. Not that he'd paid enough attention tonight to have any idea what part they were on anyway.

He carried the bowl into the kitchen and stuck a new bag of popcorn in the microwave. He stared at the window as the bag slowly inflated. Each pop reminded him of desert skirmishes. *Pop. Pop.* The shots fired at Western Outfitters a couple of days ago. *Pop. Pop. Pop.* The shots that had ended the lives of several in Corina's family. *Pop.* The shot the killer had planned for her.

He snatched the microwave door open. The bag gave one final pop before going quiet. Refusing to dwell on the slight tremble in his hands, he ripped the bag open and dumped it into the bowl.

His phone began ringing when he reentered the den. He set the popcorn aside and answered, putting his friend on speaker so Corina could listen in.

RJ didn't waste any time getting to the point.

"Here's what I've got. Espinoza's crime ring centered around money laundering and extortion. Blackmail. Like I said before, he was involved in a lot of stuff, but those were his big money-makers. Those crimes didn't reappear on a major scale for a long time." He paused to take a breath. "What local cops did notice was an uptick in other types of cybercrime about six months after Espinoza's conviction."

Bryce did the math. Based on the timeline he'd come up with, Corina and Will had fled the state about four months after the conviction. If whoever was responsible for the cybercrimes had been the one after them, it would fit that he wouldn't get back to work until after he'd lost track of them. And it could have taken the police a bit of time to notice the pattern and realize the new crimes were connected to each other.

Based on her sharp intake of breath, Corina had come to the same conclusion. He gave her hand a light squeeze.

"Was there anything to connect the cybercrimes with Espinoza's previous activities?" she asked.

"Hard evidence? No," RJ said. "But Espinoza used technology to his advantage in gathering blackmail and moving dirty money around. Experts saw enough similarities in that and the new crimes to speculate whether a common brain was involved."

"Did the police ever catch the person behind the cybercrimes?"

RJ sighed. "No. Every time investigators got close, things got quiet and the leads dried up."

Bryce's enthusiasm deflated. "What about suspects?"

"I can't tell you that, man."

That meant there were some. "Come on, RJ. This could be life or death in our situation."

RJ was quiet for a moment. Finally, he blew out a breath. "If this gets out, my job's toast."

Bryce waited out another pause.

"Fine. But you didn't hear it from me."

"Deal," Bryce said.

"A security system designer by the name of Jerry Davidson. He'd be in his late forties by now. Very successful guy but made some bad investments. Lost nearly everything, then suddenly he was back on his feet with plenty of cash about the time Espinoza's online activities started blossoming."

Jerry Davidson. Bryce silently repeated the name to memorize it.

"Never got anything solid on 'im though. Might be totally innocent."

Big might. "Where is he now?"

RJ cleared his throat as if uncomfortable. "Nobody's seen him since the beginning of July."

47

THEY WERE IN THERE.

He couldn't see them, but he'd crept close enough to the window to distinguish their voices, if not their words. Satisfaction filled him as he retreated to the area where he'd left his men. He'd watch until the house was quiet, its inhabitants asleep.

Then he'd strike.

His men were already present, so he'd use them. Up to a point. Once he had Corina away from Jessup, he'd have no further need of them. This would all be finished soon.

Thirty minutes later, lights began to go out in the front of the house. He skirted the perimeter of the lawn for a better vantage point. Light appeared in two windows, but the one between them remained dark. The bedrooms must be there. And Corina and her protector weren't sharing one.

Perfect.

48

CORINA JERKED AWAKE to a hand covering her mouth. Almost instantly, she heard Bryce's voice next to her ear. "Shh. We've been found. I dead-bolted your door when I came in, but we need to get out of here—fast." Despite his nearness, she could barely make out the words. If he had been standing two feet away, she wouldn't have heard him.

At her nod of understanding, he removed his hand and allowed her to sit up and reach for her revolver. Noiselessly, she slid out of bed and slipped her sneakers on. She still hadn't heard anything from outside her door, so she took an extra moment to buckle on the ankle holster with her backup gun and shove a knife and her burner phone into her pockets.

"Let's go," Bryce hissed. He already had the tunnel entrance open. She pulled in a last breath of fresh air and lowered herself carefully into the darkness below. As soon as she was clear, Bryce followed, lifting the drawer back onto its track and sliding it shut above them.

She grabbed a flashlight and flipped it on. The sudden light made them both blink. His face was grim.

"Did you see him?" she whispered.

"Them."

She caught her breath. There was more than one? That was something they hadn't counted on.

Bryce's voice hardened. "I caught a glimpse of two silhouettes. They were leading with their guns, and I heard one whisper your name. I don't know if there's more." Bryce pulled out his phone and dialed 911. His voice was almost inaudible as he gave their information to the dispatcher.

If they were searching the house, they'd get to her room soon. The dead bolt would slow them down, but then what? Once they were through, they'd have to know someone had locked it. She only hoped they'd think she had gone out the window.

The window! It was locked. They'd know she hadn't gone out that way. If they knew someone had been in the room and hadn't left through the window or door, it would only be a matter of time before their escape route was discovered.

She touched his arm, but before she could voice her concern, a crack sounded overhead. They both froze. Had one of the intruders kicked the door in?

Bryce ended the call and slid the phone into his pocket. He motioned for her to enter the tunnel ahead of him.

"We didn't unlock the window. They're going to figure it out," she whispered.

In a second's time, Bryce's face flashed from comprehension to fear to determination. He set his jaw. "You go. I'll wait here. They won't find the entrance right away, and I'll ambush anyone that tries to follow us. Get to the deer stand and wait for the police."

She stared at him. "No. You have to come too."

He locked eyes with her, and she could see he wasn't going to back down. Before she could react, he leaned down and planted a whisper of a kiss on her lips. "I can't. This is the best chance we've got."

Light footsteps crossed the room and reclaimed their attention. They didn't have much time.

Go, he mouthed. She hesitated only a second more, then

ducked into the crawl space, placing the end of the flashlight between her teeth. She thought she heard the words "I love you" behind her, but they were uttered too softly for her to be sure.

A tear trickled down her cheek. She felt as if she were leaving half her heart behind. *Jesus, please protect him!*

She shook her head and tried to formulate a plan. Once she made it to the barn, she could run for the trees and take shelter in the woods like Bryce wanted her to. Or she could circle around and try to take the intruders—and possibly her stalker—by surprise. But first she had to get out of this tunnel.

She counted the wall studs almost subconsciously as she maneuvered through the tunnel, absently reciting Bryce's directions. *Five to the magnolia, fifteen to the halfway point, thirty to the barn.*

This morning, Bryce had reminded her to keep careful track of where she was and where she needed to come up. The tunnel went a bit farther than the barn because it was originally designed to have a second exit in the woods, but that portion hadn't been repaired and would leave her at a dead end.

As her adrenaline tapered off, the ache in her chest started to rise. Crawling on her hands and knees didn't help. She was thankful the space was large enough to allow for that, though. If she'd had to worm her way through—well, there was just no way.

She stopped to catch her breath. Her biceps burned, and her knees were scraped. She looked ahead, trying not to despair. *Fifteen to the halfway point.* She was next to the twelfth—maybe?— but there was still a long way to go until the end. She started moving again, but her muscles were slow to respond.

Around the twenty-third stud, the glow from her light began to dim. *Don't go out! Please don't go out!* Yes, she could find her way in the dark, but she sure didn't want to. She quickened her pace as much as possible.

It wasn't going to be enough, Corina realized, as the flashlight beam rapidly degenerated. She could barely see now. She debated just shutting it off and tossing it, but she couldn't bear the thought of total darkness just yet.

Her hand landed in a spider's web strung between the floor and stud number twenty-six. She grimaced but refused to acknowledge the possibility that the eight-legged creature had been at home. If she didn't see it, it wasn't there, right? Unless it bit her. That thought made her pause long enough to swipe her hand against the hem of her shirt.

In the dim light, she could just barely make out the trapdoor ahead of her. A few feet farther, her flashlight battery finally gave out. She stilled for a moment, then dropped it and pressed on toward the exit she knew was close by.

Just as she reached for the latch, a yell followed by a gunshot sounded from the other end of the tunnel. Her heart leaped into her throat as indecision warred within her. She waited, listening, but all was silent.

Who had pulled the trigger? And had the bullet found its mark? *Please, God, don't let Bryce be hurt.*

A faint rustling met her ears. Someone was following her through the tunnel. Bryce? Or someone else? She had to get out of here and figure out how to find out. If it was Bryce, they could escape together. If it wasn't and Bryce was hurt, she had to help him, but she couldn't do that with an enemy between them.

Carefully, she pushed upward on the trapdoor and slid it out of her way. She lifted her head above the opening and scanned for threats. Everything appeared as it should, so she climbed out and stood upright. Her body screamed in protest at the new position.

But she didn't have time for the pain. Gritting her teeth, she looked for a place that would conceal her while allowing her to watch the tunnel exit.

A slight movement to her left caught her eye. She drew her gun and spun to face a shadowed figure.

49

DREAD SETTLED in her stomach at the sight of a masked intruder standing barely three feet away. How many of them were there?

She stared at him, but the man made no move toward her. Slowly, he lifted his hands in a nonthreatening gesture. "Take it easy with that thing," he said softly.

"Who are you?" She kept the gun leveled at his chest and took a step backward to widen the distance between them. Too late, she remembered the tunnel entrance was behind her. In her effort to avoid it, she tripped over the trapdoor and dropped her gun as she fell.

A booted foot kicked it out of her reach. Corina looked up to see the intruder standing over her, his own gun visible and aimed at her heart. The nice guy routine was over. "Get up."

She hesitated, grasping for a way out of this. He had the upper hand. Literally. She resisted the urge to glance at her backup gun. There was no way she could get to it in less time than it would take him to pull the trigger.

"Now," he growled.

Slowly, she rose to her feet. A cloud shifted, allowing moonlight to filter through a window and illuminate the room.

"Hands on your head."

She complied, mind racing as he stepped behind her. She felt the muzzle of his gun press against her back. "Don't move." A second later, something pierced her skin, and she jerked.

"I said don't move." The gun jabbed harder, and she caught her breath, forcing herself to be still. A chill ran through her as he injected something into her system and yanked the needle free.

She didn't have time to think about what had been in the syringe. A second man was exiting the tunnel. The pressure of the weapon eased slightly as her captor moved to the side to see the newcomer.

It was now or never. She dropped to one knee and twisted an arm behind his left leg. Leaned backward, pulling him off-balance. He stumbled back, roaring his displeasure. The gun went off, but the shot went high.

She scrambled away from him, groping for her backup weapon with shaky hands. It took less than a second to draw the semi-auto and aim it at her attacker.

But before she could fully recover her feet, the second intruder lunged at her.

She swung the gun his direction.

Squeezed the trigger.

He grunted but didn't change his trajectory. The impact knocked the air from her lungs. Pain lanced through her as her body was sandwiched between her attacker and something solid on the floor. She felt and heard the crack from her rib cage.

For a long, agonizing moment, she lay beneath her attacker. Feeling his breaths. Unable to take her own.

Finally, the man rose partway, lifting his weight from her chest. She groaned. Struggled to refill her lungs as he straddled her, hands pinning her upper arms to the barn floor.

Wetness seeped through her sleeve. Blood?

Despite the pain, she didn't think it was hers. Her shot must have wounded him, although there seemed to be no lack of strength in the arms holding her down. She might still have a chance, an opportunity for escape.

But running was out of the question. She tried to think through the pain.

She flexed her fingers and realized she hadn't lost her gun in the fall. She could still shoot.

Just as that thought occurred to her, a boot landed hard on her wrist. She gasped and tried to twist her arm away. The pressure increased, nearly crushing the bones. Rough fingers pried the weapon from her grasp and shoved the muzzle against her skull. She winced but stilled.

The man on top of her fixed her with a stern look. Practically daring her to attempt an escape now. When she didn't move, he stood. Her body crawled under his scrutiny. Without taking his eyes off her, he nodded to a third intruder.

"Search her."

None-too-gentle hands probed her body for other hidden weapons. She sucked in an agonizing breath. *God, help me!* She bit her lip until she tasted blood. Tried not to squirm. Failed as his hands traveled up her tender sides.

When he ended his search, he stepped back, holding her cell and the pocketknife.

"This is all she had on her."

"Good." He motioned to the man holding the gun to her head.

The first intruder muttered a curse meant only for her ears. "Do not try anything else," he whispered. The gun dug into her skull once more before he stood to join the others.

"Did you inject the drug?" There was no mistaking the authority in the second man's tone. This was the leader of the group. Her primary enemy.

"Yes, sir," the first man bit out. He swayed, and she blinked, resetting her vision. He hadn't moved. Whatever they'd injected her with, it was fast acting.

Despite the pain, she tried to conjure a means of escape. She came up empty. Even without her injuries, the odds of taking on three men unarmed weren't in her favor.

"Good." Contempt dripped from the leader's words as he finally turned his laser gaze away from her and looked fully at his subordinate. "I'm glad to hear you were able to do something productive before getting pushed down by a woman." He motioned the third man forward again.

Corina tried to make out their plan as he gave them instructions, but the words made little sense to her brain. The only thing she was fairly certain of was that they were parting ways. Everything else, including her surroundings, was blurring. The pain eased as her eyelids grew heavy. She fought the effects of the drug, but darkness enveloped her, pulling her into its embrace.

Someone lifted her from the barn floor as she faded into unconsciousness.

BRYCE SLOWLY BLINKED AWAKE, his shoulders cramping. The blackness surrounding him didn't recede. It took him a moment to realize he must still be in the tunnel entrance.

But if the intruders had gotten away—*Corina!*

He thought she'd had enough of a head start to make a successful escape, but he couldn't guarantee that. The stalker hadn't come back to get information from him, which likely meant he was either still searching or had already caught up to her.

Slowly, Bryce stood and immediately felt tremors run through his body. His head pounded its protest at whatever had taken place, and the light-headedness nearly did him in. He refused to sink back to the floor and instead leaned forward to brace himself against the wall.

He vaguely remembered the crash of the dresser being pushed over, revealing the hole in the floor. And then?

His brain was still too foggy.

But he knew he had to get to Corina. The tunnel would take too much time. Its purpose was stealth, not speed. He would do better to climb out and exit the house through a door.

With as little movement as possible, he felt around for the shelf. Relief washed over him. The intruders hadn't taken the last flashlight. He switched it on and swung the beam around the tunnel area. He spotted his gun, which had apparently been kicked beneath the shelf. Keeping his hand on the wall, he worked his way down to retrieve it. His light bounced off something else, and he turned the flashlight that way.

A syringe? He picked it up. No label, but the plunger was only partially depressed and some liquid remained inside. Had he been drugged? He didn't remember being injected with anything, but now he remembered the choke hold. He must have fallen unconscious. Had they drugged him afterward to keep him out for a while?

How much time had passed?

Did Corina have enough time to escape?

With trembling arms, he managed to lift himself into the bedroom. It was a wreck. The intruders had torn it apart before finding their escape route.

Bryce staggered over the upturned furniture and back to the hall. He made his way to the back door in darkness. He opened it cautiously, glad it didn't creak on its hinges. Once outside, he paused to listen. He could faintly hear approaching sirens. Good. He wasn't in any shape to handle this alone.

50

SHE WASN'T HERE.

Bryce stared at the empty deer stand, fear racing through him. Nothing inside was disturbed. The realization sickened him. She hadn't made it this far.

He scrambled down the ladder and cupped his hands around his mouth. "Corina!" The woods swallowed his shout and returned no response.

"She was supposed to wait here." He shot a frantic look at Jason Smith, the county deputy who'd accompanied him into the woods.

"What if she had to choose a plan B? Where else might she have gone?" Jason continued to turn in a slow circle, scanning the ground and trees around the small clearing. He bent and poked something on the ground with a stick.

Bryce took a deep breath and forced himself to think. "If she was being chased, she might have tried to lose him in the woods." He lifted his hands and called for her again.

"If she thinks her stalker or one of his men is close, she's not going to answer your calls," Jason pointed out, starting back in the direction of the house.

"Where are you going?"

Jason looked over his shoulder at him. "Nobody's been in this clearing recently." He pointed his flashlight at the dark spot he had been looking at. "Fresh deer droppings. They haven't had time to start drying." He resumed a brisk walk. "If she's in these woods, we need to figure out where she entered so we can track her."

He was right, and Bryce followed him. But the more he thought about it, the less Bryce believed they'd find another trail leading into the woods. Corina should have had enough time to escape before whoever knocked him out made it to her end of the tunnel. His stomach twisted, and he quickened his pace.

His mind shouted self-recriminations. They'd gotten past him. Even if the stalker didn't have Corina, he was still at large, which meant she was in danger either way.

As the drugged feeling continued to wear off, he'd remembered the confrontation in the tunnel, and in the silent walk back to the house, it replayed in his mind with a vividness that wasn't going to fade anytime soon. He balled his fists but didn't try to push the memory away.

To avoid being a sitting duck, Bryce had hidden in the tunnel's mouth until the intruders found the entrance. Hardly daring to breathe, he waited for them to climb down before showing himself.

As soon as he saw the second intruder's feet hit the ground, he had taken aim and commanded the men to freeze. He'd had the advantage—they'd holstered their weapons before lowering themselves into the hole. At sight of the gun, they'd obeyed.

Stepping forward to where he could stand fully upright, Bryce had quietly ordered them to put their hands in the air. One did, but the other just glared at him, as if daring him to pull the trigger. Despite his anger over what had been done to Corina and her family, Bryce had held his fire, firmly repeating the order. He couldn't shoot anyone in cold blood.

And the man had taken that moment to lunge at him, forcing the muzzle of the gun upward, where it could do damage to nothing except the ceiling of the room above them. As plaster fell, a short struggle ensued. Bryce had managed to land a punch to the man's left ear but was quickly outmaneuvered when the second man joined the fray.

A painful blow to the solar plexus stole his breath and distracted him long enough for one of the intruders to get behind him. The last thing he remembered was an arm around his neck, cutting off his blood supply.

Bryce could feel his fingernails biting into the skin of his palms. He would never forgive himself if his moment of hesitation had cost Corina her life. But what else could he have done? Could he have killed a man—a civilian—never knowing if it was an unnecessary shot?

The sight of red and blue lights pulled his mind back to the present. They were nearing the edge of the woods.

When they came within sight of the house and barn, Bryce could see that several squad cars still surrounded the area. Every indoor and outdoor light was on in both buildings. The other officers were searching for any scrap of evidence that might have been left.

He dashed to the barn. A couple of the deputies had gone through the tunnel right before Bryce and Jason headed for the woods. No one had been inside, and the tunnel entrance there had been exposed, so they knew Corina had exited in the barn.

But she hadn't made it to the rendezvous point. Somewhere between the tunnel and the woods, something had gone wrong. As the site of Corina's last known location, the barn would be most likely to offer clues to her current whereabouts.

A deputy stopped him at the crime scene tape just outside the doorway. "You can't come in here."

Bryce tamped down the urge to slug him and chose instead to survey what he could of the scene from the entrance. Thankfully, he wasn't asked to step back any farther.

One officer was dusting for prints, and another, whose back

was to him, crouched next to the area around the trapdoor, taking pictures.

"Hey, I've got something over here." Bryce recognized Eric's voice. They were out of Kincaid's normal jurisdiction, but apparently the county was allowing him to remain lead since it was already an active case in town.

He craned his neck to see what they'd found, but Eric's body was blocking his view. After photographing its location, the officer lifted it in a gloved hand and turned around. Spotting Bryce, he walked toward the door.

"Do you recognize this?" He held up a revolver.

Bryce's mouth went dry, and his heart sank to his toes. "It's Corina's. She had it with her tonight." And if she'd left it behind, then she hadn't gone willingly. "She never made it to our rendezvous point."

Eric turned to the other men. "Escalate this to a probable abduction. We need this area turned upside down," he barked.

"There's blood over here." Another cop interrupted.

Bryce stopped breathing. "How much?"

The officer looked to Eric, apparently asking permission, then he met Bryce's eyes. "Not enough to worry but definitely fresh."

"All right. I'm calling in an alert and requesting backup." Eric turned back to him. "We'll do everything we can to find her."

Bryce swallowed. Tried to tear his gaze from the area the officer had indicated. Whose blood was it? Corina's?

"How can I help?" he asked Eric.

"You can start by praying. We'll be organizing search parties soon."

He opened his mouth to protest, but Eric had already turned away and was giving further directions to his men.

Praying he could do. Waiting for an organized search party? Not good enough. He felt in his gut that they didn't have time for a normal search and rescue. There were just too many back roads, wooded areas, and old barns nearby. Not to mention the river.

This guy wanted Corina dead, and as far as they knew, he'd never abducted a victim before. It had already been nearly an hour since the altercation in the tunnel. Time was not on their side. If they had any hope of rescuing Corina, they were going to have to outsmart this guy. And fast.

Bryce paced away from the barn, needing to get away from the activity. *Think, man!* He pressed his hands to his forehead.

If this were a normal abduction, the stalker could have taken her anywhere, and they wouldn't have a clue where to start unless they knew his identity. But this wasn't a normal abduction. This guy was good—really good. But he had established patterns with his previous victims. The types of clues he left, his stalking method, even his mode of execution had been eerily similar in the earlier murders.

And he seemed to have followed it in Corina's case. Until tonight. The live abduction was a new twist. It may not have been planned, though. There was a possibility they may have forced that variation on him by alerting the police to his presence. Or he could have intended to move her for another reason.

Which was it? For the sake of a starting point, Bryce chose to believe it had been planned. If the plan had been to kidnap Corina, then what was the reasoning behind it?

He just didn't know. He kicked at the gravel in the driveway, sending rocks flying. One of them pinged off a squad car. The officer standing at the barn door cleared his throat.

"Sorry," Bryce muttered. Losing his temper wasn't going to help anything. He sucked in a deep breath, then another.

God, I don't know where to go with this. I need you to help me figure this out. Keep Corina safe until help can get there. Please, Jesus.

The prayer helped to calm him. He took a minute to just breathe and gather his focus. Then he resumed pacing as he thought through possibilities.

He pictured the crime scene photos from the previous murders and cringed at the vision of Corina in place of one of the other victims. He shook the paralyzing image from his mind and tried to instead recall the settings, the notes, anything that might shed light on where the killer had taken her.

He froze midstep. All four victims had been murdered in their own homes—in their kitchens. A fact determined by convenience or by design? He shook his head. The odds that four out of four murders would be committed in equivalent locations were too great to chalk up to coincidence. As precise as this man was in his planning, it only made sense that location would be important to him too.

Bryce glanced toward his uncle's house. It was swarming with law enforcement. Corina wasn't being held here. But this wasn't her home either. Conviction flooded him as he ran back to the barn's entrance. "Eric! I think I might know where she is."

51

BRYCE STOOD ON THE STREET and stared at Corina's darkened house. When he'd explained his theory, Eric had immediately radioed the alert. A nearby patrol car had come back with a negative response within minutes. But Bryce needed to see for himself, so he'd driven into town to check things out while Eric and the others continued to search for a lead at the farm.

Had he been wrong? Maybe, but he didn't think so. If he was wrong, they were back at square one. If he was right, then Corina and her abductor were either in there somewhere or would be soon.

Officer Moore, who'd responded to Eric's call and waited for Bryce to arrive, adjusted his duty belt. "I looked through the windows when I got here. There's no sign anything's been touched since the vandalism the other day. I've been watching, but the place has been dead." He grimaced. "Sorry. But they're not here."

"I can't see him taking her anywhere else," Bryce said. "Can't you go inside and check it out?"

"I'm sorry. Without a reason to believe she's there, I can't go in. And I've been watching since I arrived. There's been no activity."

Something about that assurance bothered Bryce as Moore climbed back into his car. Just the fact the officer hadn't even suggested Bryce leave the area indicated he wasn't expecting any-thing to happen here. All the more reason to keep watch himself.

He slipped into his borrowed car and fixed his eyes on Corina's house. His brain was busy pulling everything to the surface that he knew about her abductor. There had to be a clue they'd missed.

Besides the man's obvious obsession with Corina's family and his propensity to murder people in their own homes, one char-acteristic stood out: he planned ahead.

A watchdog, motion-sensing lights, and a security system hadn't deterred this guy when he'd broken into Will's house. Sure, he'd gone through a window, but he'd found a way to do it undetected. Bryce didn't believe for a second that this guy would be unable to get into Corina's house without being seen if he really wanted to.

Bryce straightened. Had that been a flash of light in the front window, or was it his imagination? He squinted but didn't see anything else. He looked toward the patrol car, but the officer was leaning forward, adjusting his scanner.

His heart skipped a beat as his phone rang. "Hello?"

"Bryce." Eric's voice came across the line. "I just got an update. They picked up a couple guys outside Butler."

The patrol car pulled onto the street and aimed toward the main road. Moore activated his lights and turned out of sight. Where was he going?

Eric was still talking. "A deputy tried to pull them over for speeding and they wouldn't stop. Wrecked their car and took off on foot, but he got them. There were ski masks in their back seat as well as prefilled syringes that look like the one you found. Analysis of the contents will show if it's the same drug."

His throat dried up. "Any sign of Corina?"

"No, and they aren't talking." His voice hardened. "That's about to change. Just wanted you to know."

"I thought I saw a light in her house a moment ago."

"Where's Moore?"

"He just took off."

Eric muttered something he couldn't make out. "I'm on my way. I'll have dispatch send someone your way ASAP too."

He stared at Corina's house as he hung up. He could have imagined the light, but he didn't think so. How long would it take for another officer to get here? Eric was probably fifteen to twenty minutes out even if he sped to get back, and there might not be another officer close and available. Kincaid's force was small. If Bryce was right and Corina was in there, she probably didn't have time to wait.

He exited the car, rounding the vehicle to search the trunk for something useful. He shined his phone's flashlight inside. Relief flooded him when it landed on what appeared to be an emergency kit. He rummaged in it until he found a screwdriver and a few other small hand tools he could carry in his pocket.

The late-fall wind bit into him as he crossed the street and hurried up Corina's driveway.

52

THE FOG LIFTED SLOWLY, pain rushing in to take its place. Her head and shoulders ached, and the slightest breath was agony. Corina's eyelids fluttered, then squeezed shut again. The light, though dim, still hurt.

"Waking up, are we?"

The chill in the slightly familiar voice pulled her further toward consciousness. She forced her eyes open, blinking away the haze. Her surroundings came into focus. Her kitchen. Someone had righted the table and chairs and hung a blanket over the back window, but the rest of the mess from the break-in lay as it had a few days ago.

She shivered. Her face felt flushed, but she was freezing.

She tried to shift positions and found she couldn't move. A wave of panic swept over her. Her ankles were tied to the legs of her chair, and her wrists were securely fastened behind her back. She attempted to wiggle her fingers but couldn't tell if they actually moved. They had lost all feeling. How long had she been unconscious?

The memory of the struggle in the barn rushed back to her. *Bryce!* Was he even alive? Obviously, he had lost the fight on his end of the tunnel.

One of the intruders had to have brought her here. She turned her head in search of him. Nausea threatened to overtake her at the motion. Swallowing hard, she closed her eyes in hopes the feeling would pass.

"Come on. I haven't got all night." The rough words were followed by a splash of ice water in her face.

She gasped, and the muscles in her chest spasmed. The sound that escaped her lips sounded more like a groan than the scream she'd expected. Blinking the water away, she met her abductor's gaze. He stood in front of her now, a ski mask pulled over his face. Only his mouth and eyes showed. Her blood chilled at the undisguised hatred staring back at her.

"Who are you, and why are you doing this?" She recognized the pleading in her tone but couldn't bring herself to care.

The slightest flicker of pain glinted in the man's eyes before he firmed his mouth and walked behind her. She tensed and turned her head as far as she was able, but it wasn't enough. She could hear him—his heavy breathing, the unmistakable ripping of a Velcro flap, the soft shink of metal sliding against metal—but she couldn't see him.

She tried to gather her thoughts. Tried to figure out how long she'd been out and if there was anything even remotely familiar about her captor. Other than the vague sense of having heard his voice before, she drew a blank on both counts.

The man circled her again and met her gaze. The hatred was still there, but it was shrouded in something else. Determination.

"An eye for an eye." His words were deliberate, measured.

She blinked, then realized he was answering one of her earlier questions. "What do you mean? I was thirteen when you started this. I haven't ever done anything to you." Had she?

"Not you," he scoffed. "You are the eye."

"I don't understand." The pounding in her head didn't help her confusion.

The man shook his head. "Your *father*"—he spat the word— "and his partner cost me my family."

"How?" Dread coiled itself in her stomach.

"By sticking their noses in places they didn't belong. Soliciting information from my men that was better left alone. Using that information against my superiors." His composure slipped, and he bent down until they were nose to nose. The fury in his eyes unnerved her.

"They blamed me! I had to watch my wife and children die because of your father's meddling!" he screamed. "They shot my family around our kitchen table. Every. Last. One."

Tears welled in her eyes. "I'm so sorry," she whispered.

He reared back as if she'd struck him. "Sorry? Sorry isn't good enough!" He started to turn away, then swung back to face her.

Corina's brain registered the coming backhand, but she was unable to dodge it. She braced herself as his knuckles connected with her mouth.

Dizziness again washed over her. As soon as he stepped away, she closed her eyes and rested her head against the back of the chair. *Jesus, please, please help me*, she pleaded silently as hot tears escaped her lashes. Her lip was already swelling. She tasted blood, could feel it dripping down her chin to mingle with the tears she was unable to wipe away.

She tried again to move her fingers but with no success. Somehow, she had to regain feeling in her hands, had to get moving. It was her only hope of getting out of this.

She flexed her shoulders, and white-hot pain shot through her chest. It was all she could do to hold back the scream that tried to launch itself from her throat. Her breaths turned to irregular panting as she turned her eyes to her captor, hoping he wasn't paying attention.

He still had his back to her. She let her eyes travel down his figure, memorizing his height and build. And registering the makeshift bandage on his left arm. So that's where her bullet had hit. That weak spot could be important.

And if she had any hope of escape, she needed to get moving. She bit her tongue and forced her breathing to slow. Gritting her teeth, she tried again—slowly this time. More tears filled her eyes, but she blinked them back. Pain or no pain, she had to do this. She squeezed her eyes shut and continued the movements until a tingling burn started in the fleshy part of her palm.

A burst of light startled her, and she opened her eyes to see a camera and tripod now standing between her and the back door. The man's eyes were focused on the screen—the edges of a smile disappearing under the fabric covering most of his face.

"Perfect. I'm sure your father will enjoy that one. Let's try some without the flash now." The conversational tone of the words stilled her. All traces of agitation had disappeared. Her captor sounded pleased—almost friendly. And more familiar, though she still couldn't place him.

Bile rose in her throat. She renewed her struggle, trying to hide her actions as the camera continued to click.

As he played with the camera, Corina thought she saw a flicker of movement behind him. Not daring to draw his attention, she slowly leaned her head back again and let her eyelids drop to mere slits. In the darkness outside, she could just barely make out what appeared to be someone peering through the sliver of windowpane where the blanket didn't completely reach the edge. Her captor shifted, and the person dropped from sight.

Her pulse increased even as she fought to hide any reaction. Someone was here. *Hurry. Whoever you are, please hurry!*

THEY WERE IN THERE. Adrenaline rushed through Bryce as he dropped out of sight of the window. The lack of response from the motion-sensing lights had been Bryce's first clue that there really was something going on here. The windowless front door had been no help, and none of the front windows afforded him much of a view, so he'd moved to the back of the house, where light now peeked through a mostly covered window.

In the short time he'd dared to look inside, he hadn't been able to process much, but it was enough to know that Corina was there and in immediate danger.

There wasn't time to wait for the police, but if they arrived while he was inside, he and Corina could both end up in the crossfire. Perspiration broke out on his forehead. He had to take that risk. If he didn't, she would almost surely die.

Angling his phone toward the ground so it wouldn't give him away, he shot Eric a text.

They're inside. Going in.

He willed his racing pulse to slow. It didn't work. "Please be with me, God," he breathed. "I'm sure gonna need your help."

He gently tested the doorknob. Locked. He might be able to pick the lock with the tools he'd brought, but he was too close not to be heard. Besides, if the dead bolt was turned too, he'd have double the work. The front door was out of the question. It was a straight shot from there to the kitchen. He'd be spotted immediately, but he wouldn't be close enough to intervene before the killer had time to react.

He'd have to go through a window, preferably one here on the back of the house.

Other than the window he stood under, only two windows remained on Corina's side of the building. One large window on the far side probably led to a bedroom, but there was a moderately small one closer to him. He made a quick decision. The larger one would have double locks, the smaller only had one. It would be a tight squeeze but doable. And if he remembered correctly, it should lead to a pantry adjoining the kitchen. Not much maneuvering space, but it would have to work.

CORINA GLANCED BACK at her captor just in time to be blinded by a spotlight he had positioned on the counter next to the door. Two steps forward and he was at the tripod again, adjusting something.

A slight scratching sound from behind met her ear, as if someone were in the pantry. Or trying to get in a window. The masked man didn't react, though, so she wasn't sure if she had imagined it. No, there it was again. She tried to remember if there was anything in front of that window that might fall and give her rescuer away. Normally there wasn't, but destroyed remnants of her belongings had been strewn everywhere during the break-in. Had the pantry been vandalized too? She couldn't remember.

Realizing silence was not on her side, she scrambled to think, to get her captor talking again. Anything to buy time and keep him from hearing anything suspicious.

"Why are you doing all this now? It's been over a decade since you murdered my mom and brother. You left us alone all these years. What changed?"

The man sniffed. "It took me that long to find you. Your father hid you well, but I knew you couldn't hide forever. No one can."

"What tipped you off?"

"A newspaper article about your little shop's grand opening. And the dedication to your *family*." He said the last word with a sneer.

Her dedication caused all this? A pang shot through her heart. What she'd meant as a gesture of honor had endangered lives. Cost at least one. Possibly more. *God, forgive me! And please let Bryce be all right.*

Alarm filled her as her captor began to walk toward her—toward the pantry—but he stopped just behind her chair. Not much of a relief. She recoiled as his gloved hands brushed her arm, but the touch only lasted a second as he freed her watch.

The other crime scenes flooded back to her. He was leaving his signature.

Panic threatened to cut off her airway. But another barely audible sound came from the pantry, and she forced her emotions back. She had to keep her head and do her best to distract this man.

"What are you doing?"

He didn't answer immediately, so she cleared her parched throat and tried again. "What are you doing with my watch?"

"Setting the time."

"Why?"

"Brenna died at 11:47."

Corina barely heard the muttered answer, but her heart chilled at the significance of the words. That's why each crime scene clock had a slightly different time. He was setting them to correspond with the deaths of specific family members.

"You know we'd bring them back if we could." She clenched her teeth as he returned the watch to her wrist, yanking the band too tight before fastening it in place.

"Shut up," he said quietly, his tone lethal.

But she couldn't do that. She had to keep him talking.

"What do you really want?" She winced as the words exited her mouth. Of all the questions she could have asked, that was probably not the best choice.

Circling to stand between her and the spotlight, he stared at her. At least, that's what she assumed he was doing. With the brightness still burning her retinas, she was unable to focus on the visible portions of his face. Without answering her question, he returned to his camera and ignored her.

No more noises came from the pantry. Had her rescuer made it inside or given up? A shiver ran through her. She was running out of time.

When the masked man finally spoke, his voice was calm, the words simple. "What do I really want? I want your daddy to see you die." He pressed a button on the camera and pulled out a suppressor-equipped pistol.

53

"I WANT YOUR DADDY TO SEE YOU DIE."

Bryce was halfway through the window when the words reached his ears. His stomach tightened. The blood froze in his veins.

"Don't do this."

The barely controlled fear in Corina's voice spurred him on. He dropped noiselessly to the floor. He took a step, and a can of something rolled away from his foot. He'd forgotten about the mess. Treading carefully, he slid his gun out of its holster and stole a glance around the corner.

The masked man was standing behind Corina now, a gun drawn and angled halfway between her and a camera set up on a tripod across the room. Bryce was out of his peripheral vision but not by much. A red recording light blinked on the camera. *What kind of person records a murder?*

"This is all your fault, William." The man's voice was much hoarser than before. It threw Bryce until he realized the killer was trying to disguise it for the video.

Bryce lifted his pistol and aimed, finger tightening on the trigger. But the man stepped closer to Corina and grabbed a fistful of her hair. He yanked her head backward as he shoved the gun against her skull. She let out a stifled cry that sent anger flowing through Bryce's body.

"Please stop," she whispered. "You don't have to do this."

The man ignored her and looked directly into the camera. "Your daughter needs your help," he taunted. "But all you can do is watch."

Bryce clamped his teeth to avoid giving himself away. He could feel the heat rising in his neck and face, but he couldn't shoot now. The killer was too close to Corina. Bryce was a good shot but not that good. Even if he were, he couldn't guarantee the killer wouldn't reflexively pull his own trigger before he fell.

An idea popped into his mind. It was risky, but not as risky as taking a potshot and hoping he hit the right person. He ducked back into the pantry and felt around on the floor for anything heavy enough and hard enough to do the trick. His hand closed over the can he'd nearly tripped over. *Perfect.* He tightened his grip and stepped into the kitchen.

"I've waited a long time for this. You've defaulted on your debt for years. Now it's time to pay." The man roughly released Corina's hair and stepped back slightly. His finger still hovered over the trigger. "Say good—"

Bryce sent the can flying. It connected solidly with the man's outstretched hand, sending the gun clattering to the floor. With a cry of pain and rage, the man spun to face him.

"Don't move." Bryce held his weapon steady, aiming at the man's chest. "It's over."

"Bryce!"

"You okay?" Bryce directed the question at Corina but kept his eyes on the masked man, who was glaring at him and cradling his right hand. Bryce hoped it was broken.

"I—will be." Corina's voice hitched. "Please cut me loose." His gaze flicked to her bound hands.

Taking advantage of the fraction of a second of inattention, the killer lunged toward him, brandishing a knife he'd pulled from somewhere.

Bryce had no choice and only a second to act. The first bullet found its mark in the man's chest, but it didn't even slow him down. Bryce's gun barked out another round, this time aimed higher, and the man dropped to the tile floor. Corina's screams merged with the gunshots.

Ears ringing, hands shaking, he stepped away from the body that had fallen far too close to him. He wasn't sure if the man was alive or dead. The police could figure that out when they arrived.

The police. If they weren't here yet, they would be soon. He needed to let them know what was going on before they came in with weapons aimed at him.

But first he had to calm Corina down. Her breaths were coming far too quickly, and they sounded painful.

"It's okay. Take deeper breaths, slower." Fighting the trembling in his own hands, he pulled out his pocketknife and cut the zip ties from her wrists and ankles. She tried to stand, but her legs refused to support her, and she fell into his arms, biting back a cry of pain. He pulled her close and held her loosely against him since he didn't know where or how she'd been hurt.

"I was so afraid he'd shot you," she choked out between ragged gulps of air.

"Shh." He smoothed the matted hair away from her face. "We're okay. Everything's okay." He looked over her head at the body lying on the floor. Even if the man was still alive, he wasn't going to bother her ever again.

It was over. This horrible twelve-year vendetta was finally over.

54

LATE-AFTERNOON SUNLIGHT filtered into Corina's hospital room. They'd admitted her this morning, and she hadn't argued. What she did argue against was their recommendation to stay overnight for observation. She still hadn't seen her dad since he'd regained consciousness, and an overwhelming need to do just that had been hounding her all day. Worse, this wasn't even the same hospital, so it wasn't like she could sneak out and visit him.

At least she'd had Bryce to keep her company, though she'd much prefer to enjoy time with him in any other setting. She smiled, thinking of the feel of her hand cradled in his. She'd be glad when he returned from his coffee run—and not just for the caffeine.

A knock sounded at her open door, and an exhausted-looking Eric stepped inside. When he caught a glimpse of her, he hesitated.

She waved him over to her bedside. "Come on in."

He claimed the chair Bryce had just vacated and gave her a quick appraisal. "Man, I hope you don't feel as bad as you look."

She nearly laughed but managed to keep it to a short huff. Even that hurt. She couldn't take offense at Eric's assessment. The hospital room's bathroom mirror had not revealed a pretty reflection today. Her face was swollen, lower lip busted, and cheek deeply bruised. Her wrists and ankles were worn raw from the zip ties too. She covered one bandaged wrist with her other hand. At least Eric couldn't see her ankles. Or the two broken ribs from the tackle in the barn. They made a nice addition to the earlier hairline fracture. All in all, she probably felt about like she looked.

"About time you stopped in," she said, only half teasing. She was sure the day had been a lot more boring for her than for him.

"Just wanted to keep you in suspense," he said dryly, apparently willing to let it slide that she had neither confirmed nor denied how bad she felt.

She shook her head. "I've had enough of that for a lifetime, thank you very much."

"Well, I'll cut to the chase, then. Your stalker didn't make it. He died around noon."

She felt guilty at the relief that flooded her, but she felt it just the same. "Who was he?"

"His real name was Jerry Gustav Davidson, a well-known security system designer."

The guy RJ had told them about. But Eric had said that was his *real* name. She raised an eyebrow.

"We knew him as Gus Ramey."

Her breath caught painfully in her chest. "Gus?"

"Yeah." Disgust dripped from the word. "Masquerading as an older man, he was able to move in and operate under our noses, and we never suspected a thing."

Not Gus. He was one of the sweetest guys she knew. He'd been a model employee since she hired him after he'd moved to her dad's neighborhood in . . . July. The same month Jerry Davidson had disappeared from Texas.

But that didn't make him the same guy. There had to be a mistake somewhere.

"Gus isn't a killer," Corina insisted. "You've known him as long as I have. There's no way."

"I identified him myself. It's him."

"No. He's . . ." She scrambled for a valid argument. "He's the wrong age. RJ said Davidson was in his late forties. Gus is almost seventy."

Eric shook his head. "No, he isn't."

"I've seen his ID. I verified his identity when I hired him, and I saw his birth date." Since he didn't want to work with the firearms, she hadn't bothered to run a background check on him, but—

"It was forged. He was about twenty years younger than he looked. Thinner too, but there's no doubt it's him. He wasn't wearing his full getup when he snatched you last night, but enough of it was there that I could easily recognize him." His frown deepened. "He already looked older than we expected—must have aged fast over the last decade or so. But he enhanced that to become Gus. Dyed his hair gray, wore colored contacts, added some padding around his middle, a subtle fake tan, some makeup. Wouldn't have held up under a close examination from someone who knew the real him, but for strangers? Pretty effective."

"I can see that working for a day or two, but I've known him for months. Nobody gets their makeup the same every day. I think I would have noticed something at some point." She would have, wouldn't she?

Eric didn't budge. "He was good at what he did. We found a printed photo of him as Gus alongside an impressive set of professional-grade makeup when we searched his house this morning. My guess? He was very careful to match his daily appearance to that picture. The hair and tan would have been easy to maintain. He'd only have to touch them up occasionally. And his makeup use was strategically minimal—a few wrinkles and age spots, a little contouring—good-bye, Jerry, and hello, Gus."

"But . . ." She wasn't sure why she was still arguing. The guy taken to the hospital had definitely been her stalker, and Eric had identified him as Gus. But she couldn't wrap her mind around it.

Eric's voice softened slightly. "Corina, we found more than evidence of his disguise in that house. He had pictures of his wife and kids next to both old and current photos of you. His computer was streaming feed from your dad's security setup, and from the history, it looks like he had the same access to yours and to Western Outfitters'—he'd been watching you from your own security cameras." He paused for a second, and she just blinked at him, hardly able to process that. "There was also body cam footage of him cutting your hair."

She raised her palm, not wanting to hear any more, but Eric didn't seem to notice.

"We also got the local police in his home and office in Texas, and they uncovered quite a bit of additional evidence of his obsession with your family and of his other criminal activities. Both the Houston and Dallas departments are revisiting their cold cases involving your family's murders. It'll take some time to confirm everything—and we may never know all the details—but between what Gus told you last night and what your dad was able to come up with back when this first started, I think we have a pretty good idea of what went down.

"Back before the murders, Davidson led two lives. He had a legitimate job in Dallas that he was good at, and he and his family lived nearby. But after a financial setback, he began to dabble in some less legitimate activities. He got involved with the Espinoza crime ring and quickly rose through the ranks thanks to his technological genius.

"Then your dad and his partner took on a case involving a branch of the organization in Houston. They were able to expose Espinoza, and Davidson was blamed for the breach. Even from prison, Espinoza ordered the hit that took out Davidson's wife and four kids."

Corina winced at the memory of Gus's distress last night when he talked about watching his family die. She rubbed her bandaged wrists as Eric continued.

"The murders were all over the news for weeks, but by the time Davidson began his revenge, public interest had died down. He borrowed the location and method of execution but added the stalking and victory notes as his signature. With the murders occurring in different cities and the investigators' focus on his signature, the connection between his family's deaths and your family's was never made."

Corina let his words sink in. Everything made sense. Well, almost everything.

"Why wouldn't Gus have been killed with his family?"

Eric lifted his shoulders in a slight shrug. "Who knows? We captured two of his men last night. They seemed terrified of Davidson and refused to talk at all until they heard he was dead. They don't seem to know a whole lot, though."

She nodded, recalling what she'd seen of them in the barn last night. Gus—Davidson—had treated them with contempt, not as equals. And with his firsthand knowledge of the damage loose tongues could cause, he probably didn't tell his underlings anything more than they absolutely had to know.

"Without Davidson alive to speak for himself, we can only speculate on a lot of the details," Eric said. "A couple of possibilities come to mind. His family's deaths would have served the double purpose of punishing him and making him an example to others in the organization. Leaving him alive to suffer could have been part of that example. Another possibility is that whoever carried out the hit messed up, or maybe Espinoza thought he was more useful alive than dead, as long as he didn't fail again." A muscle twitched in his cheek. "If that's the case, he was wrong. Davidson probably orchestrated the prison riot that killed him."

A shudder rippled across her shoulders. *He's gone*, she reminded herself. But that didn't make her feel better. His betrayal hurt. And so did his death. She'd cared about Gus as an employee, and other than Allye, he'd been the closest thing she'd had to a friend in a long time.

It was hard to reconcile Eric's revelation with the man she thought she'd known. And as much as his betrayal ached, she couldn't help but pity him for the loss he'd suffered. She knew how it felt to watch the death of a loved one.

But each time she'd faced the grief of death, God had been with her, helping her, even when she'd been too emotionally closed off to recognize it. Gus hadn't had that support in place. Without it, there had been nothing but vengeance to fall back on.

"Knock, knock." Corina looked past Eric to see Bryce reentering her hospital room door, clutching a cup of coffee in each hand like they were literal lifelines.

Eric stood. "Well, I'm going to head out of here."

"Am I supposed to take that as a compliment?" Bryce asked.

He snickered, a sound she'd never heard Eric make. "You take it however you want to. The kind of day we've just had, I'm not going to sit around smelling someone else's coffee when I could get my own." He looked down at Corina, all business again. "We'll let you know if we find out anything else."

"Thanks, Eric. For everything."

He gave her a curt nod and moved toward the door. Halfway there, he stopped and turned back to them.

"I almost forgot. I checked on your bodyguard on my way in. He said being in here is driving him batty, but they expect a full recovery if he cooperates, so he's trying to behave."

Thank God.

"Does he remember anything about that night?" Bryce asked.

"No. He remembers going to his car and feeling drowsy. Nothing else."

"Did you ever find the pizza delivery guy?"

Eric's face darkened. "Yeah. A family a couple of streets away got back from vacation yesterday and reported a car parked behind their garage. Plates matched the vehicle registered to the delivery driver. We found his body in the trunk along with a crowbar we think could have been used on Mike." His voice wavered on the other officer's name. He stood there a minute, flexing his hand. Finally, he shook his head and left.

Corina let her tears fall. Tears for Officer Mike, for Eric's grief, for the teenager she didn't know. For everyone else she'd lost.

Bryce found her hand. Held it gently between his until she was all cried out. When the storm settled, he placed a box of tissues on the bed next to her.

"I'm sorry." She sniffed. Great. Her nose was running too. She grabbed one of the tissues and blew.

"Nothing to be sorry for." He pulled a tissue out for himself, and she realized he'd been crying with her.

"So much death," she whispered, gingerly wiping her face.

"Too much," he agreed. He ran his thumb lightly down her less-bruised cheek. "But it *is* over now, and we're going to face healing together this time, right?" He swallowed as if unsure she would agree.

But she wasn't going back on her decision. No more hiding. No matter how much it hurt to face her losses or risk another, she was done with that lonely life. And between Bryce and God, she was in good hands.

She gave him as big a smile as her split lip allowed. "Right."

Epilogue

"YOU SURE YOU'RE UP to this, Dad?" Corina hovered near her father as he moved from his wheelchair to his recliner.

"I'm fine." He gritted out the words, then finished the transfer and sat panting.

"Mm-hmm." She fluffed a pillow and helped him work it into a comfortable position behind him. Standing back, she surveyed his slightly pale face. "We don't have to have the party tonight. The Jessups will understand if we need to cancel."

He grunted. "After you spent Christmas babysitting me in rehab? No way."

She didn't mind. She was just glad they'd gotten to spend the holiday together. And once visiting hours were over, she'd spent the rest of the evening with Bryce. Overall, it had been a lovely day. And now her dad was home—that was celebration enough.

Seeing the futility of arguing, she conceded. "Fine. But if you start feeling ill, you tell me. Okay?"

"If I feel bad enough." Which meant he wouldn't.

She crossed her arms. "You're incorrigible." That earned her a grin.

"That's why I'm sitting here instead of in that whitewashed prison."

She couldn't help returning his smile. He wasn't wrong. Once the doctors had been able to evaluate the extent of his brain injury, they'd cautioned against hopes that he'd be able to come home anytime soon—especially with Corina's injuries limiting her ability to assist him.

But her dad was nothing if not determined. He'd opted for the most rigorous inpatient rehab available and pushed himself hard. He had his bad days, for sure. And even on the good ones, his fine motor skills didn't cooperate well and walking was still a distant hope. But he'd progressed enough to convince the doctors to discharge him. Yesterday, she and Bryce had moved him home.

"If you're okay here, I should probably start pulling out the food." Allye and her mom were bringing the hot dishes, but Corina and Allye had spent the last couple of days putting together a spread of snacks, dips, and desserts to enjoy throughout the evening.

Before she could step away, her dad took hold of her hand. His eyes filled with tears as he met her gaze. "I'm sorry, baby girl."

"For what?"

"For everything you went through. And for not telling you the truth years ago."

She lowered herself into a nearby seat, her hand still in his. She'd been dying to have this conversation with him but hadn't wanted to bring it up during his recuperation.

"Why didn't you?"

He took a deep breath. "Thirteen was too young to handle the full truth. I didn't want you any more traumatized than you were." A pained expression settled on his face. "I was an adult, and I couldn't close my eyes without seeing their bodies. I still see them as clearly as when I found them that night. I didn't want that for you." A tear slipped down his cheek. He squeezed her hand.

"And later?" she asked gently. She hated to push him, but if her dad was talking, she needed to take the opportunity. It wasn't that she couldn't live without knowing why. The anger she'd once felt about being kept in the dark had faded. But it still hurt, and she needed to face this with her dad. Resolve the issue, not sweep it under the rug like she used to do.

He sighed. "I don't have a good reason. I guess things were going so well—you were happy and had friends—I hated to spoil that when we seemed to have safely escaped. Then when Derryck died and you retreated into yourself . . . I couldn't bear to put more on you."

"But I deserved to know."

"I know. I was wrong. I didn't realize how wrong until Eric debriefed me." His hand trembled. "I'd never be able to forgive myself if Davidson had succeeded."

"But he didn't. By God's grace, Bryce showed up in time."

A knock sounded, and Houston let out a woof from the hallway. Speaking of Bryce.

Corina stood, her hand still in her dad's. "I forgive you for not telling me. I love you, Dad."

"I love you too, baby girl. If you want to know more later, I'll tell you whatever I know." He let her go and swiped at his cheek. "Now go let that young man in."

"Yes, sir."

FIFTEEN MINUTES BEFORE MIDNIGHT, Corina followed Bryce into the kitchen to retrieve the sparkling cider and chocolate torte they'd saved to toast in the new year. While she sliced the dessert, Bryce began filling champagne flutes.

"How is it having your dad back home?"

"It's great. He's cantankerous, for sure, but only because he hates his limitations."

"Good thing you're here to keep him in line."

"You mean *try* to keep him in line." She grinned and swiped the excess chocolate off her spatula and popped it into her mouth. *Yum.* "I do miss my place, but being responsible for only one residence during all this has been much simpler."

After the insurance company had evaluated the damage done to her house, her landlord had offered to break the lease and give her first option once it was livable again. All things considered, she'd decided to take him up on it and had officially moved back to her dad's for the time being. Bryce and Allye had done most of the moving for her due to her broken ribs. More things had gone into the dumpster than to her temporary home, though. Most of her stuff had been a total loss after Davidson's rampage.

But it was just stuff. A few of her childhood mementos were irreplaceable, but she'd grieve the lives lost much longer. Her family, Derryck, Officer Mike—even Gus. As much as she had to fight hating the man he really was, she grieved the man she'd known. The one he could have been if he hadn't allowed crime and hatred to destroy him.

"You okay?" Bryce's voice drew her back to the present.

She blinked hard and reached for a paper plate. "Yeah." The word came out breathy and not at all convincing.

"Hey." Bryce pulled her into a hug like he had so many times over the past six weeks.

She let the plate drop and rested her head against his chest, drawing comfort from his strength. "You'd think I would expect the gut punches by now."

"Healing takes time." He rubbed her back and repeated the words her grief counselor had drilled into her the past couple of weeks.

She nodded against him. "I know. And I am healing." Just more slowly than she was happy with. But in between the gut punches, she'd become more alive than she had been in years. She'd been intentional about reclaiming her faith, and she finally believed—

really believed—she was in God's hands. Although she'd probably have to fight her hiding tendency again in the future, she was prepared to do so with his help. She wouldn't let fear rob her of the chance to live and love.

And she loved Bryce. She wasn't afraid to admit that anymore.

She drew back and pressed her fingers to her eyes. "I've got a long road to travel, but I'm going the right way now."

"Corina, I want to travel that road with you—more than I have been." Bryce dropped to one knee in front of her. "I know you may need to take things slow, and that's fine. I'll wait as long as you want—I'm not going anywhere. But I can't wait any longer to ask you to marry me. Will you?"

He pulled a small box from his pocket and opened it to reveal a ring. She caught her breath. A single heart-shaped diamond glittered as he pulled it from the box. The rose gold band was fashioned to look like a lasso, twining twice around the finger. Simple, but with a touch of the West about it. It was perfect. Was this the one he'd had designed years ago?

"Of course I'll marry you." Her voice softened to an almost whisper as he slipped the ring onto her finger. "I love you, Bryce."

"And I love you so much." He pressed his lips to her hand, then stood without letting go. He pulled her close again, this time leaning down for a kiss.

She wrapped her arms around his neck and rose on her tiptoes to meet him halfway. This kiss wasn't their first, but it was one she'd never forget. Full of promise and hope and dreams of the future.

"About time, you two."

Corina pulled away and turned. Allye stood in the doorway with her camera, smirking as she snapped another photo.

"Go back in the living room, Allye," Bryce practically growled.

"Sure. But you'll thank me for these later." She winked at them and retreated down the hallway. "Don't take too long, or you'll miss the fireworks."

"I was already enjoying them," he murmured, drawing Corina into his arms once more.

"Me too." She tugged him down for another kiss. Cheering erupted from the other room.

Fireworks indeed.

Acknowledgments

In acknowledging those who played a part in making this book a reality, I have to thank my Savior first of all—for true life and peace in him, and for the words, friends, mentors, and everything else he worked according to his will to bring about this story. To him be the glory.

My family, who didn't complain when I holed up in my room for so many evenings that first couple of weeks or months, working on a "project" I was afraid to tell anyone about. Thank you guys for your support and love throughout this journey and for being some of my earliest readers!

The Sycamore Sisters from Mount Hermon, who adopted me for a night at my first writers' conference and supported me ever since. I will always claim you as my four extra "moms," and I'm so glad I can call you friends. You ladies are the best!

Hannah Davis and Jessica Kate, the extroverts to my introvert. Your friendship and encouragement those first years of writing were (and still are) so precious to me.

My agent, Wendy Lawton, for taking a chance on a new writer and not holding our first appointment against me. You were so gracious despite how green I was. I appreciate your encouragement and prayers and all the work you did to find a home for *Secondary Target* and its sisters.

The amazing people at Bethany House—editors, marketers, designers, and everyone else—you've made this book sparkle in a way I never could have alone. Thank you!

And, of course, a huge thanks to my writing group, the Masters of Mayhem—Crystal Caudill, Liz Bradford, and Voni Harris. I love writing and doing life with you ladies. Even if none of my books had ever seen the light of day, your friendship would have made every step of this journey more than worth it. Here's to many more books from all of us, more memories than we can count, and a never-ending list of shenanigans to pull off together!

There are so, so many more I could thank. Those who prayed for me, followed me before I had anything to follow, sent messages of encouragement, taught at workshops and conferences, freely shared your hard-earned wisdom, and in other ways walked alongside me. I can't mention you all by name, but you all have my thanks.

Read on
for a *sneak peek* at
the second book in

THE SECRETS OF KINCAID
SERIES

Allye Jessup is certain she witnessed a murder in progress and that the killer attacked her. But she's still alive, and there's no body or any evidence of what she saw. Maybe the brain fog surrounding her inexplicably deteriorating health has progressed to hallucinations, but she isn't so sure.

Police detective Eric Thornton knows he can't rid the world of illicit drugs, but he is determined to at least wipe out the trade in his hometown. When Allye Jessup insists that she witnessed a murder, he's skeptical—until it becomes obvious that someone doesn't want her to tell what she knows.

Available May 2025

LIGHTS? CHECK.

Camera? Check.

Three bags and a purse? Check.

Allye Jessup looped all four sets of straps over her left shoulder and stepped out of her small second-story photography studio into a warm autumn evening. The sun had just set, but it was still bright enough out that the dusk-to-dawn light above the landing hadn't kicked on yet. That wouldn't last long.

Tightly gripping the rail, she started down the metal stairs. She didn't need another fall, and the way her equilibrium had been off lately, she wasn't taking any chances. When she was nearly at the bottom, a dull thud sounded from behind the building. Someone stifled a cry. Another thud.

Allye hurried down the last few stairs toward the noise. She slowed before she reached the corner and fished in her pocket for her phone. She groaned silently. Not there. No telling which bag she'd stuffed it into. Or if she'd left it in her studio. Wouldn't be the first time.

As she edged toward the back of the building, she heard a louder thump, as if something heavy had fallen. The sounds changed to a muted, rhythmic pounding. She reached the corner and peered around.

Two men. One standing back in the shadows, arms crossed, watching.

The second man delivered another savage kick to something—no, someone—unmoving on the ground.

Allye sucked in a breath.

The attacker swung around, chest heaving. Looked her straight in the eyes.

Allye pushed off the building and ran, bags flopping against her back and side. Pursuing footfalls pounded the gravel behind her. She didn't dare look back. She had to get out into the open. Had to—

A heavy weight plowed into her back. She screamed. Tried to catch herself as she went down in a tangle of bags. Pain shot through her knees and wrists, but she pushed herself up. Turned to fight.

Her attacker shoved her against the side of the building. The back of her head bounced against the wall.

She screamed again.

A rough hand closed around her throat, cutting off her cry and pinning her against the rough brick. Her hands flew to his, but his grip was like steel. Too tight for another scream. Just loose enough to allow her the slightest bit of oxygen.

"What do we have here?" He studied her, ignoring her struggle. He touched her hair, letting a curl wind around his finger, then slide off. His lips curved in a predatory grin. "Pretty little thing, aren't you?"

A new wave of fear skittered up her spine. She kicked, and the tip of her shoe connected solidly with his shin. He slapped her, then shifted his hold on her throat, lifting her so her toes barely touched the ground. Rage glittered in his eyes.

And he started to squeeze.

Eyes wide, she clawed at his fingers, his arm. He snatched both her hands in his free one with a grip that threatened to snap her wrists. Her vision darkened, punctuated by pinpricks of light. She tried to kick again, but he was too close, and her strength was fading.

Someone shouted—the words garbled by the rushing in her ears. Hope flared.

Her attacker looked to the side, but the force of his grip didn't diminish.

Lungs feeling ready to burst, she jerked one last time against his hold. He didn't budge. The glimmer of hope faded.

Allye succumbed to the darkness.

Angela Carlisle resides in the hills of northern Kentucky and is a member of American Christian Fiction Writers and The Christian PEN. Angela is an editor by day and prefers to spend her free time reading, baking, and drinking ridiculous quantities of hot tea. Her unpublished works have won awards in ACFW's Genesis and First Impressions contests and placed in the Daphne du Maurier contest. Her shorter fiction works, including the prize-winning flash-fiction piece "Mansion Murderer," have appeared in *Splickety* and *Spark* magazines. Learn more at AngelaCarlisle.com.

Sign Up for Angela's Newsletter

Keep up to date with Angela's latest news
on book releases and events by signing up
for her email list at the link below.

AngelaCarlisle.com

FOLLOW ANGELA ON SOCIAL MEDIA

Angela Carlisle   @AngelaCarlisleWriter

You May Also Like . . .

Making amends for his criminal past, Christian Macleod has become one of the country's top security experts. But a string of heists brings attention from Andi Forster, an insurance investigator with her own checkered past. The two of them are drawn into a dangerous game with an opponent bent on revenge, and one wrong move could be the death of them both.

One Wrong Move by Dani Pettrey
JEOPARDY FALLS #1

Former FBI profiler River Ryland suffers from PTSD from a serial killer case gone wrong and has opened a private investigation firm with Tony, her former colleague. Their first job is a cold case, but when they race to stop the killer before he strikes again, an even more dangerous threat emerges, stirring up the past and plotting to end River's future.

Cold Pursuit by Nancy Mehl
RYLAND & ST. CLAIR #1

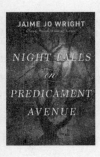

In 1910, Effie joins forces with an English newcomer to discover what lies behind the doors of the abandoned house on Predicament Avenue. In the present day, Norah reluctantly inherits the house turned bed and breakfast, where her first guest, a crime historian and podcaster, is set on uncovering the truth about what haunts this place.

Night Falls on Predicament Avenue by Jaime Jo Wright

 BETHANYHOUSE

 Bethany House Fiction

 @BethanyHouseFiction

 @Bethany_House

 OB Free exclusive resources for your book group at BethanyHouseOpenBook.com

 Sign up for our fiction newsletter today at BethanyHouse.com